A
Hustler's
QUEEN

Also by Saundra

If It Ain't About the Money
Her Sweetest Revenge
Her Sweetest Revenge 2
Her Sweetest Revenge 3
Hustle Hard

Anthologies
Schemes and *Dirty Tricks* (with Kiki Swinson)

Published by Kensington Publishing Corp.

A Hustler's QUEEN

SAUNDRA

Dafina Books

KENSINGTON PUBLISHING CORP.
www.kensingtonbooks.com

DAFINA BOOKS are published by

Kensington Publishing Corp.
119 West 40th Street
New York, NY 10018

Copyright © 2019 by Saundra

All Kensington Titles, Imprints, and Distributed Lines are available at special quantity discounts for bulk purchases for sales promotions, premiums, fund-raising, and educational or institutional use. Special book excerpts or customized printings can also be created to fit specific needs. For details, write or phone the office of the Kensington special sales manager: Kensington Publishing Corp., 119 West 40th Street, New York, NY 10018, attn: Special Sales Department, Phone: 1-800-221-2647.

Dafina and the Dafina logo Reg. U.S. Pat. & TM Off.

ISBN-13: 978-1-4967-1202-8
ISBN-10: 1-4967-1202-1
First Kensington Trade Edition: January 2019
First Kensington Mass Market Edition: May 2020

ISBN-13: 978-1-4967-1203-5 (ebook)
ISBN-10: 1-4967-1203-X (ebook)

10 9 8 7 6 5 4 3 2 1

Printed in the United States of America

Acknowledgments

I can never start my acknowledgments without thanking God. It's because of him that all things are possible. I'm so grateful. It's to him I give my praise and thanks for my two daughters, DJ and CJ, and husband, Onester. I'm thankful to my mom, sisters, brothers, and father, who all continue to support me.

Shout out to all my family, friends, and readers. I would like to thank my editor Selena James. Selena, you are the best. And that's for real. Thanks to my Kensington/Dafina family for the continued promotion of my work. I promise writing brings me joy and gives me life. Being able to share it with the world is the icing on my cake. *A Hustler's Queen* is a beast and sure to leave all who pick it up craving more. So sit back and get ready to turn the pages.

Saundra
One Key Stroke At A Tyme!!

Chapter 1

"You can't do that, Precious. No fair." My childhood friend Linda stamped her right foot and pouted. "I'm going to quit if you keep cheating."

"I ain't cheating though, just quick," I declared. We were standing outside my father's dry cleaners playing our favorite hand game, rock-paper-scissors. Anytime Linda was losing she would accuse me of cheating, but really, hands down I was just faster than she was. "Tell you what, I'll give you a ten-second head start." I stood with my arms folded.

"What does that even mean?"

"Just go." I laughed.

Smiling, Linda chanted, "Rock, paper . . ." She stalled and I followed her gaze to where we could hear yelling coming from inside the dry cleaners. We looked toward the door, but then there was silence. We glanced at each other and I shrugged my shoulders. We started playing again.

"Ha-ha, I won," Linda chanted.

"See, I knew the head start would help, but I ain't giving you another one." We both started laughing and prepared for the next round. Then we heard loud voices again. Looking at each other once again, we started running toward the dry cleaners.

We stopped in our tracks as Ava, Linda's mother, burst out the door. Walking straight toward me, Ava stopped and looked down at me with tears in her eyes. Reaching out for me, she hugged me really tight. "I love you, Sweet Pea," she whispered in my ear. Loosening her grip, she looked me over then grabbed Linda by the hand and quickly walked away. Linda glanced back at me and almost tripped.

"Where we going, Momma?" I heard Linda ask, struggling to keep up with her mother.

"Get in the car, Linda. Now!" she yelled and let go of Linda's hand. Linda glanced back at me one last time.

Confused, I watched as they drove away at top speed. When I could no longer see the car in the distance, I turned around to find my dad standing in the doorway; I guessed he had been watching the whole time. I looked up to him, hoping for an explanation, but he had no expression on his face. Slowly turning away from me, he walked back inside the cleaners.

A few seconds later, when my legs allowed me, I put one foot in front of the other and started the journey inside the cleaners. My dad came out of the back from his office just as I entered.

"Come here, Sweet Pea." That was the nickname they had for me, especially when something was wrong. I didn't move, so he motioned me over. Slowly, I walked over to him. He reached out and put his left hand on my shoulder. "Ava and Linda are moving away, and they will not be returning."

"But why not, Daddy?" I asked.

"Well, Ava has a new job in another city . . . and it's a good opportunity."

"And she's gone for good? Never, ever, coming back?"

"Yes, Sweet Pea."

I wasn't sure what to think. Ava had been in my life since I was a baby. I didn't have my own mom. Ava was the only mother I knew, and Linda was like a sister to me. Ava worked in the dry cleaners six days a week with my dad. The only time I wasn't with her was when I was home or in school. Linda and I went to the same school and were even in the same class. But just like that, they were gone.

"From now on it will be just you and me here to run this dry cleaners on our own. I mean, I may have to bring in some part-time help. But other than that, just us two," he explained, but I was still a bit confused. His emotionless facial expression suddenly seemed sad to me.

"Are you going to be okay, Daddy?" My bottom lip started to quiver.

"Of course, I'm fine, Sweet Pea." He looked down at me and smiled. "Now, don't you cry." He gently brushed his finger across my quivering lips.

"I'll help you, Dad." I hugged him tight. I would miss Ava and Linda; they were like family, but my dad belonged to me and I knew we would always be together.

Chapter 2

Ten Years Later

I still couldn't believe it; it had been two weeks since I had walked across the stage, graduated high school, and turned eighteen years old. I still felt the same, but I knew that change was going to come. Since I graduated with a 3.4 grade point average, I had received several offers from colleges out of state. While I couldn't wait to taste a bit of freedom, I didn't really want to leave my city completely, or my dad. I was born and raised in South Central, on Bonsallo Avenue, and I loved my city. Although I have to admit it is not the best side of Los Angeles, but home all the same. So instead of accepting offers to Spelman College, and a host of other out-of-state colleges, I chose to attend college on my stomping grounds, UCLA. And I couldn't have been happier.

Dad was also happy because not only did this mean I would be close to home, but I could still help out at the dry cleaners. I had chosen to stay on campus so that I could experience being an adult. Pushing the curtains back in the living room, I saw the mailman outside. Sliding into my slippers, I set my cup of orange juice on the coffee table and went to check the mailbox. To my surprise, there was a letter from UCLA. When I was back inside, I sat down on the sofa and opened the letter. As I read the words I became confused because according to the letter, my tuition was not paid. And that was shocking news to me because as far as I knew, Dad had taken care of that months ago. There had to be some kind of mistake, and I had to get to the bottom of it quickly. Since it was almost time for my shift, I got dressed, jumped in my 2005 Toyota Corolla, and headed over to the dry cleaners.

"Hey, Precious," Katrina said. Katrina was the other part-time person besides myself who worked at the dry cleaners. Dad was the only one who worked full-time.

"Hey, K." That's what I had called Katrina since day one and she didn't mind. "Where Dad at?"

"In his office, he just got back from the bank."

"Did they get the machine fixed?" One of the pressers had been down for two days and it was costing us business. Daddy had called up one of his old friends, Earl, who was a shade tree mechanic. And sometimes he could get junk to work when it still had a little life left in it. I hoped that was the case with that broke-down machine.

"Yes, Earl just left about an hour ago. I'm glad you made it in. I'm leaving early today, I got a few things I have to do. Are you going to go to that party that I invited you to? You never gave me a definite yes or no and it's tonight."

It was a good thing she brought that up because I had forgotten all about her inviting me to that party.

"I don't think I can make it, K." I shook my head because I knew she would be disappointed. "I don't
have anything to wear. And I haven't had time to do
any shopping."

"Precious, girl, you got to stop making excuses to
keep from having fun. You just graduated and
turned eighteen. That, girl, is a reason to turn up.
And don't blame your dad, because he can't stop you
now. And I already told him you were going," she
threw in.

"I know, I know, and I'm not blaming him this
time. I'm just not prepared, but next time, I promise,
I'ma go."

"A'ight. You gone miss out though. But I gotta
bounce." I liked Katrina, she was really cool. She was
twenty-one and from around Compton, so she was a
bit rough around the edges, but she had a two-year-
old daughter named Mandiee, who she credited for
changing her into a much calmer person. And she
was working hard and planned on finding another
part-time, and was just trying to get herself together.

Two customers came through the doors as Katrina
exited. After taking care of them, I made my way
back to Dad's office.

"Daddy, this came in the mail today. What are they
talking about?" I handed him the letter.

Observing the name on the envelope, he hesitated before flipping it over and pulling out the single piece of paper. I was a bit anxious, so I shifted my
weight from my left leg to the right. I watch Dad's
eyes as they scanned the words. It seemed to take an
eternity, but finally his eyes met mine. "Is Katrina
gone?"

"Yes, she left about twenty minutes ago."

"Lock up for a minute."

"What about the customers?" I asked. His request was a little unusual. Dad hated to close up on the one day he was scheduled to be closed, so to lock up on a day we were supposed to be open made me raise my eyebrows with curiosity.

"Just do it, Precious." This time I scrambled to the front door without question, then went back to his office. Dad sighed before speaking. "I've been meaning to talk to you, but it's been difficult." I saw the worry on his face and the lines in his forehead and I was alarmed.

"What is it, Dad? Whatever it is, I need you to know I'm not a kid anymore."

He looked at me as if from those words he just realized I had grown up. "Nope, you're not," he agreed with another sigh. "The dry cleaners is suffering. Business just has not been good. But I'm sure you know that much already. The equipment is declining and I need to put some money into it . . . some real money. Because without the equipment, we shut down."

I was not surprised to hear that the equipment was breaking down. And I also knew that if he could afford to replace it he would have done that a long time ago. "So what are you going to do? That equipment is expensive."

"For starters, I'm going to have to let Katrina go."

Now that stunned me. "Daddy, K needs this job." I couldn't help but think about Katrina and the goals she had. She was trying to save up money so that she could take her baby and move out of her mother's three-bedroom house, where her eight brothers and sisters all still lived with their children.

"Precious, I know that." He hung his head as if he

was ashamed. He had heard Katrina, time and time again, talk about her goals. "I have considered all of that. But I have no choice in the matter. I have to try and save the business. It's all we have."

"When are you going to tell her?"

"Tomorrow. I can't put this off any longer. I should have done it six months ago, but I have been trying to find other solutions. One more thing . . ." He dropped his head again, then he slowly raised it, his gaze fixed on me. "I know how much school means to you, and you know how much it means to me that you go. But right now I just can't afford it."

"Daddy." Tears instantly started to fall from my eyes.

"I know, Sweet Pea, and I'm sorry, but it's just for a while. I need you to sit out for one year. By then things should be back on track. I'm almost certain they will." A tear slid down his cheek and I felt bad for crying like a baby, because I knew how hard he had tried.

This dry cleaners was his life; I had spent my entire childhood here and not once had it let us down. Dad spent all of his time here, day and night, and not once had he ever complained. So this was a time for me to be strong, suck up my feelings and wants. As difficult as it was, I wiped my tears.

"I got your back, Dad. I will sit out of school and help you out full-time until the cleaners is back on track."

Dad stood up. "Thank you, Sweet Pea." He kissed me on the forehead. I wasn't worried. A year would fly by, then I would be enrolled and attending school again at UCLA.

Chapter 3

Two Years Later

"You have the whitest teeth I have ever seen." Kevin leaned on the counter. He was close, almost closing the space between us, forcing us to be face-to-face. He was close enough to smell any plaque that might have graced my teeth and given my breath a foul odor. But I wasn't worried; the spearmint gum in my mouth would kill any bad breath that attempted to attack. And I in return thanked God that Kevin's breath didn't stink either.

"Boy, you better get off this counter before my dad catches you." I giggled, but I was serious at the same time.

"Man, I swear Mr. Larry stay trippin' off me." I had known Kevin for about four years. We had graduated high school together. He had started at my school our sophomore year, but was suspended most of the time. His mother had sent him down from Oakland to live with his grandmother. Back in Oakland he'd been in and out of juvie for petty crimes. But his grandmother, Mrs. Lucy, ruled with an iron fist, and by senior year he was a model student. His grandmother had her Sunday clothes cleaned here, so he was in at least once a week to pick them up. And I didn't mind seeing him because he was fine. Dark chocolate, low-cut fade, and six two. I needed some eye candy to keep me sane from spending so much time at the dry cleaners.

"You really think my teeth are that white though?" I smiled again to showcase my teeth.

"White as snow. Real talk, you are beautiful, Precious. But I think you know that already."

Honestly, I didn't think about my looks much. I wasn't one of those girls who stood in front of the mirror and praised her looks. But I was well aware that I was considered the full package. I had stopped growing by the time I was fifteen, but the growth spurt I had between twelve and fifteen was significant. I stood five foot eight, with a waistline identical to Meagan Good's, high cheekbones, and straight teeth to match. I could have easily hit the runway as a Victoria's Secret model. But I had no interest in that. Kevin was amusing though, and I always enjoyed his company.

"Let me take you out on a date?" I was about to answer just as Dad appeared from his office. "What's up, Mr. Larry?" Kevin said.

"Hey, did you get your grandmother's order yet?"

"Yep, Precious took care of me." Turning to me, he said, "Umm, a'ight, Precious. Think about that. I'll call you." Kevin grabbed the bag with the clothes and was out.

"Dad, why you have to make him nervous?" I grinned.

"How I make him nervous? His lil ass ain't up to no good. That's why he nervous. Talkin' bout will you go on a date with him."

He had heard Kevin. I had wondered if he was eavesdropping, and I was right. "Dad, you were listenin' to our conversation?" I accused. I often wondered if he was listening to conversations because he always seemed to pop up when it got interesting.

"This is my shop, I pay attention to everything. So yes, I heard and I don't like it one bit. I don't want you going anywhere with that hood." I wasn't surprised to hear him say that. He always found something wrong with any guy who liked me. In his eyes, I was still a baby.

"Daddy, you shouldn't call Kevin names. He really is a good dude and definitely not a hood. Besides, I'm twenty, and whether or not I go out on a date with him should be my decision."

"Hmmm," he said. Before he could elaborate on his sarcastic sound, Keisha, another one of my old schoolmates, pushed her way through the glass door. Dad exited toward the back.

"What's up?" Keisha said, chewing on some gum.

"Same ol' thing. Work, work, around here." I sighed.

"Girl, for real that's all I see you do. Shit, what you need to do is get out in this sun. It's baking but it's beautiful. Ain't no way in the hell I could be in this damn shop all day." Keisha swung her sixteen-inch weave off her shoulder and pulled off her sunglasses. She was always dressed to the nines when I saw her, and she always looked like she had somewhere to go. But she was in the dry cleaners often, picking up clothes. Everything we cleaned for her was name brand. I'm talking that expensive stuff. So I always took extra special care with her things.

I felt what she had said about me spending so much time at the cleaners, but this business was our survival. And now was not the time to focus simply on myself. But I didn't have to explain that to anyone. So I replied, "I feel you. Let me get your clothes." After grabbing her order, I took her money and wished her on her way.

I watched as she bounced back out into the LA streets, where everything was possible. I briefly wondered when my time was coming. It had been two years since graduation and a year longer than Dad had all but promised I would be in college. That had not happened, though, and two years later, I was still working full-time with no mention of college. But to be honest, not much had changed business-wise, and I knew that. Grabbing the UCLA catalog off the counter next to me, I thumbed through and glanced at the updated list of classes. I was really considering changing my major from communications to business, when and if I ever did get into college. Maybe then I could help my dad with the business side of the dry cleaners, help the business thrive and be successful.

Dad came out of his office and saw me thumbing through the book. "Don't you worry, Sweet Pea, the time is coming soon. I promise you that." I knew he could tell I was restless. I tried daily to hide it, but sometimes it was difficult.

"I know . . . You know, I was thinking about maybe going for a business major when I do go."

"You changing your major?" It was apparent in his

tone and gesture he was shocked. I had been full of passion about becoming a news anchor since I was in middle school. It's all I had ever talked about. When I was only twelve, I would stand by the television with my karaoke set and act as if I was out on the scene reporting the news. "What about your dream of becoming a news anchor? You can't just give up on that dream."

I chewed my bottom lip for a minute. "I know, and it still is my dream, but I was thinking with a business degree, I could help you with the dry cleaners. Get this place to its full potential. I know it can be done, Daddy." Regardless how bad business was at the dry cleaners, I was still optimistic about its future.

"I do too. And we must never lose hope." He looked around the place like he expected it to cosign. "Listen, I know you really want to attend UCLA. And believe me, I'm still working to get you there. So I was thinking . . . how about you attend community college for a year? The tuition would be much cheaper. I could make it happen."

I had to admit the thought of starting college, period, was exciting. But I was a bit apprehensive about community college. Sometimes their curriculum was not the best. And a school's accreditation was a big deal to me. But beggars couldn't be choosers; he was giving me options. "I'll think about it" was my response.

"I know it's not ideal for you, Sweet Pea. Just do me a favor and look into it before you rule it out."

"No worries, Dad. I will." I smiled to reassure him.

"Well, I don't know about you, but I'm hungry. Why don't you head over to Italiano and pick us up some sandwiches for lunch?"

"Now that I'm game for." I reached my hand out for the cash.

Once outside in the sun, I could see exactly what Keisha was talking about, it was nice out. Hot but beautiful, and seeing all the people coming and going gave me energy. So instead of heading straight to Italiano to pick up those sandwiches, I decided to turn a few corners first and just relax. I didn't do this often because most of my time was spent at the shop. Kevin was heavy on my mind though. I was really feeling him and seriously considering taking him up on his offer to go out on a date. But it bothered me that Daddy didn't see any potential in him. Maybe if he got to know Kevin better he could see that he was not a "hood," as he described him. And even if nothing else happened, a few dates would put a smile on my face. And that would be enough for me. So with that, my mind was made up.

After picking up the sandwiches, I headed back to the shop. I would convince my dad that Kevin was a nice guy. And that I would go on a date with him. Pulling the door open at the cleaners, Dad was nowhere in sight.

"I'm back, Daddy," I announced. The door opened behind me and a customer walked in. "Hello," I greeted her.

"I'm here to pick up for Lisa Walker." The young lady laid her ticket on the counter.

"Okay, give me a minute and I'll grab that for you." I walked behind the counter to set the food down, grab her ticket, then get her order. "That will be $69.23." After I took care of the customer, Dad still had not come out of the back. Hungry, I walked toward the bathroom to wash my hands so that I could eat. "Daddy!" I yelled again.

My hand on the bathroom doorknob, I paused. There was a strange silence and Dad had yet to answer me. Turning around, I made a few strides to his office. "Dad," I said again, and my breath seemed to catch in my chest. His body was lying between his desk and the wall. I stepped forward. "*Agh!*" I screamed, as I realized he was lying in a pool of blood. "What's wrong, Daddy?" I dropped to my knees, crying. I tried to get back on my feet but my legs were weak; I reached for the phone on his desk and dialed 911.

"Please send help. I think my dad has been shot," I cried into the phone.

The ambulance arrived along with detectives. The detectives helped me to my feet. They took me to the front by the counter. They tried to ask me questions. Distraught, I tried to explain I had just come back when I saw my father on the floor. I watched as the paramedics loaded him into the ambulance, then pronounced him dead. My whole world stopped in that moment. Everything seemed distant and surreal.

"Ma'am, do you have anyone you could call?" I read the detective's lips because my hearing seemed to have stopped working.

With the biggest lump in my throat imaginable, I mouthed, "No." For the first time in my life, I realized that I was alone. I had no one. Dad was the only family or friend that I had. I was utterly and completely alone.

Chapter 4

It had been a week since I had buried my beloved father. The whole thing was so surreal. Somehow, I had found the sanity to put the funeral together alone. It was the hardest thing I had ever done. But I did what he would have expected me to do, and was strong and responsible. Thankfully, everything had turned out alright. All of Dad's friends had showed up. It was mostly his bowling partners, a few guys he served in the military with, Earl—a longtime friend—and a host of his loyal customers from the dry cleaners. Even Katrina had showed up; she cried a lot and she said that Dad had been like a father to her. I was sad to hear her say she was moving to Texas with her auntie. She had found a job out there and would be leaving in a week. I was happy for her though.

I still could not believe someone had shot my dad. According to the police, it was a robbery gone bad. I would have never thought anyone would do that to him. He was the nicest man anyone could ever hope to meet. His only flaw was that he could be brutally honest. But other than that, he would give someone the shirt off his back. I prayed the murderer would be caught and charged. I hurt so bad; I was sure I would never get over losing him.

I knew that I needed to go on, and I tried. Finally, a few weeks later, the cleaners was released from being a crime scene. CTS, the crime scene cleanup crew, had come through and cleaned it up. But I hired some cleaners to come in to clean Dad's office again. I just felt better knowing it was spic-and-span as could be. I reopened the dry cleaners as I knew he would have wanted. But being back there on a daily basis was just as difficult as I had imagined it would be. Every day, all of my thoughts were clouded with thoughts of my dad, from the time I got up until I went to bed at night. Being at the cleaners didn't help the situation. Unable to shake the sadness and pain, I did something he would not have approved of: I put the Closed sign on the door. Gathering my purse and a few papers off the counter, I prepared to leave, not certain if I would ever return. Just as I was about to head toward the door, I noticed Kevin pulling on the doorknob. Dropping low, I ducked behind the counter and hid. I had not seen him since the day Dad was murdered. And at the moment, I was in no mood to talk to anyone. I stayed down as he continued to pull on the doorknob. The noise soon stopped. Gradually, I peeked out from the behind the counter and thankfully he was nowhere in sight. Breathing a sigh of relief, I locked up and made a quick break for my car.

Back at Dad's house, I found a check in the mailbox for the insurance settlement. Inside the house, I dropped it on the living room coffee table. Feeling drained, I headed straight to my bedroom, where I threw myself across my bed and cried. The feeling of being overwhelmed was starting to suffocate me. I felt as if death was all around me and there was no relief. The sun shining through my window made me feel as if I were lying in the pit of hell. Dragging my shaky, weak body from my bed, I pulled my curtains closed. And as far as I was concerned, the curtains could remain that way. I was shutting myself inside forever.

Two weeks had all but flown by and, honestly, I was still in the same head space. The only thing I could bring myself to do was shower. Eating wasn't that important so I barely did it. Sleeping, on the other hand, was my comfort, and for a minute I was convinced I would never get tired of it, but I was wrong. For the past two days, I had become restless. With my dad's voice in the back of my mind urging me on, I realized that I could not close myself off from the outside world. As much as I hated to admit it, I still existed. Throwing on my robe, I dragged myself to the front door and then outside. The sun met me with brutal accusations, almost as if it was punishing me for trying to shut it out. Blinking my eyes several times, I had to adjust to the brightness. Slowly, I made my way to the mailbox.

Just as I imagined, it was packed with weeks' worth of unopened mail. One more day and the mailman would probably have stopped delivery. After emptying it, I made my way back inside and shut the door. With the sun on the other side of the door, I felt empty and deprived. Dumping the mail on the coffee table, I made my way over to the curtains and gladly pulled them open. Relief tingled all over me. As I thumbed through the mail on the table, a letter from Faulkner's Bank grabbed my attention. I peeled back the seal only to find out they were threatening to foreclose on the cleaners, which got my attention. Another one from Faulkner's also threatened to foreclose on the house.

"Damn!" I yelled. I threw the papers to the floor. As hard as Dad and I had worked and sacrificed, we were still going to lose. "What can I do, Daddy?" I cried out. Sitting on the couch, I felt defeated. I cried until I felt drained. I tried to clear my mind so that I could think. Then it hit me: I had a choice to make, a hard one at best, but it had to be made. I could only keep one. I had enough money to do that, and that beat losing them both. I decided to save the house I was born and raised in. I would use the rest of the insurance settlement I had received to pay it off. The cleaners would have to shut down. Just even thinking about it consumed me with guilt. What would Dad think? He would be heartbroken. But I could not worry about that now. I was here, alive, and had to survive. He had left me with no choice. I knew the business was suffering, but I didn't know the house was too. How much debt did we really have? Clearly there was no way he was ever going to be able to send me to UCLA, at least not anytime soon. Why hadn't he just been honest with me? I would have understood.

Chapter 5

It had been an agonizing process, but I was glad the day to close the dry cleaners had finally arrived. I was sad yet plainly ready to be done with it. It had taken weeks, but the equipment had been sold to a cleaners owner who swore he could repair it. I didn't argue with him; I needed the money, which was used to help pay off some of the debts. Today I had come in to finish up the last of the packing. I tried to be swift about it because the people from the bank were supposed to be bringing by some potential buyers to look at the place.

I was about to be done with Dad's office, but just looking around at the bare walls that usually displayed his business license, certifications, and the awards he had won over the years from the community was so hard. I fought back tears. I pulled out the bottom drawer of his desk and I fell into his desk chair, unable to control the tears that flowed down my cheeks, as I saw the picture he had of me. I was around five years old in the picture, outside of the cleaners, riding my big wheel. I missed my dad so much.

I wiped at my tears and attempted to dry my face as they continued to flow. "Hey, Precious . . ." I stood up in shock as I heard someone yell my name. I wasn't sure who it could be as the front door should have been locked. And the stuck-up Realtor, Nancy, who worked for the bank and had the only other set of keys, would never yell my name. I bent down and reached to the right of the desk to pick up the bat that Dad had kept for protection. He had a gun too, but I figured the bat would do.

Tiptoeing to the front of the cleaners, my nervousness quickly subsided when I saw that it was only Keisha. "Girl, what the hell you doing back there? I almost left, I thought nobody was here. I need to drop off these jeans."

I'm sure the look on my face said I was confused. Clearly she had seen the sign that we were closing up. "Umm, we are closing up. Didn't you see . . . I put the sign on the door." I pointed toward the door.

"Closing? Why y'all closing so early? I thought you stay open to like seven thirty?"

"No, we are closing for good. That door should have been locked . . . at least I thought I had locked it."

"Oh, my bad. Damn, I did not see that sign. But for real though, why is Mr. Larry shutting down the best dry cleaners in the area? What we gone do over here? Cause I refuse to fuck wit' that cleaners up the block. They be fuckin' up people's shit," she said. I could do nothing but stare at her though. I heard all the things coming out of her mouth and I had to admit she was right. Dad was one of the best and he had loyal customers. Business had only slowed because the machines were not the best anymore. But what shocked me most was that Keisha was speaking about Dad like he was still alive.

I cleared my throat because it was hard, but I had to inform her. "Keisha, I'm the one closing the shop. My dad was murdered. I thought you knew." Talking about it made me feel as if it was happening all over again. I felt sick to my stomach and I grabbed my abdomen to try to control my emotions.

"Wait, when?" Keisha seem genuinely shocked. "I ain't heard shit about it."

"It's been about . . ." I hesitated and swallowed to keep from crying or screaming out. The pain was just unbearable. I took a deep breath to finish my sentence. "It happened almost two months ago."

"Precious, I'm so sorry. Damn, I ain't heard shit about this. But I been out of town for a few months."

The tears again flowed like a faucet and my body become so weak I had no choice but to lean up against the nearest wall. But I could no longer hold myself up and I slid to the floor.

"Hey, hey. Everything gone be cool." Keisha dropped to her knees and hugged me.

Keisha sat with me until I felt better, and I really appreciated it. I had no one that I could share my emotions with. But it had started to get late and I realized that I really needed to finish up before the Realtor showed up. The last thing I was in the mood for was to watch potential buyers scout the place. That I could live without.

"Well, I guess I'll get up and finish packing up the last few things. The Realtor is coming by any minute now."

"A'ight, but look, you should come by my apartment sometimes; we could hang out."

"Yeah, maybe once I get everything taken care of."
I was apprehensive. I really wasn't used to hanging
out with anyone. And with my emotions being all
over the place, I wasn't sure if it was such a good
idea. But she had been nice to me, so I didn't want to
be mean.

"Tell you what. You put your number in my phone
and I'll put mine in yours."

"Okay," I agreed as she handed me her phone and
I handed her mine. After retrieving the last few
things from Dad's drawers, I packed his Ford F-150
with his stuff. I walked around the dry cleaners one
last time. I tried as hard as I could to pack the memories safe in the back of my mind. I locked up the
place and I walked away without looking back, because if I looked back I was sure I would throw up
again from regret.

Chapter 6

Being at home all day every day was turning out to be a challenge for me. Not that I had a life before, but at least I'd had the dry cleaners to look forward to. To keep busy, I cleaned the entire house from top to bottom, nothing in the house was left unturned. I welcomed the sun as I pulled back the curtains in every room. It gave me energy. Suddenly, I had the taste for my favorite type of doughnut, Krispy Kreme. I slid into some shorts, a tight T-shirt that read *Girl Beat*, and a pair of flip-flops. I was out. By the time I reached Krispy Kreme, my taste for a doughnut had risen to a craving.

I walked out of Krispy Kreme carrying a full dozen of hot and fresh doughnuts. Before I could even get out of the parking lot, I ate two of them. I was about to go in for number three, but my ringing cell phone interrupted me. Between trying to shut the Krispy Kreme box and balance the hot doughnut, I almost dropped my phone.

"Hello," I managed to answer in the midst of my struggle.

"What's up, Precious?" I recognized Keisha's voice right away.

"Oh hey, Keisha." I was shocked that she called me.

"What you into right now?"

"Nothin' really." I gazed at the doughnut in my free hand.

"Sounds like you being bored?" It sounded more like an answer than a question. "So why don't you meet me at Baldwin Hills mall? I'm headed over there now."

I knew it should have been an easy yes, but I wasn't sure if I was ready to hang out. Especially in a mall full of strangers. The doughnuts were enough happiness for me for now.

"Aye, what's up? You rollin' or not?"

"Why not?" came out of my mouth. It's not what I wanted to say. But Keisha's tone told me she wouldn't take no for an answer.

"A'ight, bet. I'll see you in a bit."

Now I had plans, something I was not used to having. Biting off half of the doughnut, I placed the other half in the box, then wiped the fast-drying icing off the tips of my fingers. I jetted out of the Krispy Kreme parking lot and headed for the mall. Finding a parking space outside, I made my way inside Macy's. Keisha had texted me and told me to meet her there in the women's shoe section.

"What's up wit' cha?" Keisha greeted me. By her statements over the phone and her greeting, you would have thought we were old friends.

"Nothin' really," I replied dryly. I hoped I didn't sound mean, but I really wasn't sure of what to say. I wasn't in much of a mood to be conversing.

"I had to get you out that damn house. I'm sure you been locked inside."

"Something like that. But actually, when you called I was over at Krispy Kreme picking up some dough-nuts."

"For real. Were they hot and fresh?"

"Yes, and good." I smiled. It had been a long time since the last time I smiled. But it felt good.

"You gone have to share them shits, hot or not. I love Krispy Kreme."

"Cool, you can have some."

"Bet. Look at these Tommy Hilfiger heels. Bitch, they are cute as shit."

"They are," I agreed. "The question is, how much are they?" I reached for the opposite shoe and looked at the bottom. Just like I thought, they were over two hundred dollars.

"Fuck the cost, that doesn't matter." Keisha was blunt. I wasn't sure why, but I liked that. "I'm getting these." She gestured a sales person over and asked for the shoe in her size. "Precious, I'm a shopaholic. I try to control myself, but sometimes it's hard." The saleslady handed her the box.

"I used to love to shop too, but over the last cou-ple of years I had to slow down while Dad got the fi-nances back on track." I wasn't sure why I shared that with her. Maybe I needed to get it out.

"Sounds like when I was growing up. Except I just didn't have shit at all."

I was shocked to hear that, because in school she always wore the most updated styles. "In school you were always rockin' the new stuff."

"Yeah, see, you met me in high school—that's when I was just getting my fresh on. Before that I was a bum. I'm talking about dingy pants and busted shoes."

"I had no idea." My tone was sad.

"It's cool though, because in high school, like you said, I was fuckin' 'em up with the gear. See, I took matters into my own hands. I promised myself then that shit would only get better. Fast forward to a bitch dropping stacks on whatever." A grin spread across her lips.

After paying for her Tommy Hilfiger shoes, we made our way over to the jeans in the women's department.

"These are cute. I got a blouse that would go great with that." I was starting to thank myself for coming. Even matching things up that I was not going to buy felt good.

"You gone cop them Guess jeans or what?" Keisha asked.

"Nah, I'm good. I'm just window shopping today."

"Why not? Maybe you can put that blouse to use. Go on, try them on," she encouraged. I really didn't want to spend any money, but the jeans were just hard to resist. I skipped off to the dressing room and returned to model the jeans for Keisha. "See, I told you, you hot in that shit. Precious, you need to get those." Keisha boosted my ego.

I double-checked myself in the mirror and the pants were indeed hot on me, I had to admit it. "I really do like them. But I can't see myself paying one hundred and twenty dollars for these."

"Hey, just think of all the heads you gone turn . . . I'm gone get me a pair of these." Keisha pulled out another pair of Guess jeans that were ripped completely at the knee. "I'm getting these too. My booty gone be lookin' delicious in these." Keisha turned her butt to the mirror and looked at it sideways. "I might wear these to the party. Aye, why don't you go to a party with me tomorrow night?"

"I can't."

"Why not? You got plans or some?" Keisha was still staring at her butt in the mirror.

"No, I don't . . . it sounds fun though."

"And it's gone be fun. Off the chain fun at that."

We both grabbed the jeans and headed toward the counter. As much as I wanted to put the pants back, I had to have them.

"Let's grab a bite from the food court," Keisha suggested.

Hunching my shoulders, I said, "I'm good with that." Inside the crowded food court, we grabbed some Japanese, then found a seat.

"So, please, tell me what you do for fun."

"Fun . . ." I repeated. Her question was truly something for me to think about. I racked my brain for at least a minute, but there was nothing. "Fun." I sighed. "I have to say I don't have too much of that. I mean, I had fun with my dad; we used to laugh and we did everything together. But I didn't really hang out with friends and all that. I was my dad's only child, so he was always protective of me."

"I guess that explains why I can never remember seeing you at a school game or dance. Hell, when I think about it, I only ever seen you at that damn dry cleaners."

The way she said that, it made it sound bad, like I'd been locked away. But I never saw it that way. Then I remembered I had went out with a friend a few times in high school. "Actually, I went to a few games with my friend Liza Petro, but she moved away in tenth grade."

"Liza? You were cool with her? I took a few classes with her in ninth grade. I remember her ass was a little bougie."

I laugh. "Yep, that's her." Everyone thought Liza was stuck-up, and she could be at times, but she was nice and we got along great.

"But real talk, Precious, you can't just sit in your house and rot. I know you don't want to do anything right now, but you need to get out and live life. Hell, at least a little." She was right, I knew it in my heart. But I felt as if I was not ready. And I didn't know when I would be. "What are your plans now? You need to have some."

"Yeah, I do. My plan since graduating high school has always been to attend college. And I still want to go. I thought UCLA was gone be it for me. But like I was trying to say earlier, things had changed for us financially before Daddy . . ." I paused. I couldn't bring myself to say it. "Daddy was still trying to get things on track." I wrapped it up.

"You know it ain't too late to sign up for community college. Believe it or not, once upon a time I researched college. They have grants and all that to help you. You should sign up."

Her mentioning community college made me think of what Dad had said. Community college may have not been the best option, but it was an affordable chance for me. "What about you? Why didn't you ever sign up?" Keisha chuckled at my comment. "What's so funny? If you put in the time to research, you must have been interested." I had to know.

"Bitch, really, does it look like I'm about to sign

up for school?" I couldn't answer, but she finished her point. "Look, school's great and all, but I gets money. I ain't got time for that bullshit. When I re-searched that shit I was bored." She spoke matter-of-factly. "But check this out, you need to come to the crib and hang sometimes. We gotta get you some fun in your life. And I mean ASAP." She had changed the subject, just like that.

I couldn't do nothing but smile. Keisha was fun. Being around her would keep my spirits lifted. Maybe hanging out with her was what I needed.

Chapter 7

It had been a full four months since my dad had been murdered and two months since I had started hanging out with Keisha. And honestly, it seemed that hanging with her was for the best. She was cool people and we had a lot of fun. It kept my mind off my dad too. If I wasn't doing anything else, I would have thought about him twenty-four-seven. I had made my way down to the community college and signed up for classes just in time for the new semester. To my surprise, I was really liking community college; all of my professors were great. I wished I had signed up a long time ago. But it was too late for regret, so I wouldn't waste time on the thoughts.

Today I had no classes, so Keisha had invited me over to chill at her apartment. After gassing up the Corolla, I pointed it toward Brentwood, where Keisha and her boyfriend owned a three-bedroom condo. I loved going on that side of Los Angeles; it was really nice. Dad and I used to drive down to Brentwood and he would take me shopping. This would be the first time I had ever visited someone in Brentwood though.

"What's up, Precious?" Keisha's boyfriend, Quincy, greeted me as soon as he swung the front door open. I had only met him once a few weeks before, when he came to Starbucks to give Keisha some money. He seemed really nice and she always had good things to say about him.

"Hi, Quincy," I said.

"Come on in. Keisha in the kitchen." Stepping inside the condo, I admired how elegantly it was decorated. They were living really nice, to say the least. When I was outside, I had noticed they had a three-car garage attached. Keisha drove a Mercedes, so I could only imagine what else they had behind those other two doors.

"Girl, you were supposed to be here two hours ago," Keisha said as she came out of the kitchen.

"No, you said four, remember?" I reminded her.

"Fuck it, you know I don't remember much." Keisha chuckled. "Come on in the kitchen and help me out."

"You want me to help? I told you, I ain't a cook," I joked. Inside the kitchen, I was loving the spread Keisha had set up. Turkey roll-up sandwiches, chicken Alfredo, hot crescent rolls, and sweet tea. "Keisha, you don't need my help, this looks delicious. Pass me a plate." I wasted no time digging in; I was hungry. I had skipped breakfast just so I would have an appetite.

"I got you." She passed me a plate from the cabinet. "I can't wait to dig into that pasta. I love my Alfredo." She reached for a plate for herself.

"This place is really nice," I commented, then took a bite off my roll-up. It was so good, the cream cheese that she had rolled the turkey in was to die for.

"Thank you. It's a long way from where we come from, right?"

I looked around the kitchen at its decor. Nothing was cheap. "Yes." I had to agree.

"I mean, your dad's house is nice, but I came from the straight roach-infested side of South Central." Her face was sad for a moment. "But I guess it was all worth it. Look at me now." She tried to sound happy. But I could detect a lot of sadness. "So how is school going?"

"Good. Actually, better than I thought, with it being community college."

"What's wrong with community? Shit, it's college ain't it?"

"Yeah, but I always had this bad perception of community college based off other people's experiences. Thinking it wouldn't be organized and all that. But it's been great. All the advisers got me going in the right direction with my courses. And the professors are great. So either I was lied to or I'm just lucky." I shrugged my shoulders. "But now it's the work I'm concerned about, the assignments. I think I forgot all about the thought that went into school-work. Now I remember why I couldn't wait to gradu-ate." I laughed.

"Shiiit, you could have asked me and I could have reminded you. That, I won't ever forget. I couldn't wait to be out that motherfucker."

"Right." We both laughed.

"So what's next though? You can't put everything into school."

"True, so I been considering getting a job. Some-thing part-time."

Keisha burst out laughing. "Bitch, doing what? Dry cleaning or some shit." She continued to laugh.

"Ha, ha, whatever. You ain't no comedian, just know that." I gave a fake sarcastic laugh. "No, for real I was thinkin' an office job or something. I can type like sixty-five to eighty words a minute. And I'm the bomb with Excel and different computer programs, period."

"Ahh, damn, you ain't tell me you was professional material. That's what's up. But see, me, I can't go to nobody's job. Motherfuckers can't pay me enough to put up with them tryin' to boss me around."

"I feel you. The only boss I'm used to is my dad. But see, you are lucky, you living in a nice house, driving that nice Mercedes. How you do it?" I had to know. Keisha didn't have a job to think of, but she was living it up.

"I would think you should have the answer to that." She looked at me like I was naïve. "My man," she blurted out. "Hell, Quincy takes care of me. But I been gettin' money on my own for most of my life. Until Quincy came into my life, ain't nobody ever gave me shit. The hustle. That's got to be your motivation."

I nodded my head in agreement, but I wasn't sure if this advice suited me. The doorbell rang before I could respond.

"You wanna ride wit' me over on Crenshaw? I have to pick up my friend Buffy."

The mention of Crenshaw kinda had me pressed. I mean, I rode over to Crenshaw like to a business or something. But never did I venture into socializing with the neighbors. I'm from South Central and it was no joke. But sometimes other hoods didn't welcome outsiders. I guess my facial expression revealed how I felt. Keisha started laughing.

"Aye, you ain't gotta be scared, most of my family live over there. So you ain't got shit to be worried about. You cool?"

"Yeah, I'll ride," I decided.

"Me and Buffy about to check on some hair with a wholesaler that she got a connection with. Cause I'm thinkin' about opening up a hair store. Get some of that good Brazilian and Persian hair and it's gone be on an' poppin'."

"That's a good investment," I agreed. I glanced at the kitchen door, where I could hear Quincy laughing with someone.

"Girl, that's Quincy and his boy in there bullshittin'. Hold up for a minute while I grab my bag." Keisha exited the kitchen and I followed her out.

Quincy's laughter led me to the living room, but I didn't go in. I could see them from the hallway. And damn, was Quincy's "boy" fine as ever. They instantly stopped talking as I unwittingly grabbed their attention. Feeling uneasy, I tried to walk away.

"Aye, Precious. Come back, it's cool." I felt embarrassed and worried that if I turned around they might figure out what I was thinking. But I stopped and turned to face them. "Yo, this my nigga DaVon right here."

"Hey." DaVon dished out the cutest grin I had ever seen on a man.

"And like I said, this is Precious, Keisha's friend," he informed DaVon. But by the way he delivered it, I was convinced Quincy was not well versed in introducing anyone. Dude was hood as they came, but I was not mad at him.

"Hi." I felt so shy I could barely get it out.

"What the hell y'all doing to my friend? Precious, you straight?" Keisha grilled as she appeared next to me from the hallway.

"Ain't nobody doing nothin', she good." Quincy smiled. "Man, she swear she the boss up through here." Quincy passed DaVon the blunt they had been smoking. The room was lit up like Cheech and Chong. I hadn't been around weed smoke a lot growing up. My dad used to try to sneak and smoke it in the garage sometimes, but I knew from the school bathrooms exactly what it smelled like. So he really wasn't hiding nothing from me.

"Quincy, shut the hell up." Keisha twisted her lips up, pretending to check him. "Precious, you meet big-headed-ass DaVon." She smiled in his direction.

DaVon sucked the blunt, allowed the smoke to slowly escape his lips, and chuckled. "Hey, Keisha."

"What's up, DaVon? You know I got to give you a hard time. Pass me the smoke." She reached for the blunt and wasted no time inhaling. "Wanna hit it?" She passed it in my direction.

"No, I'm good." I waved it off.

"Pass that this way." Quincy reached for the blunt.

"A'ight, we out, we about to ride over on Crenshaw to scoop Buffy. I'll be back later." Keisha walked over to Quincy, then leaned down and kissed him.

I noticed DaVon staring at me. "Bye," I said softly before exiting. Finally, when we were outside, I was able to breathe. I don't know why I felt so nervous or even bothered by DaVon. I didn't know him, and he didn't know me. I wasn't the type to get in her feelings about a guy. And some unknown weed smoker would not be the first. No way.

Chapter 8

Finals were coming up in a week, along with all my other assignments, and I was completely beat because of it. I silently thanked God I didn't get a job right away as planned. The money that I still had from dad's insurance was saving me. It wasn't much, but it was right on time because there was no way I would have been able to hold down a job and school this semester. But this semester had definitely prepared me for the next. Now I knew what to expect, but for now, I had to ride this one out. I wasn't worried about passing, I would be finishing the semester on the dean's list. And I was proud of myself. The ringing of my cell phone pulled me away from studying.

I sighed as I watched Keisha's name light up. She had invited me to attend a party that she was having for Quincy. Now I had to tell her that I just couldn't make it. Initially I thought I might be able to swing it, and study, and honestly I really wanted to. Fun was something I needed in my life, but there was just no way.

"What's up, Keisha?" I answered reluctantly, because from what I learned from my friendship with Keisha, she was not going to make this easy. She hated the word *no*.

"Precious, what the hell are you doing over there? I ain't heard from you all week. You got a nigga over there or some?"

At that, I laughed. "Keisha, you are funny. I think you know better than that. It's school, I been preparing for finals. And on top of that I have two papers due in a couple of days. I told you school was a beast." I hoped she understood. But who was I kidding, she never did.

"Bitch, don't give me that. Quincy's party's tonight and you supposed to come through. What's up? You my girl, so you can't leave me hangin'."

"I know. And I want to come. But . . ."

"Yo, stop with the excuses, you can do both. It's going down tonight. Come on," Keisha begged. But I had set myself up for this one, because I knew when I answered the phone, Keisha would eat me alive. I wanted to hang up, but she might come over to get me.

"Keisha, you my girl, but I'm tired. I'm not sure I can even drive over there; I might fall asleep at the wheel." I pouted, not that it would help.

"Fuck them lame excuses, you need to have some fun. I ain't hearing nothin'. Get dressed. I will be there to pick you up."

"I don't know." I was still undecided. I sighed. "Well, I did buy an outfit to wear. I might as well rock it." I gave in.

"Yes, see how easy that was? I'll be there around eleven."

"Eleven?" I repeated, shocked. "Damn, Keisha,

now that is late." If I stayed out that late I would never get home in time to study.

"Eleven ain't that late. Hell, actually that's early. Now would you stop actin' like an old lady and be ready?"

I would have responded but Keisha hung up before I could. I swear I was gone fail, dealing with her. This had better be worth it. Shutting down my laptop and pushing my books to the side, I headed for the shower.

We pulled up to Club Shade, a hot spot club that Keisha had rented out for the party. The club was lit already when we stepped inside. "See, didn't I tell you this spot was the shit?" Keisha talked loudly in order to be heard over the music.

"It is." I admired the club; there were dancers in cages in the air, dancers swinging from shiny disco balls, the whole nine yards.

"There go Buffy." I pointed. She was already on the dance floor, twerking. We made our way over to her.

"Bitch, why I always got to see your ass first?" Keisha playfully grabbed Buffy by the butt.

"'Cause that's the best side of me." Buffy laughed. "What's up, bitch? I was wondering when you was gone get here. How you gone be late to the party you throwing?"

"I ain't never late. I'm a showstopper, remember?" A few people stepped up and spoke to Keisha, giving her hugs and what's-ups. She was like a ghetto superstar. "See, I told ya ho ass." Keisha laughed. "For real though, I had to scoop Precious."

"What's up, Precious? It's cool you came through," Buffy said while tugging at her tight dress.

"No doubt." I smiled and almost yawned at the same time. The music was on fire, but I was sleepy.

"Aye, you seen Quincy's ass yet? Have you been watchin' the door?" Keisha looked over her shoulder.

"I ain't seen that nigga yet and yes, I been watchin' out like you told me."

"Good, he ain't arrived yet then. Let's grab a drink. I need to sip." Keisha signaled a waitress over and ordered a shot.

"I'll take a martini, dry. And please, light on the vodka." I was definitely ready for a drink, and I silently prayed it would give me the boost I needed to wake up.

"Let me get that gin." Buffy went for the hard liquor.

"That's a strong one," I commented.

"Shit, you know I gets it in." Buffy twerked for good measure.

"See, Precious, that is a drunk ho talkin'." We all laughed. Keisha and Buffy were always taking shots at each other. But their friendship seemed to survive it. I liked Buffy, she was fun the few times I had hung around her. Sometimes, though, her behavior had me a little skeptical. I couldn't quite put my finger on it. Well, I guess I could say the girl was wild and super ghetto, but I didn't want to judge her so I didn't.

"Bitch, there go Quincy, get on your feet," Buffy announced, still dancing.

Keisha jumped to her feet and grabbed a bottle along with the four waitresses in VIP. They all popped bottles at the same time as he entered, and everyone started singing happy birthday. Quincy had been escorted to VIP with three of the baddest strippers LA had to offer and he was all smiles. They would be his private dancers all night. Keisha smiled, loving the enjoyment on his face from her gift.

"You did good," Quincy said loudly over the music, then kissed Keisha. His entourage stood back. The waitresses stepped forward with bottles. Then one of the strippers handed Quincy an unopened bottle and he popped it. "Pour the fuck up!" he yelled with his bottle in the air.

From that point on, drinks start flowing and everybody was having a good time. A few drinks later I was having so much fun that I had forgotten all about sleep. Not that I could sleep anyway. Buffy was bouncing off all our laps one by one, attempting to give us lap dances. I pushed her off me and she nearly fell to the floor. She jumped in Keisha's lap next and got the same result. Their friend Nicole, on the other hand, played along, smacking Buffy on the butt. They both worked together at the same strip club, so they were in their element.

Keisha looked at them and laughed. "I swear, you hos don't never take time off from work. But I ain't throwing my money atcha asses. My bands ain't gone make yo' ass dance."

"Don't be so sure. Ayee!" Buffy laughed then bounced her butt up and down. "Precious, if you still thinkin' about getting a part-time job, they hiring down at the club. That body look tight to me. You could get them coins. And check this, that shit easy; them thirsty niggas will spend all they bitches' rent money up there." I was surprised by her offer, but she was tripping at best. This was one option I didn't have to think about. My dad would turn over in his grave.

"No, thanks. I'm gone pass on this one. Trust me, I'm cool." I kept my reply simple. It was best that way. If I elaborated any more, it might come out offensive.

"Stop inviting people down there. Don't nobody want to shake they ass up in Shake That." Keisha referred to the club Buffy and Nicole danced at. "That shithole is dangerous. They down there stickin' niggas up and shootin' at least two times a week."

Buffy covered her mouth and laughed. "Bitch, I can't even front, you ain't lyin'."

"I swear she ain't. Them niggas gettin' worse too." Nicole threw in her two cents. "But yo, I gots to get paid." Nicole started twerking and we all laughed.

My laughing turned to apprehension as I watched Quincy's friend DaVon approach us. Quincy, standing a few steps away from him, met DaVon halfway. They did a handshake. DaVon's presence grabbed everyone's attention. We observed him hand off a bottle of champagne to Quincy.

"Damn, I swear DaVon's ass always ballin'. That's a bottle of that Krug, that shit is like twenty-five hundred a bottle."

My eyes almost popped out of my head. I could not believe what I had just heard. I tried to zone in on the bottle, because for that kind of money it had to be special. I could remember Dad complaining about buying a cheap bottle of wine to go with his dinner.

"Girl, you know DaVon got it like that. He need to

come on down to Shake That and spread them coins around," Nicole said.

"I second that." Buffy raised her right hand and giggled. "With his fine ass." She eyed him up and down, then seductively licked her lips.

"Now, bitch, I think you and I both know that DaVon don't fuck around in that shithole y'all call a strip club."

I almost laughed until I caught DaVon eyeing me. I gave him a shy glance before looking away. I was caught off guard as Keisha grabbed ahold of my right arm and pulled me up as T.I. and Iggy's "No Mediocre" blasted out of the speakers. "Let's dance, this my shit."

I was no dancer, but those drinks had me feeling good so I gave it all I got and it didn't seem like I was doing too bad. But one thing was for sure, those drinks were coming down on me because my dance confidence was on boost.

"Bitch, I don't know what's up, but ya boy DaVon got his eyes glued to you," Keisha leaned over and whispered in my ear.

"Nonsense." I sighed and kept dancing. I would have sat down, but the next song was a banger too, so I kept dancing. Usher's old-school song "Slow Jam" came on next and forced me to move toward my seat. Quincy was in Keisha's face within seconds of the song coming on. She wasted no time wrapping her arms around his neck as he gripped her butt. I couldn't help but smile at them.

I saw Buffy and Nicole each grinding on a dude. I wondered if they knew who they were. But knowing those girls, I didn't waste no time betting on it. On my way to sit I asked a waitress to deliver me a martini, this time with an extra shot. No sooner had I sat than the waitress was standing in front of me.

I took two sips of my drink, then watched DaVon take even steps in my direction. The thought of him being close had me feeling nervous. I gazed downward with the hope that he was not headed for me, but my prayers went unanswered. I looked up in time to read his lips. "Can I sit down?" He pointed to the empty space next to me.

"Well, it is a free country." I tried to sound bold. But on the inside my heart was pounding so hard I wondered if it was possible he could hear it over the music.

"Precious, right?" he said as if he was trying to verify my name. But I had to admit I was surprised that he even remembered.

"You have a good memory." Impressed, I had to fight to hold back my smile.

"Ain't no way I would forget that." He returned my smile. "So you live around here?" He wasted no time jumping to the next question.

"No, I'm from South Central," I shared proudly. I was never embarrassed about where I came from.

"Me too." He nodded his head. Knowing he was from South Central helped me loosen up. It made me feel as if we had something in common. I was glad for it. We conversed while I finished my drink. And he didn't hesitate when it came to making it clear that he was interested in me. I didn't know what to think about that, so I chose not to speak on it. But I did like his vibe; he seemed to be cool.

"Yo, DaVon." Quincy yelled over the music to get DaVon's attention. He waved him over to where he was standing with a short, stocky dude.

Keisha stepped in out of nowhere, grabbed me by the wrist and pulled me to the side. I didn't know what was so urgent she couldn't wait. "See, I told you that nigga was feelin' you."

"I wouldn't take it that far. He's just being nice." I tried to downplay it.

"Precious, do not play wit' me. I know that you know better than that."

"I see you, Precious." Buffy sucked her teeth and grinned at me. "Umm-hmm, over here puttin' your hooks into DaVon." She twisted up her lips and smacked them at the same time.

I had to look at them both; they were really feeding into whatever they thought they had seen. "It's not like that." I smiled at their assumption, but I was serious.

"Is that all he was doing, huh?" I took Buffy's tone to be sarcastic but she laughed. "Well you might want to watch out, I been tryin' to sit on that nigga face for a long time now," Buffy declared. I glared at her, hoping to understand her reasoning for putting her business out like that.

"Bitch, please. I think you also know DaVon ain't fuckin' wit' you like that," Keisha added.

"How da fuck you know with yo' hating ass?" Buffy wasted no time gathering a quick comeback.

Keisha reached out her hand and gently grabbed a waitress's arm. "Bring this bitch a shot of Hennessy, she is delusional."

Nicole burst out laughing. I followed suit, it was just too funny not to.

"Well, at least you are honest," Nicole added.

Buffy looked at us all, one by one, and playfully rolled her eyes. "I swear y'all bitches don't give me a break." She turned around and started bouncing her ass up and down to Young Jeezy's "SupaFreak." "Come on Precious, let's fuck up the dance floor."

"That's my song so let's do it." I stood up and bounced my booty like Buffy.

"Ayee," Keisha chanted.

We all made our way to the dance floor and Quincy approached Keisha from behind. She bent over and grinded on him.

Keisha walked over to us as the song ended. "Hey, Quincy's ready to bounce."

"Me too. I'm tired," I threw in. I was surprised I had made it this far.

"It's still early. I swear y'all wack. But whatever." Buffy popped her mouth. "Nicole, you feel like hittin' up another spot?"

"Nah, I'm good. The bed sounds nice." Nicole's eyes were looking droopy.

We all headed outside. Keisha was clearly drunk because she staggered several times and held on to Quincy. Buffy said, "Bitch, how yo' lightweight drunk ass gone drive home? Precious, I'm tellin' you, she gone kill both of y'all. Quincy, you better wake yo' drunk ass up cause you gone be dead in a minute." Buffy went on and on.

"Shut the hell up, Buffy. I got this." Keisha attempted to stand straight on her own. But she still showed signs of being wobbly.

"Hey, I can take you home." DaVon stepped in beside me. I looked at Keisha and Quincy. A blind man could see that Keisha was indeed drunk and did not need to be driving, but I could not ride with a stranger.

"No thanks, I'll be good, but Keisha, you shouldn't

be driving. You two just go on home and I'll take a cab."

"Nah, not cool, anything could go wrong. My man will get you home." Quincy spoke up and pointed at DaVon. I gave Quincy an iffy look then fixed my eyes on DaVon. I could tell he was enjoying his friend having his back.

"You can trust me." He smiled at me.

Keisha stepped in front of DaVon with her hands on both her hips. "She sure can, cause I'll fuck you up on sight about my friend, DaVon."

"Mane, come yo' ass on here, Keisha. Always pullin' gangsta-ass moves." Quincy chuckled. DaVon laughed.

"Nigga, shut up." Keisha playfully rolled her eyes then smiled at me.

"Aye, follow me to the crib in Keisha's ride," Quincy yelled to one of his peons, then tossed the keys over to him.

DaVon grabbed my attention. "Precious, my ride is right over this way." He pointed in the direction of his car.

Briefly, I considered sticking to my guns about the cab, but I no longer felt like the hassle was worth it. "Keisha, I will call you tomorrow." I gave in.

"A'ight." Keisha leaned in closer to Quincy. I fell into step next to DaVon and headed toward his car.

Buffy yelled out, "Don't do nothing I wouldn't do." I slowed my stride and glanced at her. I could have been overthinking it, but her tone seemed to have a bit of jealousy in it. I didn't respond though, I smiled and kept stepping. Soon we were standing in front of a Maybach. A bulky white guy stepped out and opened the back door. DaVon instructed me to climb inside. I looked at him to be sure he was telling me to climb into the Maybach. The bulky white guy smiled. DaVon noticed my apprehension. "This is my car," he clarified. "Go ahead and get inside." I was confused because I was under the impression that he would be driving me home. He never said there would be a driver. Once inside, DaVon looked at me and grinned. I guess my question was written all over my face.

"I guess I should have told you I had my driver with me tonight. See, sometimes when I know I'm going to turn up I bring him along. This way I don't have to worry about unnecessary hassle from LA's finest."

He didn't need to say anymore on that matter. Because it was no secret to anyone that LA cops were known for their petty harassment. Especially of black men. But I didn't bother to comment on that. "Okay," was my only reply. The ride home was quiet, besides me giving his driver my address. DaVon tried making conversation, but once I sat down in that luxury car, sleep came down all over me. I could barely keep my eyes open, and at some point I must have dozed off. When I opened my eyes, we were sitting in front of my house. I felt bad for going to sleep, but my reason was legit. DaVon insisted that he walk me to my door. I tried to decline, but of course he wouldn't take no for an answer. Once at the door, he requested my number. I didn't have the energy to explain why I didn't want him to have it. So I gave it to him.

Chapter 9

It had been about two weeks since Quincy's party. Even though I had been exhausted from partying, the fun had helped me relax during my exams. I passed all my exams with flying colors. Studying and dedication had paid off.

I still couldn't believe I had accepted DaVon's offer to give me a ride home and had given him my number. He had called me twice trying to get me to go out with him. But each time I had turned him down. Deep down I wanted to go, but I just didn't have the time. I wasn't sure if I was ready for dating. If I dated, what should I expect? But I also wanted to have some fun sometimes. Or maybe just more fun besides hanging with Keisha and crazy-ass Buffy. That's why when DaVon called me up for the third time and asked what I liked to do, I told him bowling. And when he offered to take me to do just that, I agreed. He wanted to pick me up, but I assured him I would get there on my own.

I had taken one ride too many from him, and that really was to benefit Keisha, but I wouldn't have him drive me twice. I didn't need him getting any ideas. As for bowling though, now that I could agree to. After jumping in the shower, I threw on a pair of jeans and a thin blouse, and hopped in my Toyota and got into traffic. I wanted to feel relaxed when I arrived, so I put on Sisqó's "Incomplete." I was crazy for old-school music and the song did the job.

I pulled up to the Lucky Strike bowling alley, and to my surprise DaVon was standing outside, waiting on me. I hadn't expected him to be outside, and while I wasn't embarrassed about my car, I wasn't sure if I wanted him to see it. Driving off into the third row I found a parking spot and scrambled out.

A huge smile spread across DaVon's face as I approached him. He spoke up first. "Hey there, Ms. Lady." Just looking at him made me want to melt. DaVon looked to be about six foot four, two hundred pounds, dark chocolate, a flat fade, and just plain handsome.

"Hey," I replied. "You didn't have to stand out here and wait on me."

"I was inside, but then I started to worry you might not show. So I came out here to wait."

"You did not have to do that. If I said I was coming, I meant it." I laughed.

"A'ight, next time I'll remember."

I smiled at his arrogance. What made him think there would be a second date?

"Come on, let's go inside." He opened the door for me.

Once inside, we got our shoes and picked our bowling balls. He said, "You don't think you are about to beat me, do you?"

"Actually, pretty sure I am. Just sit and watch." I finished typing my name on the keyboard as one of the players. "Now you take lessons." I fitted my fingers into the bowling bowl, then hit the lanes. Sizing up the pins and the distance, I set my stance and released the ball. I watched as the four pins close to the left side fell. I slowly turned around.

Just as I thought, he had a huge grin on his face. "It's okay. It's early," he joked.

"And you are so right. Plus, this medium ball is too big. I might have to try a small." I made up excuses. Picking up my ball again, I attempted another try. This time I knocked none of the pins down. I smiled as I faced him.

He grinned. "Don't worry, I'll take it easy on you this go around. Maybe I'll leave one pin for a second chance." Grabbing his ball, he made his way to the lanes. Once his ball started rolling, I watched as it slowly approached the pins; all fell but three.

"So is that the new taking it easy?" I played at being sarcastic.

"Yep. A little something, something." He pulled the tip of his shirt like he was popping his collar. I couldn't help but laugh.

Trying a few more of the small balls, I found one that fit me perfectly. "It's on now," I chanted.

"You don't really believe that's going to help you?" He referred to my ball.

"I guess we'll see." Strutting up to the lane, I sent my ball off without any contemplating. No surprise, I knocked all the pins down on the first try.

"Okay, I see you. But I'm sure it's just luck."

"You can call it that. But I assure you it's not." DaVon stepped up for his turn, but little did he know it was over for him. For the next thirty minutes I knocked down all of my pins almost every time. I was having so much fun. Until now, I hadn't realized how much I missed bowling. I couldn't help but laugh when DaVon realized I had hustled him from the beginning.

"So were you gone tell me you're a pro?"

"No, I promise you this is beginner's luck." I laughed.

"Nah, you ain't foolin' me. Come clean."

"A'ight, you got me. My dad and I bowled a couple times a week. It was our thing. He taught me since I was like nine. He was the pro. He was on a bowling team and they were like serious, competing in contests all over the city, winning money."

"Oh, so you just gone hustle me, huh?"

"Not hustle. School," I joked.

"A'ight, it's cool. I got to give you your props . . . You want to get some wings or something from the bar?"

"Nah, I'm thirsty though. I'll take a Coke."

"A'ight, sit here and chill. I'll be right back." He walked away but stopped and turned to face me. "Aye, and no cheating. That means don't take my turn." He chuckled.

"Your turn is safe with me." I laughed.

While he was off getting my Coke, I glanced around the bowling alley for the first time and took it all in. I thought about my dad. I could see him placing his bowling bag on the table, taking out the bowling ball and all but kissing it, with a gleam in his eyes. He had true love for the game.

"Coke on ice," DaVon announced as he approached, bringing my thoughts back to reality.

"Thank you." I immediately took a huge swig from the straw. I was really thirsty.

"So I take it you and your family are from here?" He also had a pitcher of beer and a frosty cold glass on a tray.

I really wasn't prepared to talk about my family, or lack thereof, mainly because there wasn't much to say. But I was enjoying myself, and what could it hurt? "Actually, I don't have a lot of family. It's just me and my dad . . . I mean *was* me and my dad . . ." I paused because the last part was just hard to say. "My dad . . . he died recently." I took another drink, but while the straw was at my lips, I caught the all-too-familiar sadness that was in DaVon's eyes.

"What about you? Where is your family?" Surely, he didn't mind me getting personal since he wasted no time checking my family history.

"Well, let me see . . ." He seemed to go into deep thought. His breathing slowed; his hurt was apparent. I pushed mine aside and braced for the sad news he was sure to deliver. "My mom died in childbirth when I was ten, leaving me the only child. I went to live with my aunt, but she died two years after my mother. My aunt didn't have kids and their parents were dead . . . all my life it had only been my mom and aunt around. From what I knew, we had other relatives, but none that we were in touch with. So with no one to claim me, I ended up in foster care." I thought I saw water fill his eyes, but he blinked and it was gone.

The mention of foster care made my heart break for him. Thankfully, my dad had been around until I was an adult. But it felt ironic knowing our backgrounds were somewhat similar: We both were the only child, no parents or family. "Wait, what about your dad?" I realized he hadn't mentioned him.

"I never knew the bastard," he said flat out. But the tone of his voice was geared more toward anger than hurt.

After that, I decided it was time to change the conversation to something else because if we kept up with this one we would both be in tears. To get back on the positive side, I grabbed my bowling ball and promised to finish my win. And I made good on the promise. We laughed and talked the entire time; his conversation was good.

I enjoyed myself so much that I agreed to go out with him on a second date. That date turned into another, and by the third date, DaVon made it clear that he was feeling me. And I was enjoying him, but I was not ready to say it. I needed time to get my thoughts together. I had a lot to focus on, and he seemed to understand.

"Damn, Precious. I know you didn't forget to get ranch with these buffalo wings. Cause ain't no way I can eat these wings without it." Like a madwoman Keisha searched the bag the wings had been in.

"They didn't put none in the bag?" I said, surprised. I had ordered a fifty-piece wing tray, so it should have been common sense for them to put ranch or some type of dipping sauce in the bag.

"Girl, you know you have to ask. These bitches are simple." Keisha had thrown down the bag, given up her ranch hunt. She bit into a wing.

"Ain't that it," I said in agreement. I shook my head from disappointment. "Check the fridge though, it's some in there." I pulled a few wineglasses out of the cabinet. Keisha had come through so that we could hang out. I had stopped off and got some wings, some wine, and a few other snacks so that we could catch up. It had been a few weeks since we had been able to kick it.

"Saved by the bell!" Keisha chanted as she pulled the ranch from the fridge. "I swear them bitches up there was about to hear from me."

I couldn't help but smile at her threat, cause I felt the same way. "Come on, grab the wings. I got the wine and other snacks in the living room." I led the way.

In the living room, we sat down and got comfortable and geared up to chat. I filled both of our wineglasses with Moscato.

"These wings are so good. Addicting is the only way I know how to describe them." Keisha's wing was dripping with ranch. I threw a few on my saucer and scooted back on the couch.

"So you gone tell me what's up with DaVon, or what? The last I heard a few weeks back you two were going bowling."

"And we did." I bit off my wing and chewed. I had known these questions were coming.

"And?" Keisha pressured me to give her more.

"The date was cool . . . DaVon, he cool too. But since that date we been on several others," I admitted.

"Shit for real? Well you mighty calm about the situation to say y'all been on several dates. Don't hold out. Spill all the juicy. Did he hit it?" Her eyebrows raised.

Her question sent me to the edge of the couch because I knew she was not asking me what I thought. "Did he hit what?"

"Bitch, *it*! That ass. Fuck, you mean it?"

"Hell no. I just met him." My mouth was wide-open from shock.

Keisha laughed. "Shit, there ain't no time stamp on sex. You feelin' him. So what's the problem? Precious, you a grown-ass woman. And he fine as hell too. Unless you blind." She didn't wait on me to answer the question and gave me reason all at the same time.

"All that may be true. But I ain't no ho." I hoped I was clear on the matter.

"Ain't nobody labeling you as no ho, but word of advice you better stop playin' around. DaVon a catch. And in these gritty streets that shit hard to come by."

That, too, was true, but in my opinion that was no reason to go jumping in the bed with him either. "You right, I might be moving too slow, but he don't need me. Buffy seemed to make it clear at the club that she wants him anyway."

"Girl, DaVon don't want Buffy's ass and she knows that. Trust. Hell, don't even take her seriously." Keisha smiled, then pulled out a small baggy with weed in it. She shook the bag in my face. "I'm done with all the small talk. Let's roll up. You gone chief with me."

"Nah, I'm cool, this the only peace I need." I raised my wineglass. "Like I told you before, I don't do that." I nodded my head at the bag.

"Hmm, I guess ain't nothin' wrong wit' that if you choose." She giggled. "But for me this offers freedom, and I need that." She pulled out a Swisher and I watched her as she sliced it open down the middle, emptied the contents, and then filled it with green trees. I really wasn't into it, but I had to be honest, the smell was enticing. After licking the blunt and making sure it was sealed to her liking, Keisha gave me a wide grin, then pulled out her lighter and lit it. I watched her inhale then slowly blow the smoke out.

"Listen, don't let DaVon's fine ass slip through your fingers. You'll regret it."

"Keisha, we only been on a few dates. I'ma just let it flow and see what happens. Besides, I can't look forward to much, school is still my main focus. I don't want to let anything throw me off that path. Enough time been wasted on me not getting my education already."

"Yo to school, I say fuck that. I ain't sayin' forget about it altogether, but hey, DaVon got money. Plenty of it." She stressed that part. "He can buy you whatever you want . . . You like my car, right? You want one just like it, right? Well, DaVon the man who can get it for you. Hell, two or three of them to be exact."

Just watching Keisha was comical, her facial expressions were serious yet dramatic. And she held on to that blunt so tight I thought she might squeeze the weed out of it. I couldn't help but laugh; she was making her point. "Keisha, you are a gold digger for sure." I sipped my wine and laughed some more.

Unfazed, Keisha hit her blunt. Next, she reached into her purse and pulled out a stack of money. From where I was sitting, I could make out they were all hundred-dollar bills. "Now you can call me what you want, but this spends." She started shaking the money in the air. That was another point she was attempting to make. And I couldn't help but agree, but that still didn't change my mind. My dad had raised me to be independent, to think for myself, to trust in myself. To him, that was an important foundation, so I didn't know anything else. Money was good, and I knew better than anyone that it was needed, that it made the world go around, but I didn't believe that it was worth everything, that you sold your soul for it. And for that I thanked my dad. But instead of saying that to Keisha, I chose to sip my wine, bit off another wing, and watched her slide that beautiful stack back into her beautiful Burberry bag.

Chapter 10

Talking to Keisha and hearing all her reasons as to why I needed to date DaVon, I came to the conclusion that maybe I was moving too fast going on all those dates with him. At first the dates were fun, but once Keisha put a price on it, it felt complicated. So I decided to just chill for a minute. Now I just had to share that with him, but I hadn't decided how to tell him. Sipping on my strawberry daiquiri, I watched my cell phone as his name ran across the screen. I had been ignoring his calls for the past few days. I didn't feel good about it, but I didn't know what else to do. This dating thing was new to me since my dad hadn't allowed it.

Then I started to wonder if my dad would have approved of DaVon. Besides knowing he grew up in foster homes and was parentless like me, I didn't know much else about him. He appeared to be a good guy. Out of everything Keisha had mentioned about him, that was the one and most important thing that she left out. But how much should I know about a guy before getting serious?

But I also knew it was hard for my dad to approve of any guy who liked me. I was his one and only precious daughter, and he didn't want anyone to take that away. Just thinking about him brought a huge smile to my face. Picking up my daiquiri, I suddenly had the urge to be close to my dad. I walked to Dad's room and started going through a few of his belongings. I had planned to go through them eventually, but it had just taken longer than I expected. The empty boxes I had planned to use to store things were scattered about the room as if they had been waiting on me. Truthfully, I just had not been ready, but now I was. I pulled out things one by one and determined what needed to go into the boxes that would go into the attic.

I fought tears as I picked up an old locket that Dad had shown me when I was about twelve years old. At that time, he had stressed to me how important the locket was to the family, as it had come from his mother. It was the one and only thing besides a few pictures that he had that belonged to her. My tears of sadness turned to tears of joy as I opened the locket and observed the picture inside of my grandmother and my father when he was a kid. I smiled as the idea entered my head to have it cleaned up. I closed the locket, kissed it, and carefully put it to the side. It would not be going into the attic. Next, I decided to go through the brown trunk that had forever sat in the corner of his closet. Pulling it out into the middle of the floor, I was surprised to find it locked. But then I remembered some keys I had found in his chest of drawers under his polo shirts. I wondered if one of those keys fit. Making my way over to the chest, I retrieved the keys.

Luckily, one of them worked and I was glad because I was not in the mood to be searching for more keys or breaking my way inside. To my shock, the trunk was full of women's clothing, petite in size. I knew right away the neatly folded clothes didn't belong to me. The style of the clothes was old-fashioned. Curious, I started to pull them out. Then I started to wonder who they could have belonged to. At the bottom of the trunk, I felt something hard. I removed the piece of clothing on top of the object and discovered a green box. Slowly, I pulled off the lid. Inside was a stack of letters. I saw that they were addressed to my dad.

I needed to know what the letters said. I removed the thick, tan-colored rubber band, took the papers from each envelope, and read the letters one by one. They were from my mother. In each one, she begged my father to let her see me, and each letter contained a telephone number where she could be contacted. As I approached the bottom of the pile, I realized that the last letter was postmarked when I was about six years old. From the looks of it, no letters had come after that, or they just were not in the box.

Confused and filled with emptiness, I folded the letters up, placed them back inside the envelopes, and put the lid on top of the green box. Suddenly all types of crazy, wild thoughts invaded my mind. What did these letters mean? Did they mean anything at all? My dad always had told me that my mother, Lacey, was dead. According to him, she had died when I was a baby. Annoyed, I become extremely agitated as I realized I had never asked how she died but also that he had never offered the information.

He had been there for me, taking care of me, for as long as I could remember. So when it came to my mother, I hadn't dwelled on it. There had been a stint in high school when I was a bit curious about her as a person and I had tried to ask him a few things. But he had been so saddened by me talking about her that I stopped asking.

But here I was, faced with these letters from my supposedly dead mother, who should have been dead when these were written. She had written on my birthdays and holidays consistently. Tears flowed from my eyes like busted faucets. My gut churned with nausea. I held my stomach and questioned myself. Had my father lied to me? Suddenly, my tears were anger. Why had my dad lied to me? I had trusted him and only him all of my life. Believed every word out of his mouth, never once questioned anything. Here I was, left alone in this world, when I could have known my mother. Why? Why lie to me all of my life?

A feeling of emptiness and betrayal took over me and seeped from my veins, because I would never have the answers that I wanted. Needed. No, I would be left alone for the rest of my lonely life to wonder why, and what if. Then I remembered that I only had my father to thank for that.

Chapter 11

I couldn't shake my dad's betrayal, no matter how hard I tried; it had consumed me. Feeling depressed, I shut myself inside the house, unable to go any-where. A new semester had started at school and I had missed an entire week. I wanted to go, but I knew I wouldn't be able to concentrate because the only thing that had my full attention was the mother that I didn't know. Was she still out there? Had she given up on me after begging for so long? I couldn't shake the constant funk I was in. To make myself feel better, I had even tried to rationalize Dad's state of mind. But I concluded that Dad was a strong man and he never did anything that he didn't want to do. So there was no excuse.

In the kitchen, I pulled a can of Sprite out of the refrigerator, popped the top, and started pouring it into a glass. The sudden ringing of my doorbell an-noyed me. I didn't have any idea who it could be. But I wished that whoever it was would just go away; I wasn't in the mood. Wrapping my hand around the cold glass, I took a swig of the Sprite. The doorbell started ringing again. I sighed and realized I might as well answer it, because whoever it was didn't seem to be taking the hint and going away.

Placing my glass on the kitchen counter, I reluctantly headed to the door. Annoyed, I didn't even look to see who it was before swinging the door open. With a scowl on my face, I was prepared to kick whoever it was off my property. But to my surprise, I came face-to-face with DaVon. Never in a million years would I have expected him to show up at my house unannounced. The first and only thing that came to mind was the headscarf that my hair was wrapped in. Without saying one word, I immediately shut the door in his face and raced to the hallway bathroom. Quickly, I unwrapped my hair and allowed it to fall to my shoulders. DaVon started to knock again. Making my way back to the door, I yelled, "What?"

"Aye, I wanted to check on you to see if you were okay."

Am I okay? I silently repeated to myself. What was this all about? But I didn't want to ask him that; it would require me to hold a conversation. So I decided to keep it simple. "Yes," I replied from my side of the door.

He didn't reply right away, so I hoped that was enough for him, that maybe he was gone. "Precious, will you please open the door?" I should have known that would be next.

"Listen, I would but I'm busy. I'll call you," I lied.

"Come on, I just want to see you for a minute," he begged.

For some reason his begging made me feel guilty. Turning the bottom lock, I opened the door halfway and stood in the gap. "What's up?" I sighed. I wished he would just go away.

"I just wanted to come through and check to see if you were okay. I been hittin' you up for a couple of weeks. Your phone been going to voicemail, so I thought what could be better than face-to-face?" He hunched his shoulders.

"Well, you've seen me, I'm fine. Now you can say goodbye. Cause like I said, I'm busy." With that, I attempted to shut the door.

He placed the palm of his hand on the door, stopping it. I paused and glared at him. He was looking so good. "Can I please come in?" he asked with a slight smile on his face. "I promise not to stay long." He was not giving up.

Opening the door wider, I stepped to the side so he could enter. I shut the door behind him, and he stared at me as if he was trying to take me all in. I felt so unsexy. I had just gotten out of the shower not long before he arrived, so I only had on a pair of sweats and T-shirt. I led the way to the den. "Go in and have a seat. I'll be right back."

In my room I changed into a pair of fitted jeans, fitted T-shirt, then pulled my hair back into a soft ponytail. Back in the den, I found DaVon looking around the room at my old pictures. Some were of me in school and some were family pictures Dad and I had taken.

"So why are you really here?" I asked.

"Like I said, I really wanted to check on you. I haven't heard from you. I tried reaching out by phone but got nothing." I really wished he wouldn't repeat that.

"Can I get you something to drink?" I offered. I

thought it better to change the conversation because I didn't know what to say to that. My life was complicated, but I didn't want to share that with him.

"Nah, I'm cool. Seeing you is enough."

I wasn't sure what those words did to me, but suddenly I was glad he was there and I was not in a hurry for him to leave. We got to talking and decided on ordering up some food and watched a movie.

That night turned into more nights, and just like that we were back to hanging out and going on dates. I was enjoying myself and his company. Turns out, his company was what I needed to begin reviving myself. Keisha had reached out. She was ready to hang, but I was too busy for that. I had returned to school and I had booked my free time with DaVon in advance.

I still thought about my dad and his betrayal daily, but I was ready to push it to the side. I was tired of torturing myself with the ifs, ands, or buts. Whatever his reasoning was, be it selfishness or for my own good, I would never know. What I did know was that he didn't have the right to lie to me. And I was angry as hell about it. But this was my life now and I could live it the way I saw fit. No one could tell me what to do with it, how to think, or assume what was good or bad for me. I had believed that my dad was a good, honest man who only sought to raise his daughter to be the best person that she could be. All lies. But now my eyes were wide open. I saw life as it really was, and I had a new take on it. And I was taking control of mine and officially becoming DaVon's lady.

Chapter 12

Although DaVon and I had fallen into the role of being a couple, we hadn't talked about it yet. We were still just having fun, enjoying each other. Especially me. I laughed as much as possible, and I needed it. I guess you could say it was therapeutic. But tonight was something different. I had finally accepted his offer to have dinner at his house. Originally, I planned on driving, but he insisted on sending a car, so I gave in. After the long ride I was glad that I had accepted his offer, especially once we pulled up to the gated community in Bel-Air where he lived. The driver slowed down so that I could take in the full sight of the mansion. Its outside beauty truly made my jaw drop. Like everyone else I knew, I had heard about Bel-Air and seen it on television a few times. I mean, who hasn't watched *The Fresh Prince of Bel-Air*? But never had I been there.

The circular driveway was unbelievable. The driver opened my door and I climbed out and made my way up to the door. I wasn't sure because I didn't want to stare, but I could have sworn there was a chandelier hanging outside the door.

"I thought you might never get here." DaVon opened the door before I could ring the doorbell or knock.

"Well, never didn't come. Cause here I am." I smiled. For a brief second, I felt nervous about going inside. Butterflies jumped around in my stomach like hot firecrackers.

DaVon reached out for my hand. I was glad he had done that. Otherwise I might have just stood there like a statue. "Come on inside." Soon as I was inside, he wrapped me in his arms. "I waited all day for this." A smile spread about my lips. My eyes captured the floors. I wasn't exactly sure what real marble looked like, but my intuition said this had to be it. And I was too embarrassed to ask. "You look beautiful, as always." He ate me up with his eyes.

"And you too," I returned without hesitation. Since he was cooking—well, his chef was preparing the meal—I had decided to wear a cute mini dress and some heels so that I looked formal. "Your house is beautiful."

"Thank you. Let me show you around. I want you to feel right at home whenever you are here." He said that like I would be there all the time. Maybe he had forgotten, but I was just there for dinner.

The house was amazing; he showed me every inch and I was wowed. Never in a million years could I have imagined it would be like this. I had never envisioned being invited to a place so beautiful. Then I realized that with all that was going on with myself, issues with school, and my dad, never once had we discussed nor had I asked him what he did for a living, but I guessed now was not the time. I was about to say forget it and ask him anyway when his chef announced dinner was about to be served. I decided to save it for another time.

"Would you like another slice of pie?" DaVon looked at me like I was on the menu.

"I can't eat anything else. I am stuffed. Compliments to you and the chef."

"It was nothin'. This is what he do," he bragged playfully. "Let's go in the den for drinks."

In the den, I was equally stunned to find he had it set up for the date. A bottle of Montrachet Chardonnay chilling on ice, chocolate-covered strawberries, candles, the whole nine. Seeing the room set up like this sent my brain cells hopping around. What was he expecting from me? My thoughts must have been written on my face.

"Don't be alarmed." He gently grasped my right hand. "I just want us to relax and unwind after our meal," he explained. "No expectations."

"No, I like it. It's nice." I took in a deep breath, thankful that he'd quickly cleared that up.

He took the lead and I followed him inside. I sat down on the huge, comfortable sofa as he poured us both a glass of wine. After handing me my glass, he sat down next to me. I took a sip, and the taste sent tingles through my whole body.

"That was good," I said. I sucked in my bottom lip to savor the taste.

"That good, huh?" DaVon grinned at me.

"Yes." I grinned. Leaning into me, DaVon came in for a kiss and I was more than willing to oblige him.

The wine had done its job and relaxed me. DaVon was such a good kisser. He had schooled me and I was getting better.

"Now that was good for me." He licked his lips like he could taste me on them. I laughed. Looking around again, I was wowed by his home. "This house is so beautiful. I can't believe you live here all alone."

"Yep, just me. I have a housekeeper named Maria; she comes about three to four days a week. I consider Maria family. Other than that, I'm always here alone."

"Well, it's spic-and-span, so she does a good job . . ." I paused as I thought about all the nice cars that DaVon drove, this big house that he lived in alone. Everything about his lifestyle smelled like money. I didn't want to be out of line. But the question was eating at me like a bedbug at feast time. I spilled my questions in his lap. "So, what is it that you do for a living? Where do you work?" I broke it down even more. I didn't want there to be any question about what I was asking.

Silence covered the room and I was not sure if that meant that I should be alarmed, so I sipped my wine and waited.

"I expected you to ask me this eventually," he finally said.

"I guess it would be only natural. And no disrespect is intended, but I would like an answer." I had not expected to say that, but at this moment in my life, I was not about to accept lies. My dad had done enough of that to last me a lifetime.

The gleam left his eyes and a serious look took over. I would have braced myself, but I wasn't exactly sure how. So I just listened.

"I deal in supply and demand . . . lots of it."

The glass in my hand suddenly felt slippery. I didn't need him to go into full detail because I knew exactly what he meant. I may have been sheltered growing up, but I was from South Central, and had attended public school all of my life. Drugs were nothing new to me. I just had never dealt with anyone up close and personal in it.

"In fact, some might say I'm on the fast track to become a kingpin. Quincy and everyone you have seen around him . . . they work for me," he went on to explain. I didn't say anything, but suddenly everything made perfect sense to me. The whole setup. "I know it's a lot, but I gotta know, are you okay with the hustle? Because that's what I do full-time. Nonstop." His question was bold and the acceptance in his tone was blunt.

"Yes." The word jumped out of my mouth so fast I was in disbelief. But I sounded bold and in control, as if I knew what I was accepting. Inside though, I was frightened as to what I was stepping into. What would my dad think? I answered that question in my head right away. I didn't care. This was my life, and now DaVon was my man. His life was my life.

Placing my wineglass on the table, I gently pulled DaVon's glass from his hand and set it beside mine. Placing both arms around his neck, I stuck my tongue in his mouth and started to suck his; he matched me stroke for stroke. A warm feeling took control of my entire body and led my every move. I reached for DaVon's shirt and tugged at it. I wanted it off and desired my clothes off as well. DaVon wasted no time helping me undress. Laying me down, DaVon took full control.

But I had to share my secret first. "DaVon," I whispered.

"Yes, babe?" he whispered back.

"I'm a virgin," I announced as if I would be charged a fee for the slight inconvenience.

Hovering over me, he kissed my lips gently. "Don't worry, I'll be gentle. Next stop, ecstasy."

And that he did. I relaxed as he continued to guide me and successfully led me to complete ecstasy, a feeling I would never be able to describe.

Chapter 13

To say my relationship with DaVon took off full speed ahead like *The Fast and the Furious* would be an understatement. And we decided right away that we wanted to be close with each other at all times. So I moved in with him and fell right into position. Even though I was still angry and confused about my dad and his true intentions for my life, I did not want to sell the house. It still held all of my childhood memories and I did not intend to lose that. I had lost enough. And since DaVon's house was so far, there was no way I would be making that long drive to keep it clean. So instead I hired a housekeeper to go in twice a week to clean. I would drop by every other week or so to check on the house and retrieve the mail.

Everything was working out for the best. I was doing well in school and looking forward to putting that accomplishment behind me. As for DaVon, I couldn't have asked for a better man. From the time I woke up in the morning until I lay down at night, he made sure I was happy and didn't want for anything. Recently, he had bought me a G-Class Mercedes jeep that I adored. I wasn't used to driving around in luxury. Sometimes I considered pinching myself to make sure it was really me behind the wheel. But while I loved my truck I was equally attached to my Toyota; it was a piece of my dad, just like the house I refused to lose. Instead I had DaVon follow me home to Dad's house and I parked it alongside Dad's vehicle.

And today was an even better day for me. DaVon and I were meeting a Realtor for the dry cleaners. A week ago, I had found out that it was still for sale; apparently things hadn't worked out with the previous buyers. When I found that out, I instantly called the Realtor and set up a meeting. I was really nervous and hoped everything worked out, so I could be the proud owner of my dad's beloved dry cleaners. It would be back in the family where it belonged. Even though the worst tragedy of my life had struck there, it was a part of me, the only family that I could revive. Because my dad, I could never get back. But his legacy was in front of me.

"This is it," I announced as I pulled in front of the dry cleaners. From where I sat, the building still looked to be the same. It had been a minute since I had seen it, so I wasn't sure what to expect. I didn't know if all the windows would be knocked out or if graffiti would be all over the building. I just worried something would be wrong. To my surprise, it was free of any harm. "That must be the Realtor right there," I pointed out. We watched a tall, skinny black guy dressed in a suit approach the door and use a key to unlock it.

"Let's do this. And don't worry." DaVon winked at me and climbed out of the truck.

My heart skipped a beat when I put my hands on the door to go inside. I felt scared when I thought about the tragedy that had happened inside and claimed my father's life. But I also knew his loving presence was inside, his love for the cleaners, and knew that he would want nothing more than for me to reclaim what was rightfully ours. I took in a deep breath, held my head high, and stepped inside with DaVon behind me. His presence gave me courage.

The Realtor greeted us, his hand extended. "Hi, I'm Dexter Raymond."

"Hi, I'm Precious and this is my boyfriend, DaVon." I instantly wondered if I should have referred to DaVon as my boyfriend. While it was true, it sounded so immature. I brushed it off though. We were here for business and at the moment that's exactly where my mind should be focused.

"What's up, man?" DaVon said, his eyes roaming around the cleaners.

"I'm glad you could make it. I hear your dad was the original owner," Dexter said.

I nodded my head yes. The mention of Dad as the previous owner touched a soft spot.

"I understand that gives you a personal interest in the place?"

"Yes," I confirmed, holding back tears.

"Well, I hope we are able to reach a closing cost that will get it back for you."

DaVon spoke up. "Never mind the closing cost." I glared at him and realized that he had walked away. He had made his way around the counter. For a brief second, I could see Dad and me standing behind the counter laughing and talking like we used to do when there were no customers. "Just get her the paperwork and keys; money is not a problem." I looked at him and tears formed in my eyes. I should have known he would make sure I got the cleaners back at whatever cost. The man was good to me.

"Not a problem. I will draw up all the papers and get the ball rolling. You will hear from me in a couple of days." The bright expression on Dexter's face told me this was the easiest sale he had ever made.

"Get the price to Precious and she will get the money right over to you."

"Will do. It was nice doing business with you." With that and to my surprise, Dexter handed me the keys, then reached out and shook DaVon's hand.

"Thank you so much, babe." I jumped in DaVon's arms. Dexter stared at us both and smiled before exiting. "I can never thank you enough." I planted kisses all over DaVon's sexy face.

"It's nothin'. Get whatever your heart desires, my sweetness. You get it fixed up in here and buy whatever you need to get it back going the way you want. Like I said, money is not a problem." Leaning down, DaVon slowly slid his tongue in my mouth. Instantly, I was overexcited. Had my cell phone not rung, there was no telling what I might have done next.

"Hello," I answered the phone. DaVon dove back in and continued to suck on my neck.

"What's up, Precious? Yo ass done went missing again," Keisha barked into the phone.

DaVon held on to me but released my tongue so I could speak. "Here you go with that. I am not missing, just busy, Keisha." I laughed. "But what's up?"

"Tryin' to see if you down to have a few drinks with me and Buffy at the bar? A lil girl time."

DaVon's phone started to ring. Reluctantly, he loosened his grip on me to answer it. I didn't want his arms to move because I knew once his call was over, he was out. The hustle kept him on the move, but I was learning to accept that. It's who he was. "Yeah, I'm down. But I have to drop DaVon at his whip first."

"That's cool. I'll text you the address. Tell DaVon's apple-headed ass I said what's up."

"You better stop talking bout my man." I chuckled and ended the call.

"Aye, work callin'," DaVon said as soon as I ended the call.

"I already know. But it's cool. I'm going to meet up with Keisha and Buffy for drinks."

"A'ight, I guess we can resume this later." He stuck his tongue in my mouth again and I had to end it quickly in order to control myself.

"What's up, bitch?" Keisha sang as I took a seat at the bar where she and Buffy were held up.

"What's up, chic?" Buffy chimed in.

"Hey, you two." I couldn't help but smile at Keisha. She was always hype. Not to mention I was getting used to being called a bitch in every sentence. In high school and in LA, that's how friends greeted you, period. It was known and very normal. But for the past couple of years, I had almost fallen out of touch with my peers and other people my age. All of my time was spent at the dry cleaners. So when I got back out into society and Keisha started calling

me a bitch every third word, I had to fight to keep
from taking it personal when I knew it was not.

"I guess it's safe to say my boy DaVon is keeping
you happy," Keisha added.

"And you would be right. He's keeping me very
happy." I gloried. I was happy and there was no need
to keep it a secret.

"Shiddd, that's what up. I'm glad to witness it. I
was worried you would turn into a nun. Let's get
these drinks poppin'. Bartender, hit me with three
shots of tequila all around." Keisha pointed to Buffy,
herself, then me.

"Comin' right up." The bartender gave us a wink.

"Yeah, you cute," Keisha flirted.

The bartender blushed and we all smiled. "I guess
you in the mood to go hard," I commented on the
shots Keisha had ordered. I didn't normally drink so
heavily so early, but I was in the celebration mood.

"Damn right. What's the need to pussy around
wit' it. Real bitches drink up." Buffy grinned, took
the salt shaker, sprinkled it on the top of her hand,
licked, and downed her drink. "Another one, bartender."

"Yo, don't be surprised this bitch a G." Keisha giggled.

"Hey, I'm in a celebration mood anyhow. So let's
do it." I followed suit with the salt routine and
downed my shot. The salt was known to lessen the
blow of the liquor. But to be honest it still burned my
chest the same. "Haaah." I breathed in from the heat
of the tequila as it punished my chest.

Buffy laughed out loud. "Don't worry, the hair
will grow on your chest soon."

"So what's the celebration you talkin' about? You pregnant?" Keisha let the words slide from her lips.

That caught me off guard. Out of everything she could have guessed, that had been her choice? I was flabbergasted. "Uh, hell to the no." My eyes bulged at her.

"Hey, I was just giving it my best shot."

I would need another shot just to get over Keisha's assumption. "No, my good news is . . . I just became the owner of my dad's dry cleaners again."

"Wait, what? When?" Keisha was surprised. "I thought it was sold already."

"Well, turns out things didn't work out with the first buyer. I found out about it and jumped right on it. DaVon and I met with the dealer today and DaVon closed the deal. I have the keys and all that." I showcased them with a huge grin. And not only was my face smiling, so was my heart. When the place was sold I never thought I would own it again.

"Yo, that's what's up, Precious. I know how much that place means to you," Keisha said.

"That place is my history . . . my dad worshipped that place," I added.

"Then he would be proud," Keisha supposed. "So now what?"

Keisha's question threw me into think mode. I could only sigh when I thought about the work ahead. Buying the business back was just the easy part. "Hiring people is going to be top of the list because with school, I can't do it. I mean I will be able to work there part-time, but I want the business to run full-time like when my dad owned it. But first I need to do a bit of upgrading and replacing the machinery.

That was the biggest part of the business decline; we didn't have enough machines that worked properly. So I got to make sure that's all taken care of."

"A'ight. Sounds like you got a plan then." Keisha nodded her head in agreement.

"Damn, bitches be meetin' them Nino Brown niggas and comin' up," Buffy said. I gave her a fake smile because I knew she was tryin' to throw shade.

"This bitch drunk, I swear," Keisha commented, laughed, then ordered another drink.

I ordered another shot also, but this time only took a sip.

"Precious, you gotta come by the hair store," Keisha reminded me. She had opened her hair store a week before.

"What happened to the grand opening? I had plans to attend."

"Girl, my cousin's ghetto ass got the dates all fucked up and it threw stuff off with the planners I was tryin' to use. So my impatient ass said forget it." Keisha waved it off.

"Keisha, we gotta go. You know we got some moves to make before I go to work," Buffy threw in all loud.

"A'ight, bitch, calm down, let me finish my drink . . ." Keisha rolled her eyes at Buffy. But their behavior was normal. Someone who didn't know them might think there was animosity between them. "Precious, we got to bounce though."

"It's cool," I said.

We finished up our drinks and headed outside. Keisha suddenly stopped in her tracks. "Damn, Precious, is that your truck?"

"Yep." I smiled proudly.

"I'm crushin' on that. That shit on spice!" she replied, while still checking it out.

"Thanks." I wore a huge grin.

"That damn fine-ass DaVon know he showing out, too bad I didn't get to suck that dick first. I could have had one of these trucks," Buffy boasted.

Stunned, I just glared at her and took in her rude comment. I know she had a big mouth and was known to say whatever. But honestly, she was starting to strike a nerve. I gave her the second fake smile I had to offer that day. I was sweet as pie and it was no act. But I was not to be fooled with no more than that. "Buffy, we cool, but you need to hit the respect button. DaVon is my man now."

"Please, let this bitch know. Cause her ass crazy," Keisha cosigned.

Buffy looked at me but had no facial expression, then burst out laughing. "My bad, bitches be getting shook about the dick." She gave a dramatic thrust forward with her shoulders. "It's cool though. Again, my bad, Precious." She smirked.

I didn't feel like she was being sincere at all, but beyond her spill I didn't have a comment. Without another word, I jumped in my Mercedes. This day was going good for me and I would not allow anyone to ruin it, especially Buffy. Trina's "Here We Go" came on my Pandora. Turning it up, the beat blasted through my speakers as I exited the parking lot feeling damn good.

Chapter 14

It had taken two months but I, with DaVon's help, had been able to get the dry cleaners up and running. The building had been cleaned, painted, updated with new pictures and seating, new equipment, the whole nine. Last but not least, we had hired two staff members and I was excited that Katrina, aka K, was back in town. When she heard about the cleaners, she came down and secured her spot. I jumped at the chance to have her back, so I gave her a full-time position. To finish off the team, I hired Regina, another young lady, to work part-time. To balance it, I was going to work part-time too. The icing on the cake was the grand opening I had thrown together for today. I was so excited. In honor of the grand opening, we were giving out coupons for 40 percent off.

I was amped to watch people arrive from the community. They were actually happy that we were re-opening, and supported the business 100 percent. Especially all of Dad's old customers. But there were plenty of unfamiliar faces.

"Dang, Precious, I can't believe you pulled this off. Your dad would be so proud." Katrina beamed. It felt so good to have her here with me. She was like family.

"I know. I'm still in shock myself, K. But here we are." I looked around and admired the place.

"Well, let me get one of these cute bite-size turkey snacks, I'm hungry." Katrina moved toward the catered food we had set up for the guests.

"What's up, babe." DaVon stepped inside, looking good enough to eat. He was late because he had been out of town on business for two days. But he had come as soon as he freshened up from the plane. He pulled me into his arms for a hug and it felt so good. Being in his arms confirmed how much I missed him.

"What do you think? Look at the turnout." I was proud to have him see the outcome of his support.

"It's nice. I didn't expect anything else. You work hard, babe, and this is your family legacy. You got this." He winked at me. Damn, that turned me on.

"This is tight, Precious," Quincy commented as he approached us, looking around. "I remember this used to be Keisha's spot, always talkin' bout drivin' all the way over here from Brentwood to drop off her shit."

"She was a loyal customer," I cosigned. "Where she at? She told me she would be here." I glanced around the room to confirm that Keisha was nowhere in sight.

"My bad, she told me to tell you she ain't gone make it, she sick."

I didn't expect to hear that. "Is she okay?" I asked.

"She cool, I guess." He didn't sound too sure. "She ate something bad, I think." I got the feeling he didn't care. I made a mental to call her later myself.

Clip stepped up beside me. "Yo, you flexin', Precious."

"Thanks, Clip." Clip was one of DaVon's younger peons, but DaVon treated him like a little brother; they were really close. Clip was really cool and I liked him. But when it came to the streets, the best way to describe him was like O-Dog from the movie *Menace II Society*: young, black, and didn't give a fuck. And the streets of LA were more than aware. But his loyalty was priceless, and that also was something you didn't find with the life they led.

DaVon grabbed me by the hand and led me toward the back, where he ducked off into my office. He closed the door behind me and pulled me into his arms. "I've waited for two days to do that, and that's way too long," DaVon whispered in my ear.

"So why are we talkin'?" I went back in for his lips. He gripped my butt in his hands and I moaned.

"Damn, I hate to release you from my arms. But I gotta make this run. Don't worry though, I'll be in early tonight." He leaned in for another kiss. "So keep it tight." He smacked me on the butt.

It turned me on when he smacked me on the butt. "I'll be ready." I seductively licked my bottom lip. We walked back out to the front. I could see a few people had left, but more were coming in. I stood back and watched everyone, and for a brief moment I wondered if Dad's murderer was in my presence. The thought of it made my stomach churn, realizing it could be any one of them. The police still didn't have a clue who was responsible. But then I thought of DaVon and Clip and comfort consumed me. I took in a deep breath, knowing security from DaVon's crew was all around me, and I knew that what happened to my father would not happen to me. DaVon made sure that everyone knew I was his girl and they knew what crossing him meant. And that alone brought me the respect that assured me that no one dared to touch me. So I wasn't worried about me. But I feared what I might do if I ever found out who had dared murder my father.

From the moment Keisha open her front door I knew what Quincy said about her being sick had to be true. Her hair was frizzy and pulled back in a ponytail, there was not a speck of makeup on her face, and her skin was pale. Seeing her this way made me feel bad that it took me so long to come by and check on her. It had been a week since the grand opening and there were a few things I had to wrap up at the bank with payroll so that I could pay Katrina and Regina. Not to mention I still had class, so I had to do my schoolwork in between. Today was the first free day I had had to myself. Therefore, when Quincy stopped by the house two days ago to see DaVon and mentioned that Keisha was still sick, I made it my business to stop by today.

"Dang, Keisha, you look awful. What bug you got? Have you been to the doctor?" I was concerned and almost scared to go inside, afraid that I might catch whatever she was battling.

"Girl, yes." She gripped the loose Nike T-shirt she was wearing closer to her body. Just talking made her look like she might be ill.

"Well, what'd he say?" Reluctantly, I stepped inside the condo and closed the door behind me. I followed Keisha into the living room, where she sluggishly sat down on the sofa. She focused her attention on the television.

"He talkin' bout I'm gone have a baby." She kept her attention on the television.

At first, I was not sure if I heard her correctly. "You're pregnant?" I repeated.

"That's what the doctor said. And I feel like I'm dying, so he must be right." She rubbed her hand across her face.

"Congratulations, Keisha." I was happy for her. But she really didn't look good at all.

"Precious, this pregnancy is fuckin' me over. I can't eat shit, I feel dizzy most of the time. And I think I got the fuckin' chills. Hell, it feels more like the flu than pregnancy."

I didn't know much about pregnancy except from what I had learned in school. And her symptoms sounded classic from what I had learned. "That's morning sickness I think. It should pass." I waved it off.

Keisha lifted herself, putting weight on her left elbow. "No, this shit last all day nonstop. Morning sickness my ass," Keisha complained.

"Did you tell the doctor?"

"Yeah, Quincy took me to the clinic this morning. I couldn't stop throwing up spit and guts. He examined me and didn't find anything wrong. The doctor gave me something for the nausea. He said the dizziness and chills should pass."

"Are you taking the nausea medicine?"

"Yeah, I took one about an hour ago, but I haven't had an appetite to eat nothin' yet. Shidd, really I think I'm afraid too, this throwin' up got me traumatized . . . I don't see how some of these bitches got all these kids if this what it's like being pregnant." Keisha stretched her legs out on the couch and covered up with a throw blanket. I felt so bad for her; I had never seen her look so disheveled. Keisha was one of those chicks that always was in beast mode.

"Let's stay positive and hope the medicine kicks in soon." I tried to be optimistic. "What Quincy say?"

"Girl, his ass amped, he talkin' about buying a big house cause he want the baby to have a backyard, with a tennis court. Can you believe that shit? That's what this nigga worried about why I'm lying up in this bitch suffering." Keisha rolled her eyes. "But I can't front. I'm wit' getting a bigger crib. Hell, maybe we'll end up neighbors." She gave a weak laugh. "Nah, I'm just bullshittin' though . . . Quincy ain't ballin' like that."

"Don't doubt that man. You never know," I added.

"Nah, but maybe one day if he stick close to DaVon. Plus my hair line might blow up." She laughed, but again it was a weak one.

I smiled at her ambition. "Aye, anything possible. Look at me with the dry cleaners that's back up and running. If you had told me this a month's ago I would have never believed it." It made me emotional just talking about it.

"I know, right. I'm sorry I couldn't make it to the grand opening. But I swear I was so damn sick that day. How was it though?"

"Everything was perfect. The community really showed up."

"So what did you do about hiring someone?"

"Oh, I didn't tell you? I got Katrina back."

"That's what's up."

"Yep, and I hired another girl named Regina for part-time. And I plan to work part-time."

"Damn, Precious, you got this under control, huh?"

"I better. It's too late to procrastinate."

"I feel you, Precious. Cause don't nothin' come to a sleeper but a dream."

I noticed while we were talking some of the color seemed to be coming back to Keisha's face. I figured the medicine must have been working. And I for one was getting hungry. "Keisha, I'm gettin' hungry. Do you feel like putting on some clothes? We can go and grab some wings."

The mention of food must have turned Keisha's stomach. The moment I said *wings*, she bolted from the couch like lightning, toward the bathroom. I raced to the closed bathroom door and listened as she seemed to throw up her entire gut.

"Can I do anything to help?"

I heard the faucet running. Keisha didn't answer, but the door to the bathroom swung open. "Yes, just don't bring up food," she requested with the look of death all over her face.

"Sorry." I hunched my shoulders and apologized.

"Just the mention of food has been making me sick. Oddly though, I have been craving Snickers bars and Sprite. And even though I throw it up, I still want it. But I can't keep eating that shit; it's gone make me fat and you know I can't have that."

"Hey, what's the fun of being pregnant if you can't eat what you crave?" I added.

"And that's true." She wasted no time agreeing with me. "Matter of fact, I sent Quincy to the store to stock up on them. Can you grab me one of each out of the kitchen? The Snickers are in the refrigerator with the Sprite. I like them super chilled."

I laughed. "I will get whatever you want as long as you don't blame me being the reason you're fat when this is all over."

I gladly went to the kitchen to grab Keisha's order. I was going to enjoy her being pregnant. And I loved babies, so I knew I would spoil her baby rotten.

Chapter 15

"Wake up, sleepyhead." DaVon kissed me gently on my right shoulder.

Slowly opening my eyes, I smiled at the sweet touch of DaVon's lips; they were so sensual. His hand roamed my body and I squirmed from the pure pleasure of his touch.

"It can't be morning already," I said. But the bright sun that was beating its way inside proved I was wrong.

"And you are right. It's not morning; it's afternoon. You snored the morning away," he teased.

Had my body not been so tired, I would have jumped straight up. "I do not snore." I pouted playfully. "What time is it?" I slowly rolled over to face him, to find that he was fully dressed.

"After twelve o'clock," he announced.

"Bae, why you let me sleep so long? I got things to do."

"I figured you needed to get some rest. I know your night was long." He grinned, then kissed me on the lips. We had been up most of the night jumping each other's bones. And he was right, I was tired as hell. My limbs felt too heavy to lift.

"Yes, and I have you to thank for that." I smiled. I may have been tired, but I was completely satisfied. DaVon didn't hold back anything in bed and I made sure to match him.

"But listen, I brought you something." He went under his shirt and pulled out a handgun.

"What's that?" My eyes bulged at the black steel in his hand. That was the last thing I expected him to pull out.

"It's a Ruger GP100. Just a small piece that I want you to keep on you at all times. It's a must you stay strapped." He was serious.

"DaVon, I don't do guns." I shook my head in disagreement at his comment.

"Babe, this is not up for negotiation; you have a new lifestyle now. Shit has changed. I been thinkin' about this for weeks. You my girl, and shit out here can get real and fast. Now I know you ain't no killer. But it's a fine line out here in these streets. And if the time comes you might have to bust, and if that means taking a motherfucker's life, then it's just that."

I just stared at the gun in his hand. He was so blunt and nonchalant about what he had to say. Was this what my life had come to? Being with him?

"These niggas out here thirsty in these streets, and anytime they see what they think is an easy score, they'll try it. You from LA, so I know you ain't blind to the way shit work out here." As much as I hated to admit it, he was right. But I couldn't stand to think of the harsh reality. Somehow, I thought evil couldn't strike in my life again.

"You're right," I admitted. "I just don't know if I'm

ready for this." I had never considered even holding a gun, much less owning one.

DaVon approached me and gently stroked my right cheek, and looked me in my eyes. "The moment you accepted me and my life, you were ready. You took on this life. With that came risk, and you can't ever be vulnerable . . . Now you take this and use it to open and close doors, if and when you have to. And never think twice about it, because this holds no hearts." He gently placed the black and silver steel into my hands.

"I trust you, so I'll keep it close. I promise," I added to reassure him. Relief was carved on his face. He had probably worried I would flat out refuse. "But I do have one question. Who's going to teach me to shoot this thing?"

"I took care of that too. I set you up for lessons at the shooting range. And I plan to show you my skills as well."

"Ohhh okay." I glared at the gun, full of uncertainty.

"Well, sit up and eat." He reached to the foot of the bed and picked up a tray that held buttermilk pancakes, eggs, bacon, sliced Polish sausage, sliced watermelon, strawberries, grapes, and orange juice. My stomach growled at the sight of it.

"Aw, bae, breakfast in bed."

"Yep, I had Maria fix you up a spread. So I want you to eat before you get moving."

"Thank you." I continued to smile.

"A'ight, I'm about to be out. I got to hit these streets, but I'ma hit you up later."

"Okay," I puckered up for a kiss and he delivered.

After breakfast, I lazily climbed out of bed and strolled into DaVon's massive bathroom, opened the shower door, turned on the water and allowed it to heat up. Sliding the straps of my silk night gown, I let it slide to the floor, then stood under the hot water. The water felt so good as I allowed it to soothe my muscles and wake me up.

Turning off the water, I climbed out, dried off, put lotion all over my body, then walked into the closet and picked out a romper and a pair of sandals. Dressed, I headed downstairs with my tray, found Maria, and thanked her for preparing me a wonderful breakfast. After grabbing the keys to my truck I was out the door.

I didn't have any classes so I headed over to the dry cleaners.

"Hey, Katrina," I said once inside.

"What's up, Precious? I was wondering when you might come by today."

"I wanted to come by earlier, but I overslept."

"Them schoolbooks be kickin' your ass, huh?"

"You already know. But I'm handling it."

"That fine-ass DaVon got you tired too, I guess." She grinned.

"He straight," I replied.

"Good, you need to let loose. I'm glad to know you finally tapped into that fun I used to tell you about. You'll be glad to know that business has risen another forty percent since last week alone. Precious, the cleaners kickin' straight ass."

"For real?" I guess the advertisement was paying off. I had invested in advertisement hoping to boost sales. I never really thought it would work.

"People been piling in and the machines are the best. People been coming back saying they stuff was on point. You should be proud."

"I am. Just trying to take it all in. Thank you so much for coming back, Katrina," I replied, full of gratitude. "I know it was hard when Dad had to let you go."

"It was okay though. The business had been struggling for a while and I knew it was coming. I was really surprised he had been able to keep me on that long. But he's smiling down on you. I bet he's saying *My daughter is a boss.*" She tried to mimic my dad.

I couldn't help but laugh because she actually had his body language down. "You do that quite well." But I hoped she was right; having him proud of me would be the icing on the cake.

Heading back to the office, I counted the cash from the day before and got the deposit ready for the bank. I had to stop by and drop that off. The ringing of my cell interrupted me. I started to ignore the call so that I wouldn't get off track, but it was DaVon. "Hey, babe," I answered. I was always in the mood to hear from him.

"What's up, babe? I was just checkin' to see if you good."

"Yes, I'm over here getting the deposit ready for the bank and I'm telling you, business is great. Katrina says the people are piling in, business up forty percent, and from the looks of the deposits, she is right."

"That's what's up, and it will only get better. I gotta wrap up a few things, then I'm free. Let's meet up downtown and have dinner."

"Sounds great. I need to get this deposit dropped off, then check the house out while I'm out this way."

"A'ight, I'll see you soon. I'll text you the address to the restaurant once I decide where. Unless you have someplace in mind."

"Whatever you pick is fine with me."

"Cool."

After hanging up the phone, I finished the count, filled out the deposit bags and slips, and bid Katrina goodbye. As I pulled up to the bank, Keisha's name lit up on my phone. "What's up, Keisha?" I answered, but the phone line was dead. The phone lit up that the call had ended. Assuming Keisha had butt dialed me as she has done several times before, I decided not to call back. Turning up my radio, I got into Tamar's "Love and War." Keisha's name lit up on my phone again. I turn down the music.

"Aye, Keisha," I answered again. I heard what sounded like crying on the other end. "Keisha?" I repeated her name. I could hear that she was trying to speak, but I couldn't make out what exactly she was saying. But I thought I heard her say something about pain and that she tried to call Quincy.

"Keisha, where you at?"

"Home." The word came out but it was very weak.

"I'm on my way." Ending the call, I tried to call Quincy but got no answer. I tried DaVon but got the same result. Jumping on the interstate, I drove eighty all the way to Brentwood. Thankfully, the front door was unlocked when I arrived. Inside, I found Keisha balled up in a knot on the floor with her cell phone tightly gripped in her hand.

"Oh my God, Keisha. What's wrong? What happened?" I asked as I dropped down on the floor beside her.

"I'm in so much pain, Precious," she cried.

"Listen, I'm going to call the ambulance for help." I pulled out my cell phone but Keisha grabbed at my hand.

"No," she cried. "Don't call anyone to this house. Just take me to the hospital. I can walk to your car."

"But that might not be safe, Keisha. We don't know what's wrong and we could harm the baby. The paramedics will know what to do." I tried to reason with her. The last thing I wanted to be responsible for was something happening to her unborn child. These types of things could be sensitive. "Please let me call for help."

"Precious, no!" She yelled this time and sat up, holding her abdomen. "Quincy would not want any law enforcement of any kind in this house."

"But it's the paramedics."

"They the same damn people in our world. Now help me up."

Against my better judgment, I stood and helped her up. Time was wasting and the last thing we needed to do was waste any more time. I just hoped that Keisha and her baby were okay. I didn't see any blood so that gave me hope. But I thought it was some straight bullshit that she had to risk her baby to please Quincy. However, it was their house and their business; now was not the time for me to figure it out.

Chapter 16

Almost a week had passed and I still could not believe Keisha had lost her baby. I felt so bad for her, and to make it worse, the doctor said if we had been able to get her to the hospital at least thirty minutes earlier, they might have been able to save the baby. The doctor went on and on about something rupturing, therefore causing Keisha to miscarry. She had to stay in the hospital for two days for them to get her straight. She was trying hard to be strong though, and even though she was only three months along, I knew she was still experiencing a sense of loss. And for that I felt bad for her, because I knew that feeling all too well.

Lying in bed, I thought about the emptiness she might have been feeling from her loss. It brought on my emotions about the loss of my dad. People say time heals all, but I still was not convinced how true that was. Nothing about my loss had healed; in fact, it was stronger than ever.

"Babe, when you gone get out this bed?" DaVon strolled in the bedroom and sat down next to me. I had gotten up, taken a shower, and climbed right back into bed. I really didn't feel like doing much.

"I don't think I am. I just want to sit here and relax. Can you have Maria bring me a turkey sandwich?"

"You know I will. Are you feeling okay?" he looked me in the eyes.

"I'm fine, babe. Nothin' for you to worry about."

"A'ight. Well, I have to go out to Miami on business."

"When are you leaving?"

"Tonight, but I should be back in a day or so."

"Aww, babe, I'm going to miss you this time. I don't feel like being alone. Can I come with you?" Normally I didn't trip about him being away. But that empty feeling was back and I needed him around me. He made me feel whole.

"Babe, it's business."

"I know, but I can't be without you right now."

He smiled. "A'ight, pack your bags. I'll call and book your flight."

"Thanks, babe." I smiled, feeling relieved. Climbing out of the bed, I didn't waste no time packing my things.

Arriving in Miami had been just what I needed to pull me out of my rut. It was beautiful from the time we drove out of the airport. Palm trees were everywhere; the air even felt different. Either that or I was just amped to be away from Los Angeles. I loved home, for sure, but being in a new city seemed to just give my life a boost that I craved. And the hotel was to die for. DaVon had booked the Four Seasons, and it was grand. Upon arrival our room was filled with fruits, wine, and chocolates.

"Babe, this is so nice." I bit into a chocolate-covered strawberry. I couldn't resist.

"Nothin' but the best for you. For me I just would have stayed at the Hilton or some."

"You're so good to me." I reached up and kissed him deeply.

"Ummm, that chocolate tastes good on you."

I smiled and took another bite of my strawberry.

"Real talk, babe, I could get used to this hotel."

"Well, I'm glad you happy." He reached in his suit-case and pulled out two stacks and passed them to me. They were ten thousand apiece. "I got to make a few runs. I got you a driver-slash-bodyguard down-stairs waiting to take you wherever you want to go. So you shop and get you something nice. We got a social gathering to attend tonight."

"A'ight, what time should I be expecting you?"

"Probably around nine, but I'll text you. I have to get back to get dressed."

He didn't have to tell me twice; shopping was sec-ond nature. I had always liked to spend money. Daddy always teased me about marrying someone rich. And now that I actually had money to spend, I did. DaVon made matters worse when he specifically dropped money on me and said shop. Neiman Marcus was my destination. I loved that store with a passion. There wasn't nothing inside that I didn't desire. I could spend ten thousand dollars easy, and I did.

DaVon's jaws dropped when I stepped out of the bathroom and I knew my choice for the night was a winner. "Babe, you so damn fine." He complimented me and I blushed. "Turn around, let me get a good look at all that." I slowly turned around and modeled my outfit, and I had to admit I was bad in my Badgley Mischka ivory jumpsuit topped with a stunning pair of Gianvito Rossi Portofino velvet ankle high-heel sandals. It was my first pair of shoes by Gianvito Rossi, but it would not be the last; they were comfortable. In fact, I had picked up another pair while shopping. "Come here, let me touch you." DaVon tried to wrap me in his arms.

"No, babe, you're going to mess up my ivory." I took two steps back from his reach. "I can't be going nowhere dingy," I joked.

"A'ight, I don't want to mess you up. But tonight, I'm ripping it off." He laughed.

"You do that." I blushed again.

"Let's jet." He reached for my hand.

"Who was it you said that lived here?" My eyes bulged at the sight of the mansion we pulled up to.

"One of my business partners."

"It's beautiful." I was mesmerized and it was clear that everyone inside must have been laced. The driveway was lined with Maybachs, Ferraris, Bentleys galore. So there was no question that there was some majors inside.

We made our way up the massive steps that led to the front, where bodyguards secured the door. DaVon gave them a code and we were inside like that. As soon as we were inside, a waitress carrying a tray of drinks approached us. We grabbed a glass. I needed it because I was suddenly nervous. The house was something to see; the mosaic tile that lined the floor was to die for. My eyes were glued to it.

"DaVon, my guy," said a man with a neat accent that I could not describe.

"Aye, what's good?" They shook hands. Whoever the guy was, he was fine. He was tall and he looked to be Hispanic. He had his long, dark, silky hair in a ponytail. He reminded me of one those guys off one of them mafia movies.

"Who is this beautiful young woman?" He smiled at me.

DaVon turned to me and grinned. "This my lady, Precious. And, babe, this my favorite Spanish friend, Pablo." DaVon chuckled.

"Don't pay this fool no mind." Pablo laughed. With his accent it sounded weird when he said the word *fool*. But his words were just sexy, so it was easy to ignore. "Nice to meet you, Precious." Pablo reached for my hand and kissed it.

"It's nice meeting you too, Pablo." I smiled.

"I can't wait for you to meet my wife." He glanced around the room. "Aye, baby. Come over here." I loved Pablo's accent. A tall Victoria's Secret–type, clearly Spanish woman turned to face us. She wrapped up the chat she had been having with three females and headed our way.

"DaVon." She announced his name, stepped in his space, and kissed him lightly on both cheeks.

"How are you, Ms. Lady?" DaVon greeted her.

"Baby, this is DaVon's lady, Precious."

"Hi." She glared at me. "This is the first time I've met someone with that name." Her accent matched Pablo's. "Precious, I'm Penelope." She extended her hand to me.

"It's good meeting you, Penelope."

"Why don't you ladies have some more drinks so me and my guy DaVon can talk," Pablo suggested.

"Sure, babe." Penelope leaned in and kissed Pablo on the lips. Their vibe was so sensual, a blind man could see they were in complete love with each other.

"I'll be back." DaVon winked at me before walking off with Pablo.

"Penelope, I just want to say this house is beautiful."

"Thank you. Come on, I'll take you on a tour." For the next half hour Penelope showed me around. The house was off the charts. Penelope shared that it was fourteen thousand square feet and some change. And I believed her. The house had ten full bathrooms and three half bathrooms, along with two elevators, not to mention a two-story round glass wall that overlooked the pool and waterfront. To put it mildly, the house was ridiculous.

"So, Precious, what is it you do?" We had just finished the tour of the house and were having a drink.

"Well, right now I'm actually in college, my major is business. And I own a dry cleaning business."

"That's good. Sounds like you have a love for business."

"I guess you can say so. I helped my dad run his dry cleaning business since I was a child. What about you?" I asked.

"I have a few business ventures. My most successful is my chain of designer shoe stores. I even have one in Saint-Tropez."

"Oh snap." I was surprised to hear that. I read about Saint-Tropez all the time in the magazines and on the blogs. It was a hot spot for the rich and famous. "Ain't that the place where all the celebrities vacation on yachts and whatnot?"

Penelope smiled and sipped her wine. "That would be it. Pablo surprised me with a house out there about five years ago. And once we had that, it was a must that we buy a yacht. It's simply beautiful there. Business was going good with the other shoe stores, so two years ago I opened a shoe store there. And business is booming over there."

"Wow, that's what's up. I can only hope to be so successful one day." I was really impressed with her accomplishments. Never had I met anyone who owned a chain of anything, and in a place as famous as Saint-Tropez made it just that much more impressive.

"And if you will be in this life, you should always stay connected and loyal. For every reason." Her voice took on a more boss-like tone. "Now my other interest, besides the business, is always standing by my man," she said in a matter-of-fact tone. "Nothing should matter more than that." She looked off into the distance and my eyes followed. They landed on DaVon and Pablo still talking. Whatever they were discussing was serious, because they didn't seem the least bit bothered by all the entertainment around them. "While they build an empire, you hold it up."

"I guess I never thought of that." I was honest. The knowledge she was supplying was all new to me. "But without a doubt I would always stand by DaVon." That much I knew for sure.

"I think we have a lot in common. I see some of you in me when I first got with Pablo. Just remember that even when you are in Los Angeles, you are connected. Never hesitate to reach out, Precious."

"Trust me, I will not." The conversation had taken on a meaning of its own. Penelope seemed like no other female I had ever met. Something told me that as beautiful and elegant as she was, she was one Spanish chick that was not to be crossed. And I liked her standards. It gave me something new to think about.

Chapter 17

Back in Los Angeles I couldn't get my mind off Penelope; what she had said set off bells in my mind. Made me conscious of things that I sure wasn't conscious of before. Her style and grace were impeccable; just looking at her you would never know that she was the wife of a kingpin. Pablo was the connection from the Spanish underworld, and not known by many. How DaVon had come by him, I probably would never know. I just prayed that he stayed on his good side.

Miami had been great but we had made it back to LA. Snatching up my cell phone, I dialed up Keisha. I hadn't heard from her since I had left for Miami. I wanted to check in on her. Since the loss of the baby, she had been kind of quiet and withdrawn. After the fifth ring her cell phone went to voicemail. I hated leaving messages, so I didn't. I figured she could call me back once she saw she missed the call.

Unzipping my suitcase, I decided to go ahead and start unpacking my things. Maria was downstairs making her famous chicken tacos, and I couldn't wait to have some. I figured as soon as I was done unpacking, I could run down and have a few. Just as I pulled the zipper back on my suitcase, my cell started to ring. Keisha's name lit up on the screen.

"Where you been at? I thought you had fallen off the face of the earth," Keisha ranted into the phone nonstop. "Actin' like you can't answer nobody call, got your phone going straight to voicemail." My phone had died on the plane on the way back from Miami, so I'd waited until I arrived home to charge it up.

"See, it's not like that at all." I giggled. "DaVon and I made a trip up to Miami and on the way back my phone died."

"Damn, bitch, what's in Miami? Guess you making moves now?"

I laughed but didn't respond as I realized DaVon's business in Miami was just that, his business, so there was no need for me to disclose why we were there.

"Silence, huh?" Keisha chuckled. "Well, I guess what happens in Miami stays in Miami." And she was right about that, but I didn't feel the need to clarify, so I changed the subject.

"So how have you been?" We hadn't really talked much since she'd had the miscarriage. I wasn't sure what to say to her, but I wanted to be sure she was cool. Keisha was always playing hard, but I knew she had been happy about being pregnant.

"Under the circumstances, I'm cool. I just try not to dwell on it. I got my energy back, but I just been chillin'.

"That's good, you need to be able to relax."

"Nah, ain't no relaxin'. Buffy done had her ass over here damn near every day, gettin' on my last damn nerve. Yesterday, I threw her ass out. Told her to stay the fuck away before I kill her." I couldn't help but laugh as I imagined Keisha cursing Buffy out. "Don't laugh, that shit ain't funny." She couldn't hold back and let out a chuckle.

"I'm sorry." I continued to laugh. "Buffy just making sure you straight."

"Straight my black ass; she was naggin' the hell outta me. And as usual, Quincy spendin' all his time workin'. Day and night that's all he does. So basically a bitch alone . . ." She paused. "That nigga thinks he the only one who can bump on the street. Nigga keep forgettin' I'm grade one in these streets. Been hustlin' way before his ass. But it's cool, I'ma let him do his thing, while I relax and flex that weave."

I was glad she remembered that she had her own thing going. "Right, that's still yo' hustle. You already done made that official. "

"And I have so many more plans. That's why your girl tryin' to ride these waves steady. It's gone all work out."

"I know it will . . ." I paused. I could hear sadness in her tone but not defeat. "Listen, I'ma roll through tomorrow and we can do some shopping. Are you down?"

"Hell yeah, you know I'm always down for spending Quincy's money. Just hit me up and let me know what time. But speaking of shopping, I know you ain't went all the way to Miami and didn't drop them stacks."

"You know I did. You gone have to check me out too. Miami gone have me slayin' out here in L.A."

"Bitch, I feel you. It's cool though. I'm gone boss up tomorrow. Don't forget to hit me."

"I won't." I hung up the phone. After I finished unpacking, I realized I was tired and wanted to climb into bed. But first I had to have some of Maria's tacos. There was no way I was missing out on them. So after taking a hot shower, I raced downstairs with full intentions to fill up.

Chapter 18

I woke up with my dad heavy on my mind. Lately I had been seriously considering doing something to the house. Possibly fixing it up, doing a little remodeling. I didn't wish to sell it or anything. But I felt it really needed a makeover. But just thinking about the house forced me to think about him long and hard. What would he like, or not like? Then that brought on the feeling that I was still trying to suppress my anger at him. I was trying so hard to shake the feeling of loneliness and his betrayal. And I missed him so much.

Pulling the covers off me, I sat up on the side of the bed and contemplated fixing a cup of coffee. That could possibly get me going. I really needed to get dressed and go down to the cleaners and pick up the deposit. But it was easier said than done. Suddenly the loneliness and betrayal I felt because of my dad rushed over me. I couldn't rise from the bed as the tears rushed down my rosy cheeks. The bedroom door swung open and I quickly tried to wipe the tears away as DaVon stepped into room. The last thing I wanted was for him to see me crying.

"Babe, what's going on? Why the tears?" He rushed over to me, concerned. My attempt to hide the tears had failed. And I was not in the mood to talk about it.

I forced a smile on my face. "That's not tears. My allergies are acting up. I'm good," I denied. But the pit of my stomach was boiling over with pain. I fought to keep a straight face.

"Listen, if something's botherin' you, I'm here." Concern was all over DaVon's face.

"I told you . . ." I tried to finish my statement. I really wanted to. But the pain in the pit of my stomach boiled over until I could no longer hold it. "I can't take it anymore, DaVon," I cried.

He rushed over and put his arms around me.

"Babe, what's up? Talk to me."

Tears ran down my face. I had to take in a deep breath to control the shaking in my voice as I tried to speak. I had to calm down first.

"It's okay. Take your time." DaVon held on to me. Slowly I removed myself from his embrace. DaVon rushed to the bathroom and brought out some Kleenex.

Dabbing at my tears, I dried my face. "I'm fine now." My voice was still a bit shaky. "I was just thinking about my dad. I feel so alone in the world. You know . . ." I had to pause again to take in a deep breath so that I would be able to go on talking. "When I was growin' up it was just him and me. And he shielded me from the world as best he could, but how could he do that yet lie to me daily? Do you know that he let me believe my entire life that my mother was dead . . . that she died when I was a baby? He died with that lie. I had to discover after his death through some fuckin' letters that it was not true. Who the fuck does that!" I screamed. The pain was deeper than ever and it stung like a thousand knives. I wasn't sure if I would ever understand his motive.

DaVon hugged me tight again. "Babe, you don't ever have to feel lonely, because I'm here for you, always. You always got me, don't doubt. I love you more than you'll ever know."

"But why would he do it, DaVon? Why would he lie?"

"Ain't no way to ever know that, Precious. Sometimes people do things that simply can't be explained. Maybe he had good reason."

"Good reason?" I snatched my neck back and looked at him with attitude. How could he agree with what Dad had done? "How can you say that? No mother deserves to not be in her child's life. Especially when she is begging to be there." The letters all but haunted me.

"I don't know, babe. I wish I had the answer. Is she still alive? Have you tried to find her?" He asked valid questions. But I hadn't even thought about contacting her. I was just stunned to find out that she was not dead.

"I don't know. The last time she wrote to him, I was about six-years old. She either gave up writing to him or he hid those letters somewhere else. I still can't believe he successfully hid those letters from me all that time." The tears again started to flow. I felt like I had a bucket of tears inside me waiting to leak out.

"Babe, just know that I'm here for you. I'm your

family now, and you know that without a doubt I love you beyond measure." He kissed my forehead.

"I know." I sniffed back tears. I was so thankful to have DaVon; without him I would have been lost.

"Listen, why don't you take a ride with me?"

"I can't, babe, I got a few things to do . . ." I had got so caught up in my feelings I had almost forgotten about my busy day.

"Come on, ride with me?" DaVon repeated.

I would have given in, but I couldn't.

"I can't, I have to run by the dry cleaners to pick up the deposit. Then I have to meet up with the contractor at Dad's house. And I told Keisha we would go shoppin'." I ran down my to-do list. "And you know if I cancel on Keisha she'll talk mess until whenever."

"Aye, but I still want you to take this ride with me." I was prepared to give him the same *no* again, but he forced his handsome smile on me. "Come on, ride wit' your man."

I couldn't resist his charm, so I agreed.

Thirty-five minutes later we were pulling into the driveway at a weird location. It was back in a wooded park area with big trees, a running path, and the coolest breeze I had felt in a long time. I rolled up my window.

"Aye, you ain't got to be scared." DaVon chuckled when I let the window up.

"Oh no." I laughed as I realized he thought I was afraid. "I'm a little cold is all . . . but I'm straight. Trust," I reassured him.

"A'ight, sit tight. I'ma handle this and I'll be right back. Now give your man a kiss." Leaning in my direction, DaVon licked his lips and it reminded me of LL Cool J. Passionately and unable to control myself,

I sucked on his bottom lip, then slid my tongue in his mouth. "Damn, babe," escaped DaVon's mouth. Sitting back into my seat, I gave him a sweet smile.

DaVon climbed out of the car and walked to the back. I heard him open and shut the trunk. As he came around toward the front of the car, I noticed he was carrying two big army-type green duffel bags. I watched as he approached a money-green, old-school Monte Carlo sitting on twenty-four-inch rims. A tall black male stepped out, resembling Nino Brown from *New Jack City*. Then, suddenly, a Range Rover pulled up next to the Monte Carlo and out climbed Clip and another one of DaVon's peons who went by Mob. Mob, like Clip, carried the reputation of a beast in the streets because he had a love for knives, and he was known to butcher up his problems. And word on the streets was he was number one at it. Simply put, he was not to be fucked with.

The black Nino-looking guy approached DaVon. When they were within earshot DaVon dropped both duffel bags on the ground, and they shook hands. I was too far away to make out what they were saying, but their facial expressions and body gestures specified business only. DaVon glanced off his right shoulder at Clip and Mob and he gave them a signal. The trunk on the Monte Carlo went up and, for the first time, I noticed a tall, bulky, brown-skinned dude standing at the back of the trunk. I froze for a minute thinking something was up. But the trunk to the Range Rover also went up, and Clip and Mob immediately started loading something from the Monte Carlo into the Range Rover, with the help of the brown-skinned dude.

I sat and watched the entire transaction in disbelief, but with a hint of apprehension, and yet a bit of exhilaration. The feeling was overwhelming yet fulfilling at the same time. I had been in such a trance, watching Clip and Mob empty the Monto Carlo, that I had not even noticed DaVon walking back toward the car. He opened the door, slid inside, and startled me.

"You a'ight?" He leaned over to me, nearly closing the space between us, his cologne, as usual, soothing my nostrils.

"Oh, I'm fine."

"You saw what just happened . . ." His voice trailed off, and he looked back in the direction of Clip and Mob as they drove off. The Monte Carlo busted a U-turn and went the opposite direction. "This is my life, Precious. One hundred grand. And now it's yours," he said to me, still looking off in the direction where everything had taken place. Slowly, he turned his attention to me again. A calm seriousness, but full of sexy, was all over his face. "One day we will be billionaires living on a boat out in the middle of the ocean. You just witnessed enough kilos for us to retire ten families and make them rich. But that's just the icing on the cake, the best is yet to be seen." Again, he looked off into the distance. "And never forget Pablo and Penelope."

DaVon put the gear shift in drive, and we sped away. I felt the first rush of something I could not explain for the life of me. And I understood things that I had no idea I could. From that day forward, I would occasionally make trips with DaVon; he made sure of it. Even though I never understood why I was there, I was learning that my man was smart, and even though he already had more than anyone could ask for—hell, he was rich already—he would go farther. The sky was the limit for DaVon and me.

Chapter 19

"Precious, where you at?" Keisha yelped through the phone as soon as I answered.

"Just leaving school. I been in classes all day." My brain was tired, but it was no use sharing that with Keisha, because if she had fun in mind there would be no excuse that she would accept.

"Damn, girl, school be kickin' yo' ass, huh?"

"Without a doubt." I had to be honest. "But it's cool, I got this." I gave myself a pep talk. Because sometimes after staying up late nights, studying or doing papers, then a full day of classes, and some days straight to the dry cleaners right after, I would be drained. But positivity was the big picture, and support from DaVon kept me going. So I was good. "What's up with you though? I ain't heard from you in a few weeks."

"I know. I been busy at the hair store making sure its running the way it should. One of my orders was messed up a week ago and I had to wreak havoc in the city. But it's all good now. I was callin' to see if you could come through?"

"You got food up there? Cause I ain't ate since this morning." Sometimes I would be so busy I would skip eating until bedtime, and by then I was too tired to care.

"No, but I can order up some takeout. How bout wings?"

"I'm wit' it. Hook that up." My stomach was growling just thinking about it. Most mornings I only had Starbucks before school. I hated going to school with a full stomach; it made me fidgety and unable to think, and I did not need that. Hanging up with Keisha, I headed straight for the hair store.

"I see you're fully stocked." I gazed around at all the hair Keisha showcased throughout the store. From the looks of it, she had it set up really nice. For a minute, I thought it might look like one of those ninety-nine cent, knock-off hair supply stores that catered to the hood. But she had it looking really professional. Crystal-like glass cases showcased the hair, and some was displayed on a few full-size mannequins. "And I'm loving the setup."

"Aye, you already know I'm gone do it right. Shit gotta be right wit' my name attached. Bitches in the streets ain't gone be out here laughing at me." She looked around as if she was admiring her own store. "And business is on point. I knew this hair was gone be a gold mine. The bitches be cleaning me out. That's why I had to go straight loco when my order got messed up. I'll be damned if I miss a dime."

"What happened with that?" I could understand her frustration.

"These motherfuckers crazy. Talkin' bout they got my order mixed up with an order in Colorado. As if I cared about their reasons. Just fix my shit and fast."

She sucked her teeth. I could tell she was reliving the conversation all over again.

"Colorado?" I was shocked. "It's black girls in Colorado?" I laughed.

"Bitch, that's exactly what I said. I told them if they didn't get my damn hair here by the next day I was gone shut that motherfucker down."

"Aye, didn't Buffy hook you up with them?"

"Hell yeah, she did. So you know I cussed her ass too. They all had me fucked up." She smacked her gum.

We both couldn't stop laughing when the delivery guy came in with the order of wings and cold, two-liter cherry Coke.

"Damn, now you was thinkin' on your toes when you got the cherry Coke." I couldn't wait to have a cup.

"Bitch, I know what you like. Don't be alarmed."

"Good, let me wash my hands so I can smash. My stomach bout to snap out on me if I don't put something in it. Where's the bathroom?"

"Down there." She pointed toward the hallway off to the left of the room.

Soon as I returned, I dug in. Keisha had grabbed some paper plates and glasses from her break room and brought them to the front. We sat behind the counter.

"You ain't got no food up in here but you got dishes?" I asked as I put a few wings on my plate and poured ranch on top of them.

"Sure do. You know I'm lazy, so I'm always bringing in takeout or ordering in." She popped the top on the cherry Coke and filled both our glasses. My mouth watered as I watched the cold liquid fill my glass. I was a fool for pop. "So what's up over at the dry cleaners?" Keisha bit off a wing. "Damn, that was good," she added before I answered. I was busy chewing myself.

"You ain't lying," I agreed. "But business is really good. The advertising and new equipment are all paying off."

"Mane, I just wish your pops was here to see it."

"I know." Bringing up my dad made me emotional.

I was thankful when she asked another question that didn't involve memory lane. "How your workers workin' out? They be showing up and shit?"

"No doubt. They are doing their thing. You know Katrina about her business; she make sure everything straight. And Regina been working hard too."

"That's what's up. I been thinkin' bout bringin' in two people to help out around here. Buffy, she be helping, but you know she keep her ass down at that strip club all day and night. You damn near got to drag that bitch up outta there. That's all she know. But I can't be spendin' all my time up in here. I got shit to do." She twisted the corners of her mouth up in a dramatic motion.

"I feel you. Why don't you set up some interviews? I'll help you pick out some people," I offered. I was good at feeling people out.

"Cool, I might do that. I'll let you know so you can clear that busy schedule you keep."

"For real. But how have you really been since the miscarriage? I know you said you was good the last time I asked, but I want to be sure that you straight." Keisha was my friend, the only friend I had when my father passed. I wanted to be there for her in her time of need.

"It was a little strange at first. Getting used to the idea of having this whole new person in your life. So it's like I had to get over all that once I lost the baby and I admit it was hard at first. But honestly, I'm feeling better now . . ." She paused, so I knew something was up. "But Quincy . . . he is struggling with it still."

"Does he talk about it?" I asked.

"Nah, you know him. He plays as if he's cooler than a fan. And to keep me in the dark about it, or at least that's what he thinks he's doing. He works a lot, but he can't hide it from me. I see it in his walk, the way he talks, his whole demeanor . . ." For a minute I thought she might cry, but she kept her cool. "But we good though." She gave me a weak smile that confirmed what I already knew. She was indeed not good. "But, girl, let me tell you about Buffy."

"What now?" I laughed. I knew whatever she was about to spill was gone be full of unnecessary drama, completely animated, and probably X-rated.

"Somebody done shot up her momma house 'bout her trifling-ass brother, you know the one they call Buster. Remember I introduced you to him when we were out having chicken and waffles a while back."

"Yeah, I remember." My mind drifted back to the day she introduced me to Buffy's brother. He was what I probably would have imagined Buffy's brother to be, a hood street thug with no manners. He was walking around looking like he had just been initiated into a gang, holding his pants up with his bare hand because he didn't have a belt, with an old, stinky-looking toothpick hanging from the corner of his lips.

"You know, his ass swear he a gangbanger. Well,

them niggas he got beef with done shot up they momma house tryin' to lobby his ass. Girl, she done went bananas and threw Buffy and his ass out."

"Wait, why she throw Buffy out? She have something to do wit' it?" I was confused, but this was Buffy's family I was thinking about. I was sure this was somehow normal.

"Naw, she ain't have nothing to do wit' it, but she say fuck both of their asses. She told them to hit the bricks." Keisha chuckled. "Say she sick of both their troublemaking asses."

"That's messed up, but thank God no one got shot."

"I know, right. But that wasn't good enough for they momma. So now Buffy stayin' at my house." She playfully rolled her eyes.

"Oh, word." If I knew any better, Buffy being at Keisha's was not good. All they ever did was disagree. Soon they would be at each other's throats. Literally.

Keisha looked at me and started laughing. "But that bitch can't stay long or I will kill her ass. Or she gone kill me. You already know." It was just like I thought, soon was already near.

"I was thinkin' that." I chuckled. "But you can't put her out on the streets."

Keisha looked around and sucked her teeth. "I guess you right though. I can't have my bitch homeless. Sleeping in missions or shelters for battered women. Hell, she ain't even been battered yet." Keisha giggled. "Aye, but I called you over to talk business. For real." She had to fight to keep from laughing at her own humor.

"Hey, you feeding me, which means I can't complain. So what's good?" I would have licked the hot sauce from the wings off my hands, it was so good. But I had wet wipes, so there was no excuse.

"Earlier, I was tellin' you bout how good business was going. And you know how these bitches buying up all this hair. That got me to thinkin', 'cause you know I'm all about them coins. I was thinkin' I could keep sellin' this hair. I already got the clientele there. Then on the back end we can get this money by opening up a hair salon." I was confused about the word *we*. Did she mean me?

"Okay . . ." I stalled. "But what's the *we* stuff?"

"We as in us, me and you. I was thinkin' we both runnin' successful businesses already. How bout we put our coins together and open a hair salon? It's the perfect hustle for us, guaranteed moneymaker. I got the hair on deck; they can get the hair and have one of our potential beauticians slay, all in one whop."

"The idea ain't bad," I admitted. "But I didn't know you did hair. I know I don't." I chuckled with certainty.

"Bitch, now you know I can't do no hair. When it comes to hair, I'm only good at getting mine done. I was gone find us a few badass hairstylists right here in LA. Shit, that won't be hard; everybody round here swear they slay."

I had to agree with her on that. Also there were some bad do-it-in-the-kitchen type hairstylists all around us. Everybody had a page on Facebook claiming they could slay. Finding some stylists would be easy.

"Precious, I want this bad. I'm trying to be an experienced business owner. Have different types of businesses. Become an entrepreneur." She was hopeful.

"That's what's up. I really like the idea."

"So what's up then? Think about it—you with your schooling in business, mane, we could open up all kinds of shit. Be successful as shit out here. Soon we'll have so much cash we'll be taking trips just to get away. Hell, we could gateway to Miami. Cause networking a motherfucker these days."

The more she talked, the more I liked her idea. Everything made perfect sense. A person would be stupid not to add up on the coins that we could possibly make. But I wasn't sure I was ready to say yes just yet. As good as it sounded, I was already booked with school and the dry cleaners. "Keisha, this sounds like something I need to jump on, but with all I have going on, it's something I'm gone need to think about."

"Aye, I get it. And that's cool, just let me know."

I was glad that she understood. I had to be realistic and weigh everything out. I had chosen business initially 'cause I wanted to help my dad be successful. And since I had started the courses, I was learning a lot and I had to say I loved it. But running a business was no joke, a lot was involved, and if you put your all into it, there was nothing that could stand in your way to riches. But the one thing I had learned and trusted in was that you had to be a smart business owner to succeed. Anyone could get a loan or put up their own money to start a business; they could have a passion for it like my father did. But to stay on top and to be successful, you had to be smart. And I planned on doing just that with my degree.

Chapter 20

"Aheww." DaVon hurled into the toilet for the twentieth time since he had woke up. I stood in the bathroom doorway reading the directions on the Pepto-Bismol I had run to the drugstore to pick up. I felt so bad for him.

"Come on, babe. You have to take this now. And drink some of the Gatorade so you don't get dehydrated. Because if you do, you won't have a choice but to go to the hospital."

"No, ummm, I told you no hospital. They'll be tryin' to keep me. I got too much shit to do for that." He loosened the death grip he had on the toilet and tried to glare at me.

"DaVon, you can't worry about that. Here." I handed him a Pepto tablet.

He frowned. "How long before it works? I have to get going." He held on to his stomach. I was sure he had a stomach virus.

"Babe, you can't go anywhere like this. You throwin' up and you have diarrhea. You can't conduct business like that." I eyed him with confusion.

"Precious, I can't miss this meeting. These niggas have to know what's up. So this shit need to start working ASAP."

"Well, unless you get a miracle, this ain't gone help you in two hours. It just won't. Now come on, get in this bed." I reached down and helped him up. "Hold on to me," I suggested.

"Nah, I may crush your little weight. I got it." He took some steps that seemed like a struggle and fell into the bed. "Ahhh, this feels so much better." He breathed a heavy sigh.

"And that's where you can stay, in that bed. I'll fix up a trash can for you to throw up in." I went into the bathroom, grabbed the wastebasket, and filled it with a powder that Maria had given me to kill the throw-up smell. I set it by the bed.

DaVon tried to sit up, leaning onto his right elbow. "Listen, I have to go. This should not take long." He attempted to lift his body but fell back.

"Babe, you can't even drive. Let's be serious here." I braced myself, ready to suggest what I had in mind. "I'm going to take your meeting. I'll go."

His response did not surprise me.

"Wait, what?" He squinted at me in disbelief.

"You heard me right. And you know I can do it. Give me the layout of what you thinkin'. Call up Clip and let him know I'll be heading the meeting. You know he'll have my back. Trust me, I got this."

"Aye, that's no doubt." DaVon gripped his stomach again and I knew pain was brewing.

"So make the call." I needed him to know I meant business and I had his back. Penelope had made that clear to me. Her man and his business was also her main focus.

DaVon laid out his plans, and I took mental notes and bounced. Nothing was to be written that would leave a paper trail. When I arrived, Clip was outside waiting. Quincy was standing beside him.

Clip spoke first. "What's up, Precious?"

"Yeah, what's good?" Quincy followed up.

"Hey, is everyone already here?" I was only interested in getting down to business. I was nervous and anxious to get it over with. Inside, everyone was sitting around the table talking in somewhat muffled voices. Clip opened the door and I stepped inside first. Clearly I had everyone's attention, as their eyes went straight to me. A few of the faces looked familiar. I had been to a few spots with DaVon in the past. But the one face I was very familiar with was Mob's. He was the only one I had ever actually been introduced to. And he had been out to the house a few times.

He seemed a bit surprised to see me but said, "Hey, Precious."

"Mob," was my response. This meeting was business and I refused to digress from that. All the other guys seemed to look past me and I knew they were searching for DaVon.

Clip and Quincy both looked at me. Clip whispered, "You want me to introduce you?"

I wanted to scream yes, but I had to make it clear that I was there in DaVon's place, which meant I was in control and didn't need an intermediary. "Nah. You two can have a seat," I instructed.

A seat was empty at the head of the table. With all eyes on me, I put one foot in front of the other and made my way to the chair. I sat down and looked at them. I had a sudden urge to clear my throat and rub my both my sweaty hands on my pants. But I chilled. Clip nodded in my direction and I took the cue.

"Some of you may know my name is Precious. And you know who I am. And for those of you who don't know who I am, I'm sure you will make it your business to figure it out. DaVon won't be here today. So we'll get started. A lot is coming up in the next few weeks and months to come. We takin' new territory and we need one hundred percent clientele in those areas.

"New territory?" An unknown voice boomed across the room. I laid eyes on a light-skinned tall dude with a flat-top.

"Nigga what the fuck." Clip stood up. "Respect this shit. When she speakin' you shut the fuck up. When yo' ass can talk she'll summon you." Dude eyed Clip, then Mob and Quincy eyed him.

He apologized. "Aye, you right. I'm trippin'. My bad, Precious. I'm sorry."

I started to roll my eyes, but that would not have been a boss move and it would appear childish.

I looked at Clip and moved on. "As I said, we will conquer new territory and add some new leaders to each block. With the anticipation of the new clientele, we have a big shipment coming in. We gone flood this city. You will be expected to carry more kilos and deliver on the sales. Daily drops may shift a bit, but that information will be discussed later."

"Case." I referred to one of the leads. Case had been running a block successfully for two years, according to DaVon. And he had seen a bigger future for him, so I announced, "You will be leading two of the new blocks."

"Cool." Case nodded. "What about my old one?"

"That one will be reassigned." Case nodded again with acceptance. "Rodney." I addressed him next. Rodney was a peon, but he had mad clientele and made major plays, and was not to be fucked with. DaVon was certain he could handle running a new block and maintaining order. "You will be running one of the new blocks. You are being promoted to lead."

"No doubt." The tone in Rodney's voice told me he was proud.

"Mob, you will be leading a new block and maintaining two old ones. And you still have your other duties with pickups."

"That's what's up. I'm here for the takeover." Mob was happy.

"As for the rest of you, DaVon will be meeting with you next week to set up territory and changes. Keep in mind, taking over new territory, things can get crazy. But the plan is to step into these new blocks with as little bloodshed as possible. Gettin' the bag is the goal." With that I stood up and made my exit. Clip and Quincy followed.

"My dude good?" Clip asked as we walked outside.

"He will be."

"Yo, tell that nigga to get well soon. We got shit to handle," Quincy said.

"Aye, I'm out." I was ready to go. I had come and done what I told DaVon I would do. At least I hoped I had done a good job. Either way I was not doing it again. Or least I prayed I never had to. All those killer faces looking at me made me feel like I was next in line to be shot.

Chapter 21

"Maria, I love your breakfast steak tacos." I popped the last bit into my mouth. I chewed slow to savor the taste. There were more left, but I did not like to eat until I felt full, so I chilled.

"I like making them in the morning, it's quick and filling. I used to make those for the kids all the time for breakfast when they were in school." Maria set a tray of fruit on the kitchen table.

"Not fruit too. I can't eat any more." I rubbed my stomach. When Maria cooked, she thought of everything.

"You don't eat enough, Precious. I must make sure you eat sometimes or you'll fade. Not enough meat on your bones." She grinned at me. DaVon strolled in the kitchen on that note.

"Whatever she don't eat, I will." He chuckled, then bent down and kissed me.

"Babe, I eat enough," I declared.

"Come on over here and fill up your plate, DaDa." Maria fished a plate from the cabinet. DaDa was her nickname for DaVon.

After DaVon's plate was packed with tacos and fruit, Maria left the kitchen on a mission to clean. The house was always spotless, but she kept it top-notch. There wasn't a piece of dust that could be found on the premises. But she also took charge of the contractors for the pool upkeep, yard work, and landscaping. Maria was the glue that kept the house together.

"What you got going on today, babe?" DaVon nearly stuffed a full taco into his mouth. I watched him chew it up. Even his chewing turned me on. I so loved my man and his healthy appetite. Even though he ate well, he stayed ripped, courtesy of the full gym he had in the house.

"Well, I gotta go by the house and check up on the construction. Then I have a hair appointment, which gone clear out the rest of my day." I ate a strawberry.

"How is that going? I have been meaning to stop by the house too, to peep out the construction. You'll let me know if something ain't right?"

"It's going okay. And you know I will let you know if there is a problem," I assured him.

"Aye, well make sure you make time for me tonight. I want to take you out to dinner. I already made reservations."

"I'm lookin' forward to it." I smiled. I loved spending time with him, but we both were so busy we had to schedule each other in. "Oh, babe, Keisha presented this idea to me about opening a hair salon." I decided to share with him now before it slipped my mind.

"She do hair?" He threw a pineapple chunk into his mouth. Confusion was on his face.

I couldn't help but laugh. "I asked her the same thing when she said it to me. But nah, she don't. She wants to open up a salon and hire beauticians, but the major part of her idea is me."

"How so?" DaVon seem puzzled.

"She asked me to basically be part owner. You know, us go into business together." DaVon gazed at me as he bit into another taco and chewed. He pondered over what I said. I decided to break her vision down. "The way she put it to me is, business at the hair store is going really well. She selling so much hair she feel like if we had a hair salon we could get that clientele. Which is like guaranteed. You know, a chick buys hair, then we could have some of the baddest hairstylists on deck, and they can go right over and get they head done."

"It really does sound like a legit business point. But how do you feel about going into business with her?"

"I don't really know. But I told her that I had a lot going on with school and the dry cleaners. I didn't want to jump into anything else with an already full plate."

"That's true. You also have to be thinking about the fact that you two are friends. Sometimes that ain't the best combination. You both run successful businesses."

"Yeah, she pointed that out about us being successful, she said that was another reason she considered it, and plus I'm in school for business."

"So then the issue could be opinions about the way things are run from the both of you. And even though the idea sounds ideal, what if things don't work out? Now I ain't saying this to be negative. I just think these are things to consider before making a decision."

"This is why I wanted to talk to you about it, babe. I knew you would give your honest opinion and that's what I need. Not the money that could be had. I know that's a big part of it, but that can't be the reason. But like I said, I haven't agreed to anything because truthfully, I don't think I have time. And whatever business adventure I take on, I want to be hands-on with it. And once I'm done with school, I will eventually want to open up another business. Not exactly sure what kind just yet, but that is my goal."

"Well, whatever you decide to do, I got your back one hundred percent. No matter what."

"I know you do." I stood and gave him a kiss. I had to get going so I could check on the construction and get to my hair appointment on time. "I'll call you from the car though, babe, I got to get in these streets."

"A'ight, sexy." He slapped me on my butt as I turned to walk away. His phone rang.

"What up, my nigga? Pull up in a minute . . . Naw, fuck it. I got it. I don't need shit. You handle that. Bet."

The look on DaVon's face told me something was up, so I chilled a second.

"What's the matter, babe?" I pried.

"You still here?" He looked up at me. "I thought you was out the door."

"Is everything cool?" I stuck to the question at hand.

"Yeah, I'm straight. I gotta make this run to drop

off these bricks and pick up this money. Quincy was supposed to roll with me, but a block just got hit. So he handling that shit."

"So who gone roll wit' you? Ain't Clip and Mob in Dallas?" I was confused.

"Yeah, but it's cool. It's just that nigga Drake. I been dealin' wit' him forever, that's why I only normally take one nigga wit' me.

The look on his face was confident, but I didn't like the sound of that. "Tell you what, I'll ride with you," I volunteered.

"Babe, you got your own shit to do. It's cool. Trust me. Go handle your business."

"Well you been wanting to get down to see what's going on with the construction at the house. I can ride with you to make the drop, then we go by the house. The other Escalade is parked over there; I can jump in it afterwards for my hair appointment."

"Babe, you don't have to do this. Tell you what. I'll drop off the bricks then meet you up at the house. How does that sound?"

"DaVon, I want to ride with you," I insisted.

"A'ight, Miss Bonnie. Grab your piece of steel," he joked, "'cause I ride hard." He chuckled. I would have laughed, but instead I turned on my heels and went to retrieve my gun. I figured why not.

The ride over to Drake's spot was long, and I enjoyed it. I loved any time I spent in DaVon's company. We enjoyed each other. We pulled up to his house; the neighborhood was an old suburb in Compton. I was nervous and wondering how DaVon could deliver anything to anyone in this neighborhood and feel safe. But I knew there was a lot of old so-called kingpins that still lived in the hood.

"Listen, I want you to sit back and hang tight. I'll be right back. This won't take long." Smiling, he leaned over and kissed me on the lips. I smiled back and bit my lip seductively.

"I'll be here, lover," I teased. "'I get so weak in the knees I can hardly speak, I lose all control and something takes over me.'" I sang along with the SWV song "Weak." I loved old-school songs, or back-in-the-day songs, as I used to call them when I was growing up.

DaVon had been inside Drake's crib for at least ten minutes and it seemed like forever. "'Blood start racing through my veins,'" I continued to sing. Then I caught a glimpse of a short, brown-skinned guy, who in my opinion seem suspicious, slip around the side of the house. But he moved so fast I wondered if I had seen him. I looked around and saw no one else. Another minute passed. My gut trembled.

Reaching inside my purse, I retrieved my Ruger. Slowly I opened the car door and stepped out into the heat. The neighborhood kids were screaming and laughing. The block almost looked normal; if I closed my eyes, I could have imagined I was anywhere but Compton—until I heard the helicopter. I looked up and my reality was confirmed. Helicopters ran all day and night—it was loud and annoying, but in LA I was used to it.

I stepped onto Drake's porch and heard no movement inside. Gently, I placed my hand on the doorknob and was surprised when the door opened. Who knew people in Compton were bold enough to leave their doors unlocked? Inside, I shut the door. All I heard was silence, which I found odd. Slowly and quietly I stepped halfway down the long hallway. To the left was the living room, and opposite was the den, which opened up into the kitchen. My heart started to race as I realized DaVon was nowhere in sight.

I stopped when suddenly I heard voices. Gripping my gun tighter, I continued to walk to the left of me, toward a room where I heard DaVon's voice. "So you wit' the shit homeboy. You gone sneak a nigga." I knew then there was trouble. Leaning to the side, I peeked in the doorway and saw the short suspicious guy, with a gun to the back of DaVon's head. Drake was bent over, looking in the bag with the kilos. I hurriedly sat back so that he couldn't see me.

"You damn right. I knew you an them light-ass niggas would slip up. Slim, bust this nigga."

Taking a deep breath, I stepped in the room and put the Ruger to the back of the short guy's head. He flinched. "Don't move." I ordered.

"Wait, who the fuck is this? You brought company, DaVon?"

"You fuckin' right." DaVon seethed.

"Listen, man, tell ya girl to step the fuck off."

"Nigga, he don't tell me shit," I barked. "Now you, shorty fat, put the gun down. And I mean slowly." I pushed the tip of the gun into the back of his meaty head.

"Aye, aye, just be careful wit' that thang, lil momma."

"Nigga, watch yo' mouth." DaVon growled.

"Yo, nigga, I know you don't think yo' bitch gone come in here and save the day," Drake said, then quickly reached down, for his gun I assumed. But I didn't think about it, I just pointed the gun at him and squeezed the trigger. I watched as the bullet flew from the tip of the barrel and landed straight into his heart.

"Shit, girl," Drake mouthed. Slowly he looked down

at the smoke coming from his chest. We all watched as he hit the floor, then Slim quickly bent down to get his gun. But not before DaVon reached in his waist, pulled out his gun, and shot him in the neck, then ended him with a bullet to the center of his head.

In shock, I stood and stared at the bodies. Tears ran down my face.

"It's okay." DaVon wrapped me his arms.

"I couldn't let him shoot you." I sobbed.

"You did the right thing. Now we got to get out of here." DaVon reached down and grabbed the bag of kilos. Then he reached under the table and grabbed a bag full of money. "Now all this shit mine, you old greedy ass nigga." He pointed his gun at Drake and squeezed off a bullet between his eyes. I saw it coming but still flinched. "Let's get out of here." DaVon nodded his head toward the exit to the hallway.

I couldn't believe what had happened, but I dried my tears. I realized DaVon was with me and if I had not pulled the trigger he would be back there dead, and so would I.

"Everything is gone be alright." DaVon drove at a normal speed. We didn't need to bring any attention to us. Getting out of Compton was the new goal.

"I know."

"I'm lucky you went wit' me. I been dealin' wit' that suck-ass nigga for years. I made that nigga who he is. But you can't never trust shit. And I know that better than anybody. Guess I was trippin' today. Next nigga won't get the chance though, promise you that . . . I love you though." We were sitting at a red light and Compton was almost behind us. He leaned down and kissed me.

"I love you too." I smiled.

"Now I got to go and send some cleaners over there to get rid of that mess. I'ma drop you off at the house to look at the construction, but I can't stay."

"It's okay. You go handle business." I understood. Soon we were pulling up to Dad's house. The construction workers were out everywhere working. I kissed DaVon goodbye and he drove away.

"Yes, I really like the space. It's what I had in mind. But I was worried when you said there might be complications, so this is great," I said to Scott, the lead guy on the construction crew. One of my requests on the new design was for them to knock out the wall that separated the kitchen from the living room. Dad had always wanted to do that, but he never had time to oversee any construction because of his hectic work schedule at the dry cleaners. So I took this opportunity to help it come to life, but Scott had said there might be some complications because of the original structure of the house. But luckily, it had turned out fine.

"The demolition of the wall went off perfect. The designers you picked should be here in a few days to start the crown molding you requested." I liked the sound of that; everything seemed to be moving along smoothly.

"Good. I can't wait until everything is finished." I continued to walk throughout the house, observing the rest of the work. The dry cleaners' number stalled me when it jumped up on the screen of my phone. "I need to get this." I stepped away from Scott. "Hello," I answered.

"Precious, they came in with a gun!" Katrina screamed through the phone. She was talking so fast I wondered if she said what I thought I heard. This could not be happening.

"Wait, what? Gun?" I asked. My heart was beating rapidly and I felt as if my breaths were coming slowly.

"Two guys came in with a gun and tried to rob us. The police are here. Can you get down here right away?" Katrina pleaded.

"I'm on my way." I ended the call. I could not believe this bullshit. Instantly, I thought of my dad. He lost his life in that damn dry cleaners. I found DaVon's name in my phone. "DaVon, get over to the cleaners. Katrina says they almost got robbed." I left a message since he didn't answer the phone.

There were three cop cars and a few detective cars parked out in front of the cleaners when I pulled up. A policeman tried to stop me at the door. I looked him up and down and rolled my eyes. Now was not the time for him to play robo cop with me. "This is my business. I'm the owner." I glared at him at him so hard he stepped aside without any question. "Katrina," I said as I approached. She was talking to a tall, thin white guy dressed in a cheap suit. Looked like one of them JCPenney specials, but he thought he was clean and if you told him different, you might have to fight him.

"Precious!" Katrina looked over at me. "This is the owner," she pointed out to the detective. I observed my surroundings quickly; the other detectives and cops were investigating the scene. They hadn't found my dad's killer and I doubted they were going to waste time to find a robber.

"What happened?" I asked. But I knew the answer was that some idiot pulled a gun and demanded cash.

"Two guys came in and demanded I open the safe. I told them I didn't know the number but they didn't believe me. So I went to it and pretended to try and open it. After five minutes of trying, one of the guys pushed me in the corner of the office and fired a gunshot over my head. Then they just ran out." I couldn't believe what I was hearing. Katrina had a child. I could only imagine the fear she'd had at the moment.

"She was telling me that the cameras are not working yet." The detective gazed at his notepad and not at me. I thought that was rude because I knew even with all his notes, nothing would happen to bring the robber to justice.

"Yeah, there was a problem with the hookup, size, equipment and stuff. But it's scheduled for day after tomorrow actually."

"Well, thank God the bullet missed her." He looked at me as if he was accusing me of something. As if I had control over everything.

"Is there a problem?" I was offended. LA cops were full of shit and everybody knew it. They couldn't solve simple murders but accused me of something that was out of my control. The nerve of them. I was ready to give them a piece of my mind.

"Oh no, I was pointing it out. You know these neighborhoods are not the best and everybody needs a quick buck." His point was not being made. That had nothing to do with his insult about my cameras.

I just glared at him. My gaze read *shut the fuck up.* "Well, thank God we have you all. LA's finest," I said with sarcasm and rolled my eyes. "What do we do next?" That was hopefully a question they could answer for me.

"We wait. See if anybody saw anything. We already fingerprinted the whole place. I'm sure we will come up with something. Other than that, we will continue to investigate. I suggest you get those cameras up and runnin'. And keep your eyes open."

"We'll do that," I said with attitude. I hoped he got the hint I wanted his ass and the rest of his bull-dogs out of my cleaners. They were not good for shit except donuts and milk.

"Here's my card. Call me if you get any leads. And we will keep you posted if we hear anything."

I took the card and gripped it tightly in my hand and prayed it crumbled. "You okay, Katrina?" I asked as soon as they were gone.

"Girl, I'm shook up but I'm good. I can't wait until I'm able to take me and my child and get the fuck outta LA. This type of shit gets old."

"I know. I'm sorry this happened to you." I really felt bad for her and I felt guilty that the cameras were not working, even though I couldn't do anything about it. "I understand if you want to quit."

"Quit?" She popped her neck at me and put her hand on her hip. "Quit. What you mean? My job? Girl, I ain't about to quit my damn job over no scrubs. Shit, I mean I'm shook, but I ain't crazy. This LA. What are the odds you won't get robbed any-where you go?" She paused as if she wanted an an-swer. "Exactly." I guess she took my silence as an answer.

"I know but—"

She cut me off. "No buts . . . I'm fine. Once I get over the initial shock, I'm good. What them niggas bet-ter worry about is me tellin' dookie an' 'em about they punk ass. I remember they faces. I better not never see them again." Katrina's fear was now anger, and I felt her on that. But I knew all about dookie and 'em—her gun-toting cousins—and they didn't play. They would body anybody who crossed them and not think twice.

"Babe." I turned around to DaVon's voice. "What happened?" Concern covered his face.

"Some punk-ass niggas tried to rob me," Katrina jumped in.

"You get a look at them?" was his next question.

"Yeah, they dumb ass didn't even try to hide their identity."

"I'ma try to find them, and you can identify them before they take their last breath." He seethed. "You a'ight, though?"

"I'm cool. They tried to make me open the safe, but I couldn't so they pushed me in a corner and fired a gun over my head, then ran off."

"Them niggas pussy." DaVon gazed around.

"DaVon, I know they coming to do the cameras in a couple of days, but I want to get a security guard up in here. And ain't talkin' bout no rent-a-cop. I'm talkin' bout the ones that carry guns."

"No doubt. I gotcha. I'll make some calls right away," he declared.

"Katrina, you can go home for the day. I'll finish up the shift and lock up. And don't worry, you still gone get paid for the entire shift," I assured her.

"Good lookin', Precious." Katrina strolled off to gather her things. "And thanks, DaVon."

"No doubt." DaVon looked me in the eyes. "Babe, maybe you should just close up for the day. Ain't no use in stayin' open."

"No, fuck that. I ain't lettin' nobody run me outta my business. I get so sick of these thug-ass hoods bullying everybody's business. Well, they ain't gone bully me." I had to blink twice to fight back the tears, I was so angry.

"A'ight, I got your back. Whatever you want to do. But I'm gone hang out with you for a minute for the rest of the shift. I ain't leavin' you here alone."

"Don't you have business to tend to? I don't want to hold you up."

"You my business." He pulled me close and I felt safe as I breathed in his scent. I wished he would never leave my side.

As much as I tried to urge him to go handle his business, DaVon ended up staying until I left; he refused to leave me alone. So I closed an hour early, but only because I knew he had things he needed to do, and he would put them off for me. But I knew he still was taking care of the incident from earlier, and that was a priority. So after walking me to my car, he kissed me and promised to meet me at the house later.

At home I ran me a hot bubble bath, climbed in, and soaked. The water was so hot and soothing, I woke up forty-five minutes later still soaking in bubbles and feeling relaxed. I tried to ignore it, but honestly I was a little shook. Never had I killed anyone, and prayed no one pushed me to do that again. But I had to block the whole thing out of my mind. How, I was not sure, but I was going to try hard.

After drying off and lathering my entire body in one of my favorite Bath and Body Works lotions, I slid into a pair of my girl boxers and a wifebeater,

and headed downstairs to find something to eat.
Maria was gone for the evening. I decided to steam
up some broccoli and shrimp in my Rachael Ray
nonstick skillet. Fishing out a wineglass, I poured a
much-needed glass of champagne. I just needed the
day to be over.

Chapter 22

After all the drama with the dry cleaners being robbed, and DaVon almost being robbed and killed, which drove me to kill a man, I was at my wits' end. But I pushed past that and kept it moving. Nothing was going to stop my show. Finishing school, having a successful dry cleaners, and loving my man and having his back were all goal points for me, and I was on top of it. To prove it, tonight was going to be epic. It was DaVon's birthday and I had a surprise party planned for him.

I had rented out one of the hottest clubs in LA and didn't cut any corners. The entire thing had cost me more than eighty thousand dollars, but I was not tripping. He was worth every cent. Keeping it a surprise had been kind of difficult, but I had pulled it off with the help of everyone. Now I just had to be sure it went off as I planned. As usual, DaVon was busy handling business and making sure the streets were tight. He told me that he really wasn't into celebrating his birthday and that normally he was busy with the hustle. So, to pull him away from his hustle,

I had told him that we had reservations for dinner because I knew he wouldn't question that. But I still wanted him to go home and change his clothes. I called him up and told him that our reservation had moved up a couple of hours because my custom-made dress was late coming in, but I was on the way to pick it up. I told him that he should just go home, get dressed, and since the restaurant was close to Keisha's house I would just get dressed there once I picked up my dress. Then the stage was set for our next plan, which was Quincy trying to convince DaVon to go have a drink at the bar of the club where the party was being thrown. It was risky, but we gambled on it all playing out.

"It's on point up in here, Precious." Keisha scoped out the club. "That nigga gone love this." She admired the place. I hoped DaVon would be just as impressed.

"I hope so." I breathed a nervous sigh as I looked around, hoping everything was together. We were all at the club, along with all the guests who had been invited to surprise and celebrate DaVon's birthday. The food and every ounce of liquor in the club had been stocked in anticipation of the party. I made one thing very clear to the owner: I wanted everyone to leave happy and raving about DaVon's birthday bash. Now all we needed was DaVon to make his grand entrance.

"Aye, this bish about to be off the hook," Buffy chanted, as she bent over and shook her butt. That was her signature stance; she could never wait to shake her ass. "When he gettin' here? I'm ready to turn up," she sang with excitement.

"Bitch, first off, calm down, this ain't yo' party,"

Keisha jumped in. I giggled, then looked at my lit-up cell phone, signaling a text.

"That's Quincy. He said they pullin' up in two minutes. Get everybody in position." I got in beat mode. I wanted to be sure it went off as planned. I positioned myself at the door of the VIP lounge, waiting for him to enter.

"The time everyone has been waiting for, my man DaVon just stepped in the building. What's good, DaVon!" The DJ announced him as he walked through the crowd, balloons and party confetti falling from the ceiling. DaVon shook hands and slapped fives with almost everyone he passed. Watching him work the crowd was like watching Mitch on *Paid in Full*. He was loved, a true ghetto superstar. I couldn't help but smile. I was in awe of my own man.

Finally, he made it up to VIP, where I was waiting patiently to greet him, and he hugged me so tight my feet lifted off the ground. "You got me," he whispered in my ear. My surprise had worked.

"I hope you like it," I whispered back. "Enjoy every moment." I kissed him on the lips.

"I already have. This is dope!" he shouted over the music.

"My nigga." Clip approached and embraced him in a man handshake and back slap.

"And there is more, babe," I boasted and stood back.

The music stopped and the DJ announced, "Don't worry about the music, I'll be back atcha in a minute. But right now, welcome to the stage Young Jeezy, here to get shit poppin' for ya boy DaVon's birthday bash."

Jeezy hit the stage, mic in hand. "Shout out, DaVon,

turn up, my nigga!" Jeezy vocalized on the mic, then went in with his first song, "Me OK," which was one of my favorites from him.

Everyone started to jam to the song and DaVon pulled me close to him. "That's what's up, babe. I can't believe you put all this together for me. And I had no idea." His eyes were glowing from excitement. I smiled. It felt good knowing I had succeeded in making him happy and giving him a birthday celebration that he wouldn't forget. He had done so much for me, there was no way I could ever repay him. So when I found one of the hottest promoters in the city could hook me up with some live celebrity entertainment for DaVon's birthday bash, I jumped right on. Money was not a problem.

"I want you to know that I love you and appreciate everything you do for me." I looked up at him.

"No doubt. I got you. Always." He leaned down and kissed me again. "And damn, you look good. Let me look at you." He held my right hand up and turned me around in a circular motion. I couldn't help but blush as I watched my man eat up how good I looked. His reaction was half the reason I chose the outfit. I was wearing an all-black Brandon Maxwell V-neck jumpsuit that fit my curves just right. "Damn, Precious, bad and classy. Can't not one woman ever met fuck wit' you, babe. You a true diamond in the rough, and I mean that. Ummm," he said. His eyes were mesmerized by me and there wasn't another feeling like it.

Quincy stepped up. "Aww, break that up."

"Thanks, Quincy, I could not have pulled this off without you." I was glad for his help. Keeping DaVon out of the loop was no easy job.

"Aye, it's all good." He sipped from a bottle he had cradled tight.

I stood on my tiptoes and kissed DaVon on the cheek. "Enjoy your friends. I'ma check on the girls." I stepped away.

"Damn, bitch, you ain't no joke," Keisha sang when I approached. "You ain't tell a bitch you had Jeezy comin' through."

I smiled. I knew she would say exactly that, but I had my reasons to keep things quiet. The less people that knew, the better. I had begged Quincy not to let it slip during his pillow talk with Keisha. Looked like he had kept his promise. "I know, I know. I had to keep it a secret. I didn't want DaVon to find out."

"A'ight, bitch, I see you." Keisha continued to rock her head to Jeezy.

"Fuck all that. Can you hook a bitch up?" Buffy stepped in. She always had an agenda. "Shit, Jeezy down there lookin' fine as a motherfucker. A whole damn snack." She studied him from the distance. "And you know he got bank. Shit, I can barely keep my legs closed watchin' him."

"Bitch, the cable man come around and you can't keep yo' legs closed. Sit yo' horny, ho ass down," Keisha spilled. We all started laughing.

"Whatever." Buffy responded with a sneer. "Jeezy, baby, I comin'." Buffy screamed and zoomed out of VIP. Without question, we knew she was going down to the stage to try and get her hooks into him. Jeezy did six songs before leaving the stage. Afterwards, he and some of his crew came up to VIP to meet DaVon. He turned out to be really cool; he hung out with us for almost two hours before leaving. My guess was he left to get away from Buffy, who kept jumping on his lap. He ignored her, clearly uninterested. But I got the feeling he wanted Keisha and in a bad way, because he couldn't keep his eyes off her. And Quincy was starting to notice. He pulled Keisha away from Jeezy's eyesight and stayed glued to her until Jeezy was long gone.

Oddly enough, not long after Jeezy left, "Supa-Freak" blasted out of the speakers. That was my jam, so I wasted no time jumping to my feet. And so did the other girls. "Aye, I'm a superfreak," Buffy sang along and twerked.

We all danced and laughed and DaVon came up behind me and grinded on me. Keisha pulled me away from him, and we danced together, just having fun. DaVon, Quincy, Clip, and a few guys from the click were standing close to us, still drinking from their bottles. Buffy kept dancing and backed her ass up to DaVon like she was trying to grind on him. I watched DaVon hold his hands up and gently back up from her. But she tried again.

"Aye, chill, Buffy. Not cool," DaVon said loud enough for all of us to hear him over the music.

Typical Buffy, she laughed. I kept dancing, trying to ignore her because I knew from being around her how much she loved attention, no matter what the cost. The song ended, so Keisha, Buffy, and Nicole, Buffy's best friend, and I went to sit down. And boy, was I glad to sit. I was out of breath from all the twerking and unnecessary booty shaking we had been doing. But it was all in fun and I was enjoying it.

"Have any of you noticed, or is it just me? But is that damn Clip growing up and getting finer every time I see him?" Nicole asked. She had the look of complete lust all over her face. I turned and glanced at Clip.

"Hmm, I thought I seen you tryin' to back it up on him," Keisha commented with her lips twisted.

"Yeah, I seen ya ass too. Be careful, you might get that young dude hooked. You know these young niggas can't control themselves. He'll be knocking on your door all crazy-ass hours of the day and night." Buffy gave her two cents. "Guess I ain't the only one who tryin' to snag one of the crew. And that's good to know." She crossed her legs and took a sip of her drink.

"I swear, you are too thirsty," Keisha said, shaking her head at Buffy. "And you need to keep yo' wobbly ass off DaVon." That statement caught me off guard. Suddenly I could see a vivid slow-motion reenactment of her ass all up on DaVon. My head spun around to see Buffy's reaction to what Keisha had said.

To my aggravation, Buffy giggled and said, "Listen, I'm just tryin' to see what's up with the dick. You can't blame a bitch for that."

My mouth flew wide-open. That was the last straw. I jumped across Keisha and landed my right fist so hard into Buffy's jaw I could have sworn I heard it crack over the music. Buffy tried to grab my fist, but I managed to get my left hand on her chest and hold her down. My fist then connected with her mouth.

Keisha and Nicole tried to pull me off and they succeeded, but only for a second. "I'm gone kill you, bitch!" Buffy screamed and tried to come at me. I pushed her so hard she fell to the floor. I jumped on top of her and started pounding her face, fist after fist. I felt strong hands pull me off her and I tried to fight them off, then realized it was DaVon.

"Babe, stop. Calm down." He attempted to hold on to me. I continued to struggle against him. "Precious!" he yelled.

Buffy stumbled but finally got to her feet and reached for an empty glass and threw it in my direction; it went over my head. DaVon ducked and the glass crashed to the floor behind us. "Bitch, you better be glad that didn't hit me. DaVon, get off me. I'ma beat this nasty bitch's ass." I screamed and tussled, still trying to break free of DaVon's hold.

"Yo, get Buffy ass up outta here," DaVon ordered, his eyes fixed on Quincy.

Quincy pulled her up and dragged Buffy out of VIP as she continued to curse and say things I couldn't even make out. Gradually, DaVon loosened his grip on me.

"Let me go, DaVon." I jerked free.

"You cool?" Keisha approached me. Nicole was in the corner, trying to grab her and Buffy's things. After gathering their things, she looked at me and ran for the VIP exit.

"I'm good. Just keep yo' low-life ass friend away from me. Bitch rude as fuck!" I yelled. Then I tried to fix my frayed clothes and gathered my composure. I hated that I had let Buffy get to me like that. I was usually a calm person, and worked hard at acting like a lady. My dad had raised me to try and control my anger and emotions. I had only been in one fight, and that was ninth grade when a hood rat just like Buffy had tried to take my kindness for weakness. But I had put that to rest when I beat her weave out of her head in front of all her friends. Not only did she leave me alone, I earned a lot of respect as I was not to be fucked with. Not that that should have been a problem, because I didn't mess with anybody. But sometimes you had to use your fist to close a few doors.

Chapter 23

A few weeks had passed since the incident at DaVon's birthday party and as far as I was concerned, I was over it. I didn't even spend any time thinking about it. I had other important things to focus on, like my man, school, and the dry cleaners. The house was coming together and everything was finished. I was just waiting on the inspector to come in and declare that and I would make the final payments to all the contractors. Things were really going well for me. DaVon and I were planning to take another trip to Miami, but for two weeks this time. We were planning to have a Realtor show us a few condos on the beach. We were really considering purchasing one for a getaway crib. And I was too excited about that.

Today, I was at the dry cleaners filling in for a couple of hours because Katrina had an appointment. Things were getting back to normal. It had been a minute since the botched robbery, but we were not worried. The cameras were in and we had two ex-cops that would stop in and keep watch. Not to mention DaVon had put word out on the streets that the dry cleaners was off-limits and that anyone who even thought about holding it up was a dead man walking. Word on the street was he found out who the idiots were who did it. And all I heard about that was it was a wrap. I chose not to ask any questions. So being alone didn't bother me or the girls at all when we had a shift.

"What's up?" Keisha said as she made her way through the doors. I was a bit surprised to see her. I had not heard from her since the incident at the club. I figured she was a bit pissed about what I had done to her friend. But I couldn't care less if that were the case.

"Hey," I returned. I was filling out some order slips that needed to be tagged.

"I just came through to check on you. DaVon was over to the house earlier, and he said you were down here for a couple hours filling in for Katrina."

"Yeah, she had an appointment."

"You good though? Since all that crazy shit went down."

"Aye, I'm cool like I told you that night. And I'm not sweating that shit no more. I have moved on. I had just had enough of your friend. She just go too far with that mouth. She has no chill."

"Yo, trust me I know. But I checked her ass on that though. That bitch know better, she just go as far as she can. But I think she heard you though." Keisha chuckled. But I didn't see anything funny. "'Cause you got all up in that ass. Girl, I didn't know you had that in you. Bitch, you got mad hands."

I didn't really have nothing to say to that, so I just didn't. The last thing I needed a compliment on was me out in public actin' like a hood rat. That was just not my style. "So you still got her staying with you?" I asked instead.

"Hell no, thank God. Her momma took her and her brother back. Don't nobody want to deal with they ass. That's why they grown ass still live at home wit' they momma. Plus Buffy and her brother were the bread-winners at the crib. They momma don't work or do shit. She needs them."

"Hmm," was my dry response. I was not surprised to hear any of that. That summed up a lot for me.

"So have you thought about my proposition?" For a minute I was not sure what she was talking about, then it hit me. It must have been written on my face. "You know, the salon. Remember, we talked about it."

"Oh yes, that. I remember." I really hadn't thought about it much since I spoke with DaVon about it. 'Cause after talking to him my mind was made up.

"What's up? You ain't said nothing else about it. And I was tryin' not to bug you about it."

"Well, you know, it's like I told you. I have a lot going on and right now I just can't. I have too much on my plate."

"It's cool. I get it." Her words said she understood but a hint of disappoint lined her lips. She smiled though.

"Hey, y'all," Katrina said as she walked in. "Thanks for filling in for me, Precious." Katrina came behind the counter and clocked in.

"No problem."

"Aye, you want to grab some lunch and something to drink?" Keisha asked me.

"Sure. I could use a drink. It's been a long week.

You good, K? You need me to bring you something back?" I asked.

"Nah, I'm good. Trent comin' through to bring me lunch." Her new boyfriend was keeping a smile on her face as of late.

"Okay, call me if you need anything." I made my way to the office to retrieve my purse.

Keisha and I hit up a bar and grill that was close by. We had lunch and got bent. I hadn't planned on that. I was hoping to go home and get some studying done; instead I fell straight into bed, half drunk. I wasn't sure how long I had been asleep, but I was definitely knocked out. Nevertheless, the constant ringing of my doorbell unnerved me and I started to stir. At first, I thought I was dreaming, but my eyes popped open. Right away, my head started pounding. I slowly lifted my head and reached for my cell phone; the time read one o'clock pm the next day. I could not believe I had slept for so long. I turned to my right and realized DaVon was not in bed next to me. I yelled his name to ask him to get the door. But after six attempts with no response, I realized I had to get up. Whoever was ringing the doorbell clearly had a death wish, because I was annoyed to my limit. Sighing, I forced myself up on the side of the bed and dragged my body off of it. The pounding of my head sped up and became stronger as I made my way down the massive staircase. No longer annoyed, but now pissed off, I snatched the heavy doors open with as much force as they would allow, to find Clip standing in front of me.

Both my hands instantly went to my banging forehead. "Clip . . . why are you ringing this doorbell like you are high?" I tried to clear my dry throat. Before he could answer I turned around and yelled DaVon's name again. I wasn't sure what the hell he was doing, but it had better be good since I had to answer the door for his impatient-ass friend. On any other day, I liked Clip, but my headache was not feeling him.

Again, DaVon did not answer me. I slowly turned back to Clip. "DaVon is playing deaf for some reason. Come on in, Clip." I stepped to the side so that he could enter, but Clip did not move. For the first time, I realized that he had not said one word since I opened the door, which was odd because normally he was hype.

"Precious." For some reason my name sounded strange coming from his lips. It sounded different this time. I turned my left shoulder slightly and glanced behind me. Suddenly the silence inside was overwhelming. Turning back to face Clip, I looked past him before my eyes fell back on his. His mouth moved. "DaVon been killed." The words slid from between his lips.

I was sure I had heard him right but he was wrong. "Boy, DaVon is upstairs." I pointed behind me.

Clip fixed his eyes on the direction that I pointed toward, but confusion was all over his face. "Precious, DaVon was found shot in his car this morning. They pronounced him dead already. I went to the scene."

I felt my legs go weak as they gave away under me. I hit the floor before Clip could catch me. Rushing to bend down, he lifted my weak body up, but I was lifeless as I stared off into the distance in a daze. This was a bad dream, and for the second time in my life it was imperative that someone woke me up. But instead, I lay paralyzed, with Clip mumbling words that made no sense.

"Precious, you have to go and identify his body. They asking for a family member or someone who resides with him."

I tried to speak, but my lips could only tremble. I thought of my father and his spattered blood and I tried to fight and be strong. Shutting my eyes really tight, I balled my hands into fists and prayed for strength. I opened my mouth and took in a deep breath but my chest was heavy; it was useless. Clip called my name over and over until I opened my eyes.

"You can do this." He looked at me with reassurance. But I didn't feel reassured at all.

"Help me stand up," I managed to say. Now on my feet, I couldn't stop trembling, but I tried. With Clip's help I somehow made it down to the morgue, walked inside, and identified another man that meant so much to me. DaVon.

Chapter 24

Two days passed me by and I did what I was best at: shut myself inside. I had cried so much, I had made myself sick. I was at my dad's house because I could not bring myself to go home to DaVon's house. I couldn't face being around his things. Everything in that house breathed him, and I wasn't strong enough. Most of all, I couldn't understand why this was happening to me. Maybe I was cursed? Maybe I deserved to be alone? I wasn't stupid. I knew the life DaVon lived was risky, but not this, not this way. Everyone had been trying to call me, but I was not answering. Keisha had left over twenty messages, but I had not called her back. Clip had also been blowing me up, but I just was not ready to speak to anyone.

The only thing that had saved me from them was that they didn't know where I was hiding. I had left the vehicles at the house and had a private driver deliver me to my dad's house. I was sure they had been out to DaVon's house looking for me.

The knocking on the front door told me someone had finally found me. Reluctantly I went to the door, because the pace of the knocking told me they would not be going away. Once again, I opened the door to Clip.

"I been calling you, nonstop," he said as if I didn't know it. He had to have known I had caller ID and was purposely not answering.

"I've been gettin' some much needed rest." My eyes were swollen from all the crying I had done.

"Listen, I know this is hard, but you have to get this funeral planned. I need you to be strong. We are here for you . . . I promise you, when we get through this and I'ma take care of the motherfuckers who dared do this. And I think you know that I don't give a fuck, mamma or grandmother, I don't give a fuck. They gotta pay."

I glared at him because I knew he meant it. And at the moment, I didn't give a fuck or feel sorry for the perpetrator. Whoever had thought that it was okay to bring me life-long pain was evil. I wished it back to them tenfold and whoever in their life it affected.

More knocking on my front door interrupted us. This time, I opened the door to find Keisha standing on my porch. "Come on in," I said before she could say anything. "Clip's already here," I added.

"I have left you like thirty messages, Precious," Keisha complained as she followed me to the den, where Clip was waiting. "What's up, Clip?" she said.

"Aye, Keisha," he returned.

"So Clip is here so that I can start preparing for the funeral. I ain't quite sure I'm ready, but . . ." My voice broke and I fought back the tears.

"I got you; I'll help," Keisha volunteered. I wanted to thank her but couldn't find the words. But I knew she understood. "I know DaVon gone, but we yo' family too, and we here for you, whatever you need."

"No doubt," Clip cosigned. "Whatever it is, you just say the word."

I glared at both of them; the tears just rolled down my cheeks, but I wiped them away quickly. Now was not the time.

For the next couple of days, I put everything in motion, and true to her word, Keisha never left my side. The hardest part was taking the clothes to the funeral home for him to be dressed in. I wanted to make sure everything was as perfect as possible. I was paying top dollar, and I didn't need any screwups. But I didn't have to worry, the mortician had done an excellent job. There was not one blemish on his face.

The funeral had turned out okay. I passed out at the cemetery as they lowered the casket into the ground. I woke up ten minutes later in the funeral home limousine with Keisha fanning me. I told the driver to take me home to DaVon's house; I felt the need to be close to him. Keisha rode with me and insisted she stay with me to make sure I was okay. But I refused. I was in no mood for company. I wanted to be alone with my thoughts. I kicked off my pumps no sooner than I hit the door. Dragging my feet, I headed into the den to the bar, reached under it and retrieved the Hennessy, then a glass. I poured myself a shot. Normally, I didn't drink heavy brown stuff, but I had to have it. I was in the mood to be out of my mind for a minute.

To my surprise, a bottle of Excedrin headache pills were under the bar next to the Hennessy, and that was just what I need. I had a banging headache to die for, so an Excedrin would work miracles. I popped two of them into my mouth and swallowed the shot of Hennessy whole and fast, then poured up another one. Grabbing the bottle, I made my way over to the couch.

Thoughts of DaVon were all over me, his voice, his smile, his touch. Him, period. All the things about him that I would no longer enjoy and would miss dearly. No longer able to hold it in, I cried out his name, my gut filled with excruciating pain and there was no cure. Taking the top off the Hennessy, I took the biggest gulp my mouth could take. It burned my chest so badly I almost threw up and felt like my breath was cut off all at the same time. But I used all of my anger, hurt, and pain to fight it.

I woke up on the couch in the den later. Every muscle in my body ached beyond comprehension. The Hennessy bottle was half empty and my insides were screaming bloody murder. I attempted to sit up and the whole room swerved and my gut rose to my mouth. I don't know where the sudden burst of strength came from, but I took off down the hallway to one of the many bathrooms in the house. This was the first time I was glad there were so many. Lifting the toilet seat, I spilled my guts over and over again until I was empty. Weak again, all the sudden energy drained, I lay out on the floor, unable to move. I woke up hours later, still on the floor.

The sleep must have done me some good because when I sat up this time, I didn't throw up, but I was still very weak and my muscles were sore. Making my way back to the den, I noticed the sun was still shining outside. I wasn't sure how long I had been asleep, but I knew by now it should have been dark out. Picking up my cell phone, I saw it was the same time I took my first shot of Hennessy the night before. I had slept a day away.

Forcing myself up the stairs, I pulled my clothes off in the middle of the bedroom floor and dragged myself into the shower. The warm water soothed me as I cried all over again. I let the warm water run down my face and wash my tears away. After drying off, I put on some comfortable pajamas, slid into some slippers and contemplated my next move. I decide to go downstairs and fix me some coffee. Just as I added the sugar and cream, the doorbell rang.

Sighing, I shut my eyes tight and rubbed my forehead. Company was not on my list. If I had to bet, I figured it was probably Keisha at the door. I had given Maria two weeks off when DaVon was killed, so she was not due back yet. At the funeral she was so distraught I worried about her even in the midst of my sorrow. But I was in no shape to comfort her then, the same way I was in no shape for company now. I just was not in the mood, but something told me they would not go away unless I answered.

"Penelope!" I opened the door and was in full shock. She was the last person on earth I would expect to see at the door. "What are you doing here in LA?" I asked.

"I had to come and give my condolences. Pablo wanted to make the trip, but he couldn't. He sends his support though." The look on her face was sincere.

"Hey, I understand . . . Come in," I said.

"I was there yesterday for the service, but I sat in the back. I would have come by last night, but I had some business."

"Thank you, Penelope, for even coming." I shook my head with appreciation and again had to fight back the emotions. "I really appreciate you takin' the time to even come." I knew the kind of people Penelope and Pablo were, and they didn't do things like this. DaVon must have meant something to them. But he had that effect on people.

"Aye, DaVon was like a kid brother to Pablo and me."

I shook my head and tried to fight the strong shadow of depression that was hovering over me like a tree branch that kept growing and growing. "How about we go to the bar and I pour you up a drink?" I changed the subject before I fell over in a crying fit.

"I could use a drink."

I led the way into the den, then excused myself while I went off to the kitchen to grab my coffee; the last thing I needed was another drink.

Penelope opted to have a shot of Don Julio. I noted that she was going hard, right off the grid. My head pounded just watching her drink.

"So how have you been holdin' up?"

I looked at her and sucked back tears. I was so tired of crying, but I couldn't help it. I wondered if I would ever stop, if the pain would ever subside or ease. "I'm cool." My voice trembled a little. "Just still in shock you know . . . Shit came out of left field so, you know." I wiped the one tear that escaped my eye, which was followed by another. I sniffed back the rest.

"Listen, it's okay to cry. I know this probably sounds redundant because you hear it from everybody, but things will get better. Just take it one day at a time."

"And that's my plan. I'm just still processing it. But I'm good." I tried my best to believe the words that came out of my mouth.

"So what are your plans now?"

I sighed, full of uncertainty. "I haven't even thought that far yet . . . I might move back into my dad's house though. I can't stay here; it's too many memories and this house is so big. I can't be here alone."

"This place is your home, you can't just leave it. DaVon wouldn't want that. You remember what I told you back in Miami?" I was sure a confused look was on my face. "DaVon had a legacy, and you were here for it." I had to think for a minute. "Precious, you were DaVon's right hand at all times. No situation trumps it. This house, his legacy, the things he stood for. The fruit of his labor."

"I know, and I can feel it when I'm here. DaVon was not only my man but my best friend, and my family. The only family I had."

"He loved you, Precious." She said it as if to reassure me, then downed another shot. "I have to get back to Miami. But I want you to take some time out, open up to your grief and truly remember your man. And remember I'm here for you and so is Pablo . . . There is always the torch."

Penelope was deep. She was good for conversation, but this time I was bit confused by some of her words of wisdom. I shrugged it off and showed her out. She said her plane was leaving in a few hours and she didn't want to miss it. I had only met her the couple of times, but I would miss her. I knew she had extended her friendship to me, but with DaVon gone there was no reason for us to ever cross paths again. Especially with her living all the way in Miami. And with the life her and Pablo led, they had no time for a person as simple as me.

Chapter 25

A week had passed. I was still at DaVon's house and I had finally slept through a full night without waking up. And today I was hoping to sleep in just a little while longer. I had been sleep deprived for a while, so it was much needed. But somehow, when I saw Doug's name light up on my cell phone, I knew that sleeping in was not going to be possible. Doug was DaVon's lawyer and his name was saved in my phone because DaVon made sure that I kept him on speed dial. But the last thing I needed at the moment was for him to interrupt my sleep.

"Hello," I breathed into the phone with an annoyed tone. I was not in the mood to be polite or nice.

"Precious"—he called me by my first name as if we are old friends—"this is Doug Bates. Remember DaVon introduced us a couple times?"

"Yep, what can I do for you, Doug?"

"Well, first I would like to give my condolences. DaVon was a great guy . . . I know this might not be a good time, and I hate to bother you, but I really need you to come down to my office."

I had to fight to remain calm. He had already interrupted my sleep and now he wanted me to drive damn near an hour downtown to his office.

"Doug, can this wait?" I slowly pulled the covers back and sat halfway up.

"Listen, I promise this will not take long. Matter of fact, I'll come out to the house. How about that?" I was surprised to hear that he was willing to drive out to the house. I started to question him further, but I didn't feel like it.

Confused, I asked him what time, agreed to him coming, and hung up the phone. Still pissed that I had to leave the warm, cuddly bed, I kicked the covers back and lay in one spot and allowed the crisp, cold AC to force me awake. After taking a shower, I headed downstairs for something to drink. I was beyond thirsty. Opening the refrigerator door, I fished out the orange juice, reached into the cabinet and pulled out a glass, then poured myself a full cup.

Just as I attempted to raise the glass to my lips, the doorbell rang. Stuffing the carton back into the fridge, I cradled my glass in my hand as I made my way to the door. Doug stood in the doorway, cradling his expensive briefcase as if he was an heir to a kingdom.

"That was quick," I commented.

"My Porsche can take me anywhere in the city at top speed," he bragged. Doug was a rich middle-aged white man with more white than black in his hair, who made a fortune off drug dealers like DaVon. In return, he made them feel untouchable. And in most cases they were. Doug was connected, and if you could be cleared of any charges in the city of LA, Doug could make it happen for you. But I called him "thug passion" because he was a jack of all trades: Not only did he practice criminal law, he dabbled in family law as well. Not to mention he owned two pawn shops and two chicken restaurants where he had the nerve to sell soul food. Like I said, he was a jack of all trades.

"Let's have a seat in the den." I led the way.

"It's been a long time since I've been out here. I forgot how nice this place is." He made small talk, but I was not really interested.

"Can I get you something to drink?" I offered just as common courtesy, but I was really ready to get this over with.

"No thanks. I just finished some Starbucks. Now I'm all wired up. I really shouldn't have anything else."

Since I got that over I jumped right in. "So what brings you all the way out here?" I cut to the chase.

Doug took it upon himself to have a seat before I offered him one. Wasting no time, he popped his briefcase open. "Well, I wanted to go over DaVon's will. You are the beneficiary."

"What will?" I was surprised to hear he had a will. "He never told me anything about a will. Especially that he had one with me on it."

"Well, he didn't until recently. He came into the office and had me draw it up. He left your name on everything. The house, vehicles, even keys to several safe deposit boxes throughout the city."

I couldn't believe what I was hearing. "Are you sure? I mean why . . . why would he leave all that to me?" I knew DaVon loved me, but to leave me everything he owned was shocking to say the least.

"I'm certain, Precious. Your name is on all the paperwork." Doug looked at the document and handed it over to me.

I read my name in the document over and over again. I looked up at Doug. "Doug, DaVon and I had only been together for a short while, barely a year."

"All I can say is that when he did this, he was of sound mind and body. He made it clear to me that he loved you and that one day you would be his wife. And he wanted to provide for you in the event something were to happen to him. Thus, all this legal paperwork."

The tears followed at the sound of the words *loved* and *wife*. Now we would never have any of that. Both of us were cheated out of our God-given right to be happy. My heart was breaking all over again. "Thanks, Doug." I was ready to end the visit. I needed to be alone.

"Alright, I'll leave you to process all of this. But you call me if you need anything. We can sit down next week and finalize the documents to officially put everything in your name."

"Sure," was all I managed to say.

Doug shut his briefcase and stood. "I'm sorry about your loss. DaVon was a really good guy. And I mean that."

I nodded my head and gripped the documents. I knew he was being sincere, but there was nothing more for me to say.

"I'll let myself out."

I felt drained all over again. With the documents still in my hand, I stretched out on the couch and fought back tears. The doorbell rang and I was tempted to scream *Go the fuck away*. I knew it could only be Doug. I sat up briefly and looked around to see what he could have possibly left. Nothing caught my eye. The doorbell chimed again. Pushing myself to my feet, I answered the door.

"We need to talk," Clip said, his tone matter-of-fact.

Chapter 26

It took a few days, but I finally decided to visit the banks so that I could take a look inside those safe deposit boxes that Doug had talked about. My mouth fell to the floor each time I opened one. By the time I reached the last one, I was nervous and exhausted. I had opened in total ten overstuffed safe deposit boxes. I couldn't be sure because I had never in my life and probably never would be able to count that much money. I knew that DaVon had money, but I really didn't have any idea how much. But it was safe to say there was a bit over seven million in total in his safe deposit boxes.

By the time I pulled out of the parking lot of the last bank, my heart was racing. I had to turn up the air in the car to keep from sweating. I just could not believe it. There was no way I had access to that much cash, and it was now all mine. I wasn't sure if it was a good thing or bad, because I viewed it as blood money. But I tried not to think that way because I knew it was money DaVon had worked hard for. Hell, sacrificed his life for. I needed to get my thoughts together so I headed over to DaVon's house, which I now owned.

As soon as I got into the house, I made the bar my destination. A drink would calm my fast-beating heart and control my nervousness. Nonetheless, no sooner had I sat down at the bar and filled my glass than the doorbell rang. The unwanted interruptions I kept getting from the doorbell were really starting to get on my last nerve. In my previous frustration, I had considered having it removed. Deciding to have a sip of my drink first, I considered not answering the door as the brown liquid penetrated my throat. I mean, if I didn't answer, what could the person on the other side do? With the lingering question easing my mind, I took yet another swallow of my drink. The second ring forced me to my feet.

"Hey," Keisha said first. I glared from her to Quincy, who was standing patiently behind her.

"What's up, Precious?" Quincy threw in.

"Come in." I invited them in without question. For some reason, seeing them made me feel different. I actually didn't mind the fact that they had just popped up. Which surprised me, seeing as though just a few short seconds earlier, I had craved nothing more than to be alone.

"I know y'all want a drink, so I will not ask." I led the way to the den.

"You already know what it is," Keisha sang. She was a drinking fool and never once would she turn down a drink. And if you didn't offer her one, she would help herself to it.

"Pour me up a shot of that Hennessy," Quincy added.

"I'll take the Heeney too," Keisha cosigned.

"I guess that makes three of us. That's what I was drinking before you arrived." I grabbed the bottle and poured up two glasses. "What y'all doing all the way out here?"

I caught Quincy's eyes going to Keisha, then to me. "Aye, straight up, you already know. DaVon was like a brother to me, which makes you my sister, no doubt. I'm just concerned about you . . . want to be sure you straight." He reached for the glass that I extended to him.

"Yep," Keisha kicked in. "You been cooped up in this house; I call, you don't answer, and you not reaching out . . . we just been worried about you." Concern controlled her facial expression.

I knew exactly what they were talking about. I had been shut in, but I needed my time alone, to regroup, think clearly. "I'm good. I needed a little time to myself though." I hoped the words were convincing.

"I can understand that. I been waiting to talk to you but . . . these streets don't change, you know. DaVon gone, but this shit out here still alive and well . . . it's beast mode out here." He shook his head at me. "Things have to keep going or everything falls. DaVon got money out here in these streets, mad money. I gotta step up though . . . in order to do that, I have to take over."

Every word out of his mouth rang true. I glared at him because I understood the message behind his speech. I just did not expect it. Keisha eyed me briefly, then looked at Quincy.

"I worked for DaVon a long time, so I know mostly everything about the entire operation, but I need to get into his office, he got some information in there that I need."

I almost spit my drink out at his boldness. Quincy was DaVon's guy; he had worked for him and watched his back. There was no disputing that. But what made him think that I would allow him into DaVon's office? I understood that he was trying to help, but not this way. I could not allow it. Besides, I had my own plans, and although they were not confirmed, I was sure it was what I wanted, or least what had to be done.

"Quincy, I appreciate that you're willing to step into DaVon's place. I'm sure he would be grateful for your loyalty . . . but it won't be necessary . . . I'm taking over," I announced. Quincy's head seemed to drop, but he was still looking straight at me. Suddenly he started laughing. His laughter faded as he realized I was not joking.

"Wait, you being serious?" Keisha burst out laughing.

I just looked at them both. I didn't know if I should be insulted, or not take them seriously. But I had to admit, who would have thought I would be saying anything close to the fact that I was going to tackle being a queenpin. But even when I worked as a cashier at the dry cleaners, I was not to be laughed at.

My face was rock solid and I gave it to them straight. "DaVon and I were in love. True love. And as you both know, we spent a lot of time together as a couple. In that time, we made it all count, especially DaVon . . . he taught me the game. Everything." I wanted to be clear. "Even introduced me to the connect." I could tell Quincy was trying to keep a calm look on his face, but I could see that the wind was knocked out of him. And my words had been the blow.

Keisha's mouth was wide-open. "Ohhh . . . I didn't know that."

"DaVon was my man. I was his right hand. That makes me his queen." As far as I was concerned, nothing else needed to be said.

"Aye, I had no idea. And with you having ties to the connect, that only makes things better. But my face is known in the streets. I have that connection, and it would be better if I did it. I know all the crews and got the muscle to pull it off."

Maybe he hadn't heard me right or wasn't clear about what I had just said, but I wasn't in the mood to repeat myself. So I decide not to. "Don't worry, all that's covered. Now Clip will be my right hand. And he's going to bring Mob on board. I hope you'll be down with us. Your position will remain the same." The day Clip had stopped by unannounced and requested we talk, he revealed that he had known that DaVon had showed me the game, and that I had been personally introduced to the connect. DaVon always told Clip everything, so I was not surprised. Quincy, on the other hand, DaVon would not disclose this to information to him.

"No doubt. You know I got you. All I want to do is keep the streets working. Or all hell will break loose. And we don't need that," he stressed. I was glad to hear he was down. DaVon would want his guys to stick together.

"And you know I'm here too if you need me," Keisha stepped in to assure me.

"Thank you." Without much else to say, we all polished off what was left in our glasses and they left. Afterwards, I felt really good. I was glad that everything had gone well. With each second that ticked by, I faced the realization that I had actually stepped up. My mind hadn't been made up until I had opened my mouth. The day Clip had come by, he had assured me DaVon needed me and that he had my back. He made me understand everything Penelope had been saying to me all along. Then, suddenly, it was like a time bomb went off in my head; it all made sense and there was no turning back. It was time to put my first play into action. I picked up my phone.

She answered on the second ring. I greeted her, full of certainty. "Hey, Penelope."

Chapter 27

It was unimaginable, but I dived right into DaVon's life as far as the business was concerned. I didn't even give it a second thought. My first order of business to set things off was to head to Miami. So after ending that call to Penelope, when she calmly revealed to me that she had been expecting to hear from me, I boarded a plane. I didn't know how long I would be gone, but I was sure it would only be a couple weeks at the most. Turns out things were deep, so my short stay had turned into an entire month. But honestly, being away from LA had not been a bad idea. While there, I was able to control my grieving a little better than before. It was still hard, but somewhat manageable. And hanging out with Penelope was helping out a lot; everyday with her was a lesson.

"So what are we doing here?" I asked Penelope as the driver pulled into the parking lot of a rusty green building and came to a complete stop.

"Business as always." She glared out the window through her Tom Ford sunglasses. "It shouldn't take long. I'll wheel and deal a bit of this and that. You down?"

"Of course." I wasted no time replying. Penelope always intrigued me. I was a kid waiting on my next cartoon episode. I couldn't wait to see what she had in store. The driver stepped out of the car. Two big bodyguards who worked for Penelope approached.

Dressed in an all-white pantsuit drenched in about a hundred thousand dollars in diamonds, Penelope looked like she was about to attend a Grammy party. Inside, another dude showed us to the back of the beat-up building. The building was so run-down, I was curious as to what we might find in the back.

"P." The guy standing at the door greeted Penelope. He lightly tapped on it and I could hear what sounded like a huge bolt unlock. The door opened and she passed her sunglasses to the guy who opened the door for her. A dark-skinned dude with dreads sat at an iron picnic table. Penelope crisscrossed her hands behind her back.

"Scrap. It's been a long time." Penelope greeted him as if they were old friends.

"Well, that ain't my fault." Animosity was clear in the dude's voice.

Penelope giggled. And something about it sent a chill up my spine. "Small talk, huh. That's what you got me out here for?" She looked him dead in the eyes.

"I'on got you out here for shit. Try yo' fuck niggas on the block that you employee. Fuck Pablo at?"

Penelope brought her forefinger to her mouth, indicating for him to shut up. "Nigga, I think you know better than to question me. This conversation has one ending. Product and dollars. You and them gorilla taco-eating motherfuckers you call a crew think I'm to be tested."

"No, you a fucking disrespectful-ass bitch. You had three of my men killed last week alone. That dope was payback from a robbery, but you didn't think to ask. Just sent out orders. And it was you who made the call, I know that for a fact."

"You fuckin' pussies, I swear. Only thing you think about is money and cars. Nigga, this the game, not hide n' go seek for yo' kiddy pleasure. It's takes a bitch like me to prove that." Penelope turned around and the guy that had let us in handed her a gun.

"So you gone shoot me, you fuckin' *puta.*"

"That's what happens to niggas who try to fuck me. Miami is my house." Penelope was calm. "Stop stepping into thinkin' you can fuck me wit' no condom, cause this will happen every time." She pointed the gun. I could literally hear the bullet as it left the chamber and landed right between the dude's eyes. His brains spilled out the back and splattered in every empty space imaginable. I was stunned. I knew Penelope had her man's back. But I had no idea she put in work. And she didn't even break a sweat. Reaching for her sunglasses, she slid them on and we exited.

I didn't ask no questions; none were needed. I focused on getting my businesses handled. Pablo and Penelope had been great putting some things together for me, and we kept the LA streets rocking. Shipments were good and no problems had come up. I left Clip in charge while I was away and he made sure everyone was supplied in a timely manner. And Quincy confirmed that all blocks were locked and on point. So product was successfully moving on the streets and money was coming in at a steady flow and no one was coming up short. Clip made sure of that. With my new lifestyle, I made sure to keep the piece that DaVon had given me close. It still felt strange packing a gun with me everywhere I went. But I understood one thing very well: I was important. And I wouldn't hesitate to blow off anyone's ass who dared threaten to step to me like that.

My plane had just landed. It was my first day back in LA. The feel of the airport was welcoming because no matter how you enjoyed being out of town there was never any feeling that could describe coming back home to LA. After gathering my luggage from baggage claim, I headed outside to catch a shuttle to long-term parking where I had left my truck.

"I'm so glad you finally back." Maria greeted me at the front door with a hug. While I was away, she had stayed at the house. "I was beginning to worry that you may never come back." She reached for my Louis Vuitton suitcase.

"There was no chance of that." I smiled. Maria now cleaned my dad's house a few days a week as well as the upkeep of DaVon's crib. I really appreciated having her around; she was caring and did a wonderful job. "Besides, LA is rooted too deep in my blood. I love it here." I looked around the house. I could almost feel DaVon's presence.

"I see Florida gave you a little tan. You must have spent too much time in that heat. I have a cousin out there I went to visit over fifteen years ago, and I came back with a beautiful tan." Maria chuckled. "But my skin dried out and started to peel like an orange. I promised myself if I ever went back I'd use the sunscreen that my cousin begged me to."

"It is hot there, but I tried to stay out of the sun as

much as possible. But I love the beauty." I shut the door behind me as I dragged in my last piece of luggage.

"I made mini-wrap turkey sandwiches with cream cheese, lettuce, and tomatoes, and some fresh strawberry lemonade full of strawberries. I knew you would be hungry when you arrived."

And she was right, I was starving. I hadn't eaten nothing since the night before, besides some coffee on the plane. "Thanks, Maria."

I headed into the kitchen and grabbed two of the mini-sandwiches, poured me a glass of strawberry lemonade, and headed upstairs to my room. I needed a shower to get the traveling dirt off of me.

No sooner had I kicked off my Gucci sneakers than Keisha's name lit up on my phone. She had been calling when I was in Florida, but each time she called, I was busy. But she shouldn't have been surprised, I was on a business trip. I didn't have time for chatting. If it wasn't about the crew, I wasn't picking up. And since she wasn't a part of that, the conversation was off-limits. But I had texted her two days prior to let her know I would be back in town today.

"What's up, Keisha?" I answered, prepared for her complaints that were sure to come.

"Damn, well it's about time you answered a bitch's call." She was sarcastic.

"Don't be salty. You know I been handling business. So what's up?"

"Nothing, been working my ass off. I need a break. You tryin' to chill? Let's go have some drinks or some."

No was on the tip of my tongue, but she would only complain, and whine, until I gave in. "Cool. Just hit me with the place. I can meet you in about an hour."

"A'ight bet."

After ending the call, I jumped in the shower, got dressed, and headed out.

"Girl, shit, I'm glad you finally back from your long mini vacay." Keisha stood up and gave me a hug. "How was it down in Florida? You know I been tryin' to get my ass down there."

"It was cool, I almost didn't come back," I joked. "Nah, forget that, nothin' beats Cali." The waitress approached the table and I ordered a Long Island Iced Tea.

"Aye, I can't even hate. I can't wait to get down there. I keep tellin' Quincy's punk ass to take some time off. Shit, work, work, work. I'ma end up going without his ass. I ain't gone miss out on fun, fuckin' wit' him. I'm too young."

I laughed. I didn't have anything to say to that. Quincy worked for me now and we were going through a bit of a transition right now. And I needed him to be all about work for a minute. "I looked at a few cribs though." I picked up my Long Island Iced Tea and took a sip. "Ahh, now that's good."

"Tell me about it. I had two before you even got here."

"You might want to slow down then. If you ain't tryin' to come in contact with LA's finest." I chuckled.

"Shit, I'm good. You know I can toss them back and still walk a straight line. Fuck LA's finest." She spat with laughter. "But anyway, back to this Florida crib. I hope you cop one soon because I can use a vacation spot."

"Well, you know once I get it, you can use it anytime."

"Hey, what are friends for. How did business go?"

I was surprised that she asked me straight up. It was true Keisha was my girl, but she had to understand that things were different now. My role was different. Certain things just couldn't be discussed. The last thing I felt like dealing with was her being in her feelings. But I wasn't stupid. She slept with Quincy every night, and while there was a code in the game there was pillow talk too, and I didn't believe she was totally in the dark about what went on, so I kept it simple.

"Everything is good, as you can see from the work in the streets." That much I was sure she knew.

The look on her face was blank, as if she had a question, but all she said was, "Quincy been working, so I guess it's all good."

I quickly changed the subject. "So what's up with the hair salon? Are you still tryin' to get it open?"

"Girl, yes, but it has been a challenge. Quincy was supposed to step up and help me, but like I said earlier, he too damn busy. And you ain't gone believe this one. I tried to call you to tell you, but you was ignoring my calls," she threw in, playfully rollin' her eyes.

"Don't start that. Just tell me what happened already." I knew before she shared that it was something juicy.

"I got locked up."

"For what?" flew out of my mouth.

"Bitch, I had to beat Quincy's ex-girlfriend's ass at Macy's."

"Quincy's ex?" I was shocked.

"Precious, this bitch been callin' and textin' Quincy

for weeks, and I knew it. Of course, I confronted him about it and he said it ain't nothin'. Now you know I ain't that chick that badger no nigga about no other female, so I let it go. So I go up in Macy's to grab my Mac makeup and see this thot. I wasn't gone say nothin' to her, but this ho want to jump bad, and start mouthing off bout how she still fuckin' Quincy and gone take him from me."

"Damn, she bold," I commented.

"Right, but I just laughed in the bitch's face. I told her to have at it 'cause I wasn't in the business of keepin' niggas that didn't want to be kept. So I guess when she saw I wasn't gettin' mad, she really got angry. This bitch picked up a display of Mac products and threw it at me. Mind you, I let the bitch talk shit and didn't put my hands on her because you know that's how I usually would have responded. But once she threw that shit, I attacked her ass, nobody up in there could get me off of her. So I beat that ass until the police got there and they threw me behind bars. But I wasn't giving zero fucks."

"Wow, that's crazy. Sounds like she asked for that though. What Quincy have to say?"

"That nigga ain't say shit. Talkin' bout fuck that girl, this and that."

"Did you spend an entire night in jail?"

"Damn near. They got me processed and out late that night. Bitch done made me miss hours of freedom. But like I told Quincy, if I find out he fuckin' that hood rat, I'm gone fuck him up. Round here got these basic bitches trippin' on me in public. I was embarrassed as shit walkin' out of Macy's in handcuffs."

I couldn't help but laugh at the situation. As usual, there was never a dull moment when I hung out with my girl Keisha. We sat and chatted for a bit longer before I had to leave. I had to check up on the dry cleaners. I wasn't worried, Katrina always took good care of it. I paid her well to do that. But it was my job to make sure everything was on point.

Chapter 28

Three months had passed by quickly and things were still looking up. And I was feeling good and trying to get on with my life. I kept busy so I didn't have much time to think or dwell on anything that didn't include business. And as far as I was concerned, that was for the best. Keeping thoughts of DaVon at bay was a must. I missed him immensely. Today Keisha and I had decided to go to the gun range and kick off a few rounds. Honestly, I was still not a fan of guns, but they were now a reality for me, so I wanted to be solid when it came to using them. Keisha, on the other hand, was gun crazy; she had this look in her eye when she had a gun in her hand that said so. Shoot to kill. And she equally enjoyed watching me shoot as well.

"Woo, you on track wit' that shit." Keisha was excited when I squeezed off a round. I was shooting an assault rifle and it was full of power. For every round I squeezed off I felt the full pressure, but I was on point from each angle. "I think you been foolin' us. Your ass been shooting."

I laughed at her assumption. "Nope, I guess I'm just a natural beast." I chuckled. "Real talk, DaVon used to bring me to the gun range with him sometimes. He used to say I needed to be able to lock and unload whenever possible," I admitted.

"Aye, bet, and he was right. Hell, I learned how to shoot when I was just fifteen. Look where we grew up. In these LA streets, you gotta be ready—no, let me rephrase—you gotta be ready to hit yo' target."

I nodded my head in agreement. My dad had kept me so close to him that I sometimes forgot that LA was no joke. For some reason, I had always felt protected—that was until he was murdered and reality kicked in. I picked up a Ruger and squeezed off a few rounds before we packed up and headed out.

"I think Rugers are my favorite to shoot," I shared as we walked to our vehicles.

"I don't know, the way you was up in there bustin', I would say you were a seasoned shooter and have love for all heat."

"You would say that." I grinned. My cell phone rang and Maria's name lit up. "Hey, Maria."

"Precious, I'm at your other house. I need you to come over."

"Sure, I can do that. Is everything okay?" I asked.

"Yes, but I need you to come over."

"Okay, I'll be there soon." I ended the call. "That was Maria. She over at my old house and told me to come over. So I'll call you later."

"Is everything cool? You need me to come along?"

"Nah, I think it's cool, but thanks anyway." I jumped in my new Audi and sped off.

When I arrived at the house, everything seemed normal; there was no danger, at least that I could see.

I had my Ruger on me, so I wasn't worried. I used my key and made my way inside. I yelled out for Maria and she announced that she was in the kitchen. I found her sitting at the kitchen table, shining silverware.

"Maria, what's going on?" I asked.

"You had a visitor," she announced plainly, but she looked to be curious.

"Well, who was it?"

"It was a girl." I thought for a brief second *What girl would be looking for me?* The only females I talked to were Keisha and Katrina, and Maria knew both of them. So I was drawing a blank. "Did she say what she wanted?"

"No, she didn't say. Just asked if you were here. I said no."

"Did she at least give you her name?" I was puzzled.

"No, but she did say that she would be back tomorrow."

Now I was really confused. Some unknown female showing up at my dad's house looking for me, but didn't leave so much as her name. Yet Maria called me over like it was Armageddon. Without saying much else, Maria put away the silverware and said she was tired and then left.

I dialed up Keisha. "Everything cool?" were the first words out of Keisha's mouth before I could say anything.

"Your guess is as good as mine. I get here and Maria tells me that some girl stopped by looking for me."

"Is that it?" Keisha said like she was expecting more.

"Yes, that is it, according to Maria. She didn't leave a name or anything. Just that she'll come back to-morrow."

"And you don't have any idea who it could have been?"

"Hell no. I don't have a clue. And I hate myster-ies."

"What you gone do then?"

"I guess I'll stay here tonight cause who knows what time she might show up tomorrow."

"Listen, since you don't know what you facing, I say strap up. Might be some crazy psycho bitch from your past."

I couldn't help but laugh at that, but I agreed it was definitely better to be prepared. Except for one thing: I didn't have a past that included anyone but my dad. But I was strapped anyway.

Chapter 29

I stayed at the old house the next day and the next, but the mysterious woman never showed up. But I had businesses to run, so there was no way I could stay cooped up in the house waiting on someone who might never return. So finally, I left. When I arrived at the dry cleaners, I decided to tell Katrina about the whole thing and she said it was probably one of those women from the Census Bureau. According to her, one had just visited her, asking strange questions. I had never even considered that, and oddly enough, I had forgotten they used to visit our house occasionally when I was growing up.

Keisha's name lit up on my phone just as I finished up with a customer. "Girl, it's been days and you ain't called to tell me what happened. Did the girl show up? Who was she?"

"Heck no, she didn't show, and I waited literally for two days. Maybe I was the wrong Precious."

"Either that or some shady shit is going on." Keisha laughed. "Wait, or maybe it's one of DaVon's old bitches, cause them hoes used to act up and it was hard for him to cut it off. They all loved his ass."

Surprisingly, I had never thought of that, but it was something to consider. "Well, I ain't the one that they should be lookin' for. And if that is the case, lucky for her she didn't come back, cause I don't do drama."

"I swear, bitches crazy these days," Keisha added.

"But why show up at my dad's crib though?" I shrugged with uncertainty. That just didn't make sense to me. I never knew any of DaVon's past girl-friends, so I didn't have a clue how they would even know me or where my dad lived.

"Like I said, these bitches wacko these days." Keisha sighed. "But I gotta go and take Shirley, you know, Buffy's momma, down to the bail bondsman to see about bailing her daughter's ass out."

"What Buffy do now?" I was not even alarmed to hear that she was locked up. Buffy was crazy. I could probably just pick something crazy she might have done and be right.

Keisha grinned. "Now she one of them wacko bitches I was just talkin' about. She done took her ass down to Harold's car shop. You remember that shop, don't you? It ain't too far from your dry cleaners."

"Yeah, I know Harold's."

"Precious, she done went down there and busted the window out this man's shop and chased his wife down the street with a bat."

I knew it was not supposed to be funny, but I laughed so hard. "I swear, Buffy is wild."

"No, that bitch psycho. How you gone go postal on that woman when you messin' with her husband?"

"Girl, I know. That is bold as shit."

"And that's ya girl Buffy in a nutshell. But I gotta go before Shirley blows my phone off the hook."

"Okay, hit me up later." I laughed again and ended the call.

Clip walked in the door as soon as I hit *end* on the phone. "What up, Precious?"

"Hey."

"How business going up in here?" he inquired.

"Actually, it's really good. This new equipment and the advertisements have been a hit. Sales at an all-time high." Clip was more than just my worker, he was a friend and I enjoyed talking to him. Plus I knew he really had my back for real. I never had to worry about him being a pretender.

"That's what's up."

"I been thinkin' about opening up a second location."

"Aye, I say strike while the iron is hot."

"My thoughts exactly. I just need to free up the time to get it done . . . Come on, let's step in the back." I walked around the counter and locked up. We had to talk business and I didn't want to take the risk of someone just walking in.

"Just wanted to update you on business. All the blocks are on lock, everybody meeting quota. And everybody eating, so ain't no beef . . ." He paused, so I knew something else was up.

"And?" I was not in the mood for procrastination.

"One of Quincy's spots came up short, but he handled that shit ASAP."

I glared at him. I knew exactly what "handled" meant, but money could not go missing and no weakness could be shown. Ever. I didn't really want to dwell on it because I trusted them to handle it.

"We can't be fuckin' up. Shit must stay tight," was all I had to say. "Now we got a new shipment comin' in just a few days. I know you will be on point as always, but I need you to double up for this one. Take Mob with you and have Quincy supply a few more workers because, as we talked about last week, the territory has expanded."

"Yo, no doubt. I got you," he assured me. I knew without a doubt I could trust Clip to get it done.

We touched on a few more subjects of transport and distribution, then he bounced. Time was money and we did our best not to waste any of it. I reopened the doors to the dry cleaners to get back to the business, back to the money. Not that I needed any, but it kept me busy and I needed that to clear my mind of DaVon.

"How you doing, baby?" Mrs. Maxine, one of my dad's old longtime clients said as she strolled through the door.

I smiled at the sight of her. Seeing her brought back good memories of the old days. I saw her and my dad laughing and talking in my mind's eye. "I'm fine. How are you, Mrs. Maxine?" I walked from behind the counter and into her open arms to receive one of her huge hugs that she loved to give.

"I been trying to catch you, but every time I come in, Katrina say you either just left or coming in later."

"I know, I've been so busy."

"Well, I been wanting to tell you that I love what you have done with the place. Your dad would be so proud."

"Thank you."

"Are you still in school?"

"Yes and no. I had to take a semester off recently

because I have been so busy and just kind of wore myself out. I really needed a little rest." I hated to lie to her, but I had no clue what else to say. I couldn't say *I'm now a drug dealer and have to worry about supply and demand. So I missed too much school and had to drop out.* The truth was that I really did plan to go back once I got all my businesses under control. But I didn't know when that would be.

"Well, you just make sure you finish, baby. Don't let nothing else get in your way. Your education is the most important." She continued to encourage me before leaving.

Her words sunk in. It was like Dad was speaking to me, but my reality was something to be reckoned with. Thirsty, I walked to the back to grab a Coke out of the refrigerator. I heard someone come in, then a woman's voice saying hello. I popped the top on my Coke and took a huge gulp before stepping back in the front.

"Are you Precious?" I stalled at the sight of the young lady standing in front of me.

"Yes . . ." I almost stuttered, but somehow managed to keep my words straight. "Can I help you?"

"I came by your house the other day but you were not there . . . I was supposed to come back, but I kinda got cold feet." She gave a nervous chuckle.

The Coke can in my hand was ice-cold, but my hand was sweating. "Well, how do you know me? Where I live?" I questioned.

"I'm Promise." She said her name as if I was familiar with it. But I didn't respond. I just stared at her. "I'm your baby sister . . . Well, at least by three minutes." She gave the same nervous chuckle again and suddenly I was annoyed with it. I wanted to yell at her and call her a liar. But it was like I was looking into a mirror.

I wanted to say something, but no words came. I even parted my lips to force sound, but nothing came out. The look on Promise's face begged for words but I had none. "We're twins." She announced it as if it was a secret. "Mama"—I froze at the mention of her. Promise must have sensed my apprehension, but she continued on—"She always said that you looked more like her. And that I looked like Dad."

I could not take any more. I just wanted her to stop. "Umm, you must be mistaken. I don't have a mom. My dad raised me."

"Yes, I know." She jumped right back in as if she was clearing things up.

Either she was deaf or dumb—either way, I was done. "Listen, I don't know what it is you think you know, but it's not me you are lookin' for."

"I ain't lookin' for nothin'. Now I know this is hard . . . a shock even, but I'm your sister. Not that it's not obvious, I mean we look just alike." She twisted up the corner of her mouth like she rested her case. "But you are my family, all I have left, and I would not be here if you were not . . . After being raised in different foster homes, I know rejection, and do not under any circumstances subject myself to it for fun . . . Now I found out that our dad, Larry, died not even a year ago."

At the mention of my dad's name, my heart dropped and my emotions were all over the place, but I could not deny we were spitting images of each other. I cleared my throat. "I'll have to be sure. Are you willing to take a blood test?"

"Sure, whatever makes you feel comfortable, just let me know when you are ready." She agreed without hesitation.

We stood in silence for a few seconds. "You mentioned that you have been in foster homes. Where is our . . . where is your mother?" I rephrased.

Tears instantly filled her eyes and I knew what was to follow. "She died." Reaching into her purse, she pulled out two pictures. Slowly, she handed them off to me. One of the pictures showed the face of a woman that I had never seen, with my father's arms wrapped tightly around her waist. In the other picture, the lady was holding two babies. Tears fell from my eyes as I realized it was my mother holding Promise and me. Now I understood my light skin. My mother was white. Oddly, Promise had come out milk chocolate, just like our dad. But she was one of the most beautiful milk-chocolate people I had ever laid eyes on.

"You see, you are all I have." Promise wiped at her tears.

"Well. . . . your mom must have left Dad, so it's on her." I handed her back the pictures and wiped my tears away.

Promise seem shocked by the coldness and accusation. She carefully slid the pictures back into her purse. "No, that's not how it happened. It's not that simple."

"Yeah, it is. A mother takes one child and leaves the other." I was becoming angry just thinking about it. How could she have abandoned me like that? How did she choose which one us of to take? What was her thought process?

"No, Precious, it's not like that."

I yelled from frustration, "Then what is it like then, Promise? Some kind of process of elimination?"

"She would never do that. She loved us both the same . . . she was human though, with dreams, but he didn't care," Promise cried out, sounding equally annoyed.

"He who?" I questioned. "Who is this *he*?"

"Dad. All he cared about was this place." Promise's eyes roamed the room, clearly noticing it for the first time. Again, she reached inside her purse and pulled out another photo and handed it to me. It was a picture of Dad standing in front of the dry cleaners with his hands raised, pointing at the obviously newly painted sign. And he was wearing the biggest grin I had ever seen on him. "Mom wanted to sing professionally. She had a voice as big as Mariah Carey's. It was her lifelong dream and he knew it . . . they met while she was at a club performing with her band. But she said that she loved him at first sight. So they got married right away. Two years later they had us. Dad promised that she could get back to her singing as soon as we were walking. But then he suddenly changed his mind, saying he wouldn't have a wife running around the country chasing a dream. She said they constantly fought about it. Finally, with music dripping from her veins and tugging at her soul, she made up her mind to leave him. But the night she planned to leave, you started to cry and it woke Dad up. He got up and took you into the living room to rock you back to sleep. By the time he got you quieted down and sleeping again, he had also fallen asleep holding you . . . So when her ride showed up, she had the hardest choice she ever had to make. She took me and left. But she said she would have never dreamed that Dad would keep you away from her. She actually thought he might come to his senses and we might be a family again. Instead, he threatened that if she tried to see you, he would go to court and take me from her as well. She said she could not lose us both, so over the years, through letters, she begged him to let her see you. She never gave up . . . that is, until her so-called boyfriend slash manager, who she had planned to leave because he had blown a major record deal for her, shot and killed her. But, Precious, she always wanted you. She loved you."

Tears started to fall. Everything that she had said was adding up, especially about the letters. I started to remember the heartbreaking day when I had found them, and I didn't want to think about it.

"Can you please just leave?" I asked. Promise opened her mouth, probably to protest, but I held my hand up and stopped her. "Please, I need to be alone."

She reached for one of the business cards on the counter and scribbled something on the back and slid it over to me. Slowly, she turned and walked away. Before exiting, she turned and looked at me one last time.

Chapter 30

At first, I was truly at a loss for words, first finding out about my mother and then finding out that not only did I have a sister, but a twin sister. I was numb and scared to turn any corner, for fear of finding out anything else that my dad had lied about or hidden from me. Telling me that my mother was dead was one thing; he was mad at her, hated her even, for going against his wishes. But to lie to me about having a sister? That was punishing Promise and me for something that we couldn't control. Did he hate us as well? How could he handle not seeing Promise all those years? But I was my father's daughter. Instead of embracing Promise when she came to me, I did as he had and I punished her by sending her away. It took me a few days to realize what I had done, but it was just so much to handle. I had to rationalize my thoughts and try to make some sense out of my tattered life.

"I was worried that you might never call," Promise said as she slid into the booth I secured for us. I had invited her out for Mexican so that we could talk.

"Took me a couple days but . . ." I sighed. "I hope you like Mexican. This place has the best margaritas, so I ordered us one."

"Actually, it is my favorite."

"Mine too." I smiled as the waitress set the margaritas down in front of us. She asked if we needed a minute to order, but we both said like clockwork that we knew what we wanted. Turns out, we were both crazy for chicken fajitas on corn tortillas. We giggled as the waitress walked away. "I guess we like some of the same things," I commented.

"Naturally," Promise cosigned, then took a sip of her drink.

I decided to break the ice since I had invited her out, and I had a few things I needed to say. "I know the other day didn't go well. Probably not as you had planned or hoped it would. And I apologize to you about being so rude and mean. You didn't deserve that from me. I was just in a bit of shock . . . I had to process it all."

"It's okay. I understand—"

I cut her off.

"No, I need to say this . . . It was a shock for me to hear that I might have some family left. When Dad died . . ." I stopped for a minute and tried to calm down. I could feel a lump growing in my throat and I did not come out here to cry. I took a sip of my margarita. "When Dad died, I thought I was alone. It had only been he and I for so long, I knew that I didn't have anyone else. But I tried to cope with it and get on with my life. I had to. Then a few months after he passed, I was going through some of his things and found letters. The last letter that our mother had sent was when I was around about six years old. But you see, he had been telling me that she had been dead since I was a baby."

A slight gasp escaped Promise's lips and tears began to flow as she listened to the last words that slipped from my tongue. I was sure the thought of our dad telling me that our mother had been dead since I was a baby was heartbreaking for her.

She cleared her throat. "That's when she died, when we were six. Four months after our birthday," Promise confirmed.

The waitress approached our table and placed sizzling hot skillets of fajitas in front of us.

"Dad and I were really close and it hurt me so bad when I found out he had lied to me for all that time. I struggled . . . I mean I still struggle to understand why. Now I'm just . . . I don't know." I shrugged my shoulders because there simply were no words.

"Well, I guess now it's up to us. We have to somehow learn how to move forward. I can't understand why he lied either. I wonder how he could not want to see me or have me in his life. I struggled with the fact that he didn't love me enough. And as I grew older in foster homes, I resented him for rejecting me. All those times Mama reached out to him to have contact with you, never did he even ask about me. It breaks my heart knowing that he never cared for me the same as he did for you. And I would love to know why." Promise's eyes were filled with tears. "But . . ." She shrugged her shoulders and sniffed back the tears. The look on her face was defeat. We both knew that these were just things we would never have an answer to.

"I guess life will figure it out for us. Tell you what, I know what will make us both feel better for the time being. These fajitas look great, so let's eat them before they get cold."

"For real." Promise bit into her sizzling fajitas and took a taste test. "Oh my God. I love these." Promise chewed and talked.

We ate our food and actually laughed a bit. We stopped the parent talk and learned a few things about each other. It felt odd sitting across from someone who was the spitting image of me. I could hardly believe it was real. I was glad I had made the decision to call her; it felt good knowing that I was again not alone.

Chapter 31

"You sure you gone be able to stay over, K? I can come back later if you need to leave."

"Nah, I got it. I could use the extra cash; you know I'm saving up."

"You good? You need anything? You know I got you." Katrina was like family even though she worked for me. I always had her back. But she always turned me down. Sometimes I just threw her a bonus here and there; that's the only way I could get her to take the extra money. She worked hard.

"I told you I'm straight. Just fattening my pockets. I ain't got shit to do anyway. What I need is a good man. But these LA thugs won't let me be great. All they want to do is sell nickel sacks, body niggas, and end up on skid row. And I ain't got time to be visiting nobody in prison." Katrina laughed.

"Aye, I'm sure yo' true love out there." I laughed. "But I gotta go. I'll hit you later to check on things. Call me if anything comes up."

I bounced outside into the sweltering heat. The last place I wanted to be but had no choice. I had a meeting to attend. Quincy had called me a week ago with a lead on some new territory that could bring us some money. But another known crew had been trying to move in on it. The leader went by the name Black; he was known in the streets as a big player in the game. Not as huge as us—at least his supplier was not as legit—but he was making moves. Either way our crew ruled the streets of LA and everyone knew it. DaVon had paved the way and our crew was king. I didn't want to make noise where it wasn't needed. So I thought about a reasonable response. If there was such a thing. I had Quincy set up a meeting with Black. Today was the day and Quincy, Clip, and I were meeting early to go over some things. Our backup was in place just in case.

"Let's get down to business." Quincy barely let me sit down in my seat. Sometimes he could be a little edgy.

"What's up?" I gave him the floor.

"We got to get this block. The money is major and the bullshit got to be burned, now."

"Aye, fa sho' two niggas already dead over the beef last night. Shit only gone git' uglier. Them lil niggas is hotheads with no fuckin' aim," Clip said.

"That has to cease; we can't have it. The bloodshed gone stop the money. And we all know eating is the goal."

"Damn right. The block was shut down last night and still shut down. One time been patrolling extra hard."

"They tape the scene?" I asked.

"Hell naw. They don't give a fuck about them lil niggas. They just pressuring," Clip added.

"Cool. They'll probably shut that patrol down in

the next twenty-fours, and when they do we need to be ready to supply," I said.

"I'm wit' that," Quincy jumped back in, his eyes huge. "Listen, I know this ain't the norm. But like you said, the bloodshed has to stop so we can get to the money. I been thinkin' maybe we should split the block."

I thought I heard him wrong and my neck snapped in his direction. "Hell naw." Spit almost flew out my mouth. "That shit ain't nowhere on the table." I eyed Quincy with confusion.

"Mane, what the fuck is you thinkin'? Niggas gone shoot each other up just being in the same space." Clip frowned at Quincy. "Precious, this nigga must be high."

"Fuck you mean I'm high?" Quincy barked. Clip sat up in his seat. I saw them ready to growl at each other.

"Listen. Y'all calm down. Now ain't the time for this. Now like I said, we ain't splittin' no block. First off they product weak. That shit made from dust." I was being honest. "I don't want our clients buying that crap and gettin' it mixed up with our product. We distribute grade A. The streets know that. So we stand by it. That's it." I sat back in my seat. I looked at the time.

"It's time," Clip announced. Just then, Mob signaled Black's arrival.

Quincy and Clip left the room so Black could come in. They would wait outside the door. I would signal them if I needed anything.

Black was everything his name signified. I had only seen him around the way a few times. He was black as the soot around your stove. Short and stocky with dreads that started at his receding hairline. Simply put, he was ugly as fuck. I would have laughed, but I didn't have time.

"Why don't you have a seat?" I offered him. He licked his lips and I blinked, realizing he was trying to be suave.

"You just as beautiful up close as you are off from a distance."

"Really. You just as dark up close as you are from a distance," I shot back. He had some nerve.

"It's okay, baby. The blacker the berry the sweeter the juice."

"Hmmm." I twisted my lip in disgust. "Or maybe it's the bigger the ego the smaller the dick." His big eyes squinted to slits and his smile faded. I was sure that now we could get down to business.

"So why I'm here?"

"Let's see. Blocks and dead bodies." He was really starting to piss me off.

"I think I heard something about that."

"Listen, Black. I'm here on business and time is the bag. So."

"Aye, it's simple: The block is mine. We been dealing tha' shit a good week before yo' crew tried to step in. So stand down, and you can continue to make money in my city."

I laughed out loud because he was actually serious. "You a funny guy. I didn't know I needed popcorn and Skittles to attend this meeting." I smirked, then sat up and stared him down. "Now . . . if you don't stand down you will lose four of your workers a week to the cemetery. I will then sell my grade A product to your customers for half the price. And that will bring your bogus-ass business down to nonexistent." I was clear on my position. "Now you tell me. Are you ready to make a play for it?"

The fight evaporated from Black's face. He sucked on jaws for about twenty seconds. "A'ight. Calm down, you ain't got to do all that." He gave in reluctantly. "My guys dead on that block effective immediately. All I ask is that your guys don't step into any of my other territories. Shit, we gotta eat too."

I nodded in agreement and we shook on it. "But you better make it clear to your peons, the first one steps back on my block will bleed, and not for the paramedics. The morgue." I smiled to make it clear.

Black left the room and I could see his confidence roll out with him. Clip and Quincy stepped back in the room. "In twenty-four hours have my block supplied and running."

Quincy and Clip both nodded and headed out for business.

Chapter 32

The past two weeks with Promise had been busy. Without even trying, we threw each other into the mix. Promise was getting herself together in LA. She hadn't been in the city long but was learning it, and things seemed to be looking up for her. The law firm that she had interviewed with for a secretary position had finally called and she was excited. But she said that she still wanted to find another part-time job so that she could save a few bucks. So I offered her a position at the dry cleaners and she happily accepted.

But recently I found out that she was living in a hotel, and I could not have that. I owned two houses and there was no way I would have my own sister living hand-to-mouth in a hotel. I tried to offer her Dad's house, but she refused, saying she did not want to live in that big house alone. So DaVon's crib with me it was. She was due to arrive any minute; Maria was there early, getting everything ready for her. I had filled her in on DaVon, about him being my boyfriend and that he had been murdered, that he had left me his house.

I all but ran to the door when the doorbell rang. I was excited about her coming to stay with me. "Hey," I greeted her with a huge grin. Two large, plain suit-cases stood on either side of her.

"Dang, Precious, you could have told me that your man left you a mansion." She didn't even try to hide her astonishment. This had been her first time com-ing over to my place since we met.

I grinned. "It's not a mansion." But I knew exactly how she felt, since I had the same reaction the first time I laid eyes on it. Because coming from my old neighborhood, just having a four-bedroom house with two full bathrooms was considered luxury.

"Ain't no need to be modest with me. I know a mansion when I see one. You must show me the en-tire house."

"Well, I guess since you will be living here, I will give you the grand tour. Come on in." I stepped out-side and pulled the handles of her suitcases.

"I'm surprised you answered the door because from the looks of this community, I was sure every-one had a Bentley and the butler answered their door," she joked.

"Ha-ha, ain't no butlers here, silly." I laughed. "But you're right. I'm sure most if not all of my neighbors have one. But DaVon didn't have one and I don't see any need to."

We started down the foyer just as Maria rounded the corner from the den.

"And you must be Promise." Maria greeted her and reached for a hug. "I knew the first time I saw you at the other house that you were family. Such beautiful girls." Maria smiled with Promise now in her embrace.

"I remember meeting you." Promise welcomed the embrace.

"Promise, this is Maria. She's family, as you can tell."

"Only the good half," Maria joked. "I got your room all ready for you. And I cooked my famous spicy sausages with green peppers, and guacamole. You're going to love them."

"Thank you so much, Maria. I am hungry." Promise rubbed her stomach.

I chuckled. "No, you're just greedy," I joked. "Come on. Let me give you a tour and get your things to your room so we can eat."

We walked the entire house and finally landed in Promise's room; she would be down the hall from me in one of the big guest rooms.

"This room is giving me life. A full bathroom with a shower and full-sized luxury tub. I'm in heaven." Promise plopped down on her king-sized bed. "Girl, this is the life." She could not stop grinning.

"I'm glad you like it, cause I want you to be comfortable while you are here. And remember, you can stay for as long as you like," I reassured her.

"Hey, in that case I'll be here until I retire," she gibed. "Nah, for real, I thank you so much and I just need to get on my feet. Then I'll snatch me up a crib."

"No worries, you good. Just know that I got you."

"Now, Precious, what's the story behind Maria? She was the lady that answered the door at the other house when I first came looking for you. Whose family is she? Girl, was DaVon Hispanic?"

I laughed at her. "I swear, you silly. No, DaVon was very much black." I could not stop laughing. "Maria has been his housekeeper since like forever. I say she's like family because she is. DaVon treated her like family; he cared for her. I like her too. She does a good job around here. She cooks, cleans, does laundry, whatever. She even cleans the other house twice a week."

"That's pretty cool. Shit, I thought she was some kin to DaVon or some." Promise looked around the room. I could tell by the way she snapped her neck back in my direction she was not finished. "Now, dear sister, I have one last question for you. What is it that you said DaVon did again?"

I had to pause for a second before I answered the question because I could not ever remember mentioning to her what DaVon did. I had to smile at Promise, she was good. "I didn't say," I answered with a smirk.

"At least I tried." She laughed. "You showed me every inch of this house, right?"

"Yes," I answered, wondering what she was leading up to.

"Well, not once throughout this whole house did I see any doctor, law, or business degrees of any kind posted. Which probably means he didn't attend university . . ." She raised her right eyebrow in a suspicious manner with her eyes glued to me. "So I take it he was a drug dealer?"

Boy, was she blunt and straight to the point.

"Promise, I swear you are so nosy and pushy. What a few bad things to figure out about your sister in just a short time." I chuckled. I was learning really fast that Promise said what was on her mind, regardless of what it sounded like. And she did not take no shit.

"Sorry, but for me it's a bit obvious. I dated a few in my day. Unfortunately, I just never found one who cared enough not to mistreat me. They were all cheaters and assholes. From the looks of things you're lucky."

I was, without a doubt, when it came to DaVon and the feelings he had for me—blessed. But at the same time, I didn't think I was really lucky. Everything I loved seemed to get taken away from me. "Yes, DaVon was good to me," I confirmed. "There is no denying that." I was proud to be able to confess to that. I would never love again or be loved again the way he loved me. But I was in a happy mood at the very moment, and the last thing I wanted to do was be sad. "Let's get downstairs, eat, and get dressed so that we can hit the club on time. The club will not wait all night, not even for us," I chanted.

"You were supposed to be here an hour ago," Keisha complained as soon as we stepped into the VIP area. Nicole was standing beside her like a guard dog with no bite.

"Maria cooked for us, and you know she can throw down, so that slowed us down." I kept it real. And Keisha knew exactly where I was coming from; she loved Maria's cooking.

"Guess I'll give you a pass for that. Maria do be throwing down." Keisha decided to forgive our tardiness. Then she eyed Promise, who was standing right next to me.

"Keisha, this is my twin sister, Promise," I said proudly. "Promise, this is Keisha and Niki." I noticed that Buffy was nowhere in sight. And I was okay with that. I still had not laid eyes on her since I had to check her about disrespecting me about DaVon, which had been a long time ago. And she had dared not come to his funeral. I would have not been up for her on that day.

"Hey, nice to meet you two," Promise said.

Keisha and Niki both stared at Promise as if she'd disappeared in front of them then returned. "Damn, I can't believe y'all look so much alike. Just two different skin tones. That shit wild," Keisha replied, and I felt as if her comment was a bit over the top.

Promise chuckled. "Stranger things have happened." I didn't laugh though, because for some reason I figured Keisha was being sarcastic. But I was used to Keisha and I knew her mouth was like a sawed-off shotgun, so I brushed it off.

"What's up with y'all girl Buffy?" I asked. The last I had heard from Keisha, she was locked up, but she never said anything else so I assumed she was out.

"She cool, her ass was supposed to come out tonight. But her ass playin' us. Probably for some bomb-ass nigga that won't even remember her name tomorrow," Nicole jumped in, and I was shocked to hear her negative comment about Buffy. They were usually joined at the hip.

"What happened to her gettin' locked up a while back?"

"She still waitin' on a court date about that, is all she said to me. She got some wack-ass lawyer who keep gettin' the date pushed back. I don't know." Keisha shrugged it off.

"Dang, he just prolonging the situation. I would want to get it over with," I said.

"Yep, that's what I told her, but she say that he know what he doing. He told her don't worry, they probably gone dismiss that shit. If not, she might get a short stint of probation. Cause she hit that lady on the back of her legs with that bat. That shit left bruises, so it's hard to dispute that. But his dumb-ass tryin', and she cheering him on." Keisha rolled her eyes in a sarcastic manner.

"That girl crazy." I laughed.

"That's my bitch though," Niki chanted, with a drink in her hand. Now there was the Niki I knew. Always rooting for Buffy. I just looked at her. She was just like Buffy but a little toned down. Buffy was just loud, and plain nasty.

"What's up, baby?" Quincy approached Keisha and tongue kissed her, all the while grabbing and squeezing her butt.

"What's up, ladies?" Clip greeted us. He and Quincy were together.

"Quincy and Clip, this is my twin sister, Promise."

"Dang, that's what's up." Quincy smiled. "Yo, this crazy that y'all look so much alike, identical and all."

"That's why they call them identical," Keisha said mockingly.

Clip was eyeing Promise like she was the next best thing to fried chicken. Finally, he responded, "It is dope, though." His eyes never left Promise.

Promise laughed. The waitress approached with drinks for all of us.

"Hey, I just want to toast my girl Precious for bossin' up and building out this bitch," Clip boasted.

"Word is fuckin' bond," Quincy added. We all raised our glasses and let them click.

It was quick, but I noticed Promise give me a strange gaze. It was a look of confusion. I thought she was wondering about the meaning of the toast. I pretended that I didn't see her. Hopefully, I was reading something into nothing.

Chapter 33

I woke up with a major growl in the pit of my stomach and a craving for some pancakes. I made my way to the kitchen and started to cook. Maria was off.

"Good morning." Promise strolled into the kitchen. "I had hoped to smell something sizzling or brewing at least."

"I know, I woke up starving. I'm about to make some pancakes. Want some?"

"Sure, I could eat a horse." Promise walked over to the refrigerator. "I am dying of thirst." She reached for the Tropicana then walked over to the cabinet and grabbed a glass. I couldn't help but smile. It was amazing how alike we were.

"I see you finally got out of bed. I thought you might never get up."

"Ha, you should talk." Promise laughed.

"I can't believe I still have some of that headache from yesterday. I swear I ain't hanging out with them ever again," I declared.

"I know, I still can't believe we slept all yesterday like that."

We were still hungover from hanging out with Keisha the night before. I had introduced Promise to all of them and the turnup was real. We had shut the club down and paid for it dearly the next day. Promise and I couldn't even get out of bed.

"Thank God Maria wasn't here. She would have made us get up, Sunday or not, trying to feed us or some. She don't believe in rest on the Sabbath."

"No, she should have been here; we needed her. She could have nursed us back to health. I see she ain't here this morning either. When she coming back?"

"She should be back today. Unless she decides to take the day off. Sometimes she takes off on Mondays."

"Mane, I thought I was dead when I opened my eyes yesterday morning. I felt like I was stuck to the bed and my head was forty pounds heavier. Them damn Don Julio shots are a beast," Promise declared.

"I swear you are not lying," I agreed. "I wanted to get out of bed and come check on you, but I didn't have sound judgment or muscle strength." I laughed, but the slight headache reminded me that was not a good idea.

"Yeah, well I guess you must have gotten something back, since you in here bout to get this kitchen right."

"Yes, I'm hungry." I poured the pancake mix into a bowl and added water.

"But what's up with your girl Keisha though?"

"What you mean? She cool." I continued to stir the mix.

"I know that's your friend. But that bitch was a live questionnaire the other night."

"Ahh, that." I paused and giggled at her facial expression. "She didn't mean any harm. Once you get to know her, you will see. She cool people." I poured my first round of pancake batter onto the piping-hot skillet.

"If you say so." Promise sighed. "I can let it slide this one time . . . But what I'm tryin' to know is what's up? I mean what's really good?"

I smiled at her. "What now, my sister of much curiosity?" I teased her. I put the finished pancakes on a plate.

Promise placed the syrup on the table, plopped down in a chair, and wasted no time continuing the conversation. "I just want to know what was up with that toast your girl gave you? Are you like the president? And nobody bothered to tell me."

I couldn't help but laugh because she was being extra. "I wish I were the president. And if I become the president, you will be among the first to know. Oh, and by the drastic changes I would make." I giggled. "But nah, Keisha was just congratulating me on the success of the dry cleaners." I still wasn't ready to admit to her what I was sure she already knew. That was the best and fastest answer I could come up with that was half legit. "It really has come a long way. I had no idea that it could be as successful as it has been." That part was no lie.

"That's what's up," Promise agreed, then stuffed her mouth full of pancakes.

"Actually, I'm thinking about opening up a second one. Since I've discovered I'm not bad at this business thing. Keisha asked me to invest with her to open a hair salon."

"Shid, repeat that?" Promise's face lit up. "I'm a

master at doing hair," she spit out before I could actually repeat what I had said. "I been freestyling since I was about twelve years old."

"Oh, so my baby sister got them hands, huh?" I was surprised.

"No doubt. So are you going to invest wit' ya girl Keisha, or what?"

"Nah, I turned her down already . . . just not sure if I want to venture into business with a partner. It kind of changes the course of things."

Promise hunched her shoulders. "I could understand that."

"So what's up with you? Are you going in to work today?" I started clearing the dishes from the table and loaded the dishwasher.

Promise stood up to put the Tropicana back into the fridge. "Nope. Chillin' all day." She placed the plastic container in the fridge and shut the door.

"Why don't you hang out with me then?" I invited.

"I'm good wit' that."

After cleaning the kitchen we got dressed, then hit the streets. My first stop was the dry cleaners to check on business. Then we drove over to a car lot that I had in mind. It was clear they were busy. There were like five salesman in sight and they all were helping customers.

"What you doing here?" Promise questioned, her eyes gazing over the parking lot.

"About to look for something for Maria." I pulled into a free parking space.

"You gone buy her a new car?"

"Yep, she deserves it." And her car gave her trouble all the time. I turned off the ignition of my whip and climbed out, ready to spend some money. I was tired of Maria's car breaking down on her. She needed something dependable, and I would make sure she got that.

A salesman approached us. "How you ladies doing?"

Promise spoke up first. "We good."

"I would like to look at those over there." I nodded in the direction of the row of Cadillacs that had caught my eye.

"Sure . . . I can do that. I'm James." He extended his hand.

"Cool," was my response. Ready to get on with it, Promise strolled off to look at other cars. It took me ten minutes to pick out a fully loaded white Cadillac CTS. Promise sauntered back over to us. "This is it right here." I filled her in.

"Damn, this shit dope. Maria about to be killin' these LA streets in this." Promise was hype.

"This is true," I agreed. "So what is your favorite out here?" I questioned.

"That." Promise didn't hesitate to point out a sports Audi.

I chortled. "James, I'll be taking that one too," I informed him.

"As you wish." James smiled and I could see the dollar signs in his pupils.

"You really gone get it for me? Awww, thank you, thank you." Promise rushed over to me and hugged me tight. I was glad to be able to get my sister what she wanted. After all of the paperwork was complete, we headed back toward the house, Promise in her new Audi, and I drove my car behind the truck that was delivering Maria's vehicle to my house.

Inside the house, I found Maria folding some towels. "Maria, can you come outside and help me grab a few bags?"

"Sure, sweetie. I was wondering if you would make it back while I was still here. Thank you so much for sending the car for me. Such a sweet girl."

"That was nothing, Maria. I was glad to do it. Let's grab these bags." I started toward the front door with Maria behind me. We got outside, where the Cadillac was the car closest to the door. Promise was already outside wearing a huge smile. A few feet away from the car, I halted and turned to face Maria. Extending my hand, I passed her the keys.

Maria studied the keys in her hand then gazed at me with confusion.

"Maria, those keys are for you. And this is your new car," I announced with a smile.

Maria again looked at the keys, then at me. "You got this for me? This is nice." She gazed at the car for the second time. Her attention came back to me, and this time her eyebrows were raised. "But I can't take this, Precious. Too beautiful, and from the looks of it very expensive."

"Expensive is true." I nodded at the car and smiled. "But you deserve it. It's dependable and can take you wherever you would like to go."

"I really can't, Precious. Always a sweet girl." She tried to return the key to me, but I crossed my arms in refusal. There was no way I was accepting the keys back. "Maria, I ain't taking those keys back. This car is legally your vehicle. Title and all, so get used to it. You have no choice." I grinned. "Now go on and check it out." I stepped to the side.

"Come on, Maria. These leather seats in here are to die for." Promise opened the left rear car door.

"Maria, I warn you, take your whip before she does," I joked.

A single tear slid down each of Maria cheeks. "Guess I have to get used to riding in style. Cruisin'." She laughed. Walking over to the car, she checked it out. "I will never get used to driving this car. I love it . . . Thank you so much, Precious."

"No thanks needed. Just enjoy it. All you have to do is get the insurance put on it. Let me know how much it costs, and I'll add that to one of your checks each month."

Crying, Maria walked over and hugged me. It felt good doing something nice for Maria; she was good people and DeVon would have done the same thing.

"So what's up for real? No more bullshit." Promise grabbed a seat at the bar. We were at the house after all the excitement with the new cars, and I had sent Maria home early. I gave her a stack and told her to hit a few blocks to get used to her new whip and shop. But now here I was under Promise's thumb and curiosity, yet again. "I mean, I can't front, what you did for Maria was mad cool. But I gotta know."

Pulling out a bottle of Moscato, I poured us both a drink. "You, my sister, are as persistent as they come." I sipped my drink and glared at her.

Promise grinned. "Stop stalling and just tell me what's up. I mean, I been in the streets, Precious, since forever . . . and I see the way DeVon lived. The way it's set up for you to live now." She hunched her shoulders. "It ain't hard to figure out." She downed her drink.

I nodded my head in agreement but didn't speak. Instead, I took a free moment to fill our glasses. I knew Promise was smart, that was clear from the first time I met her. The lies were dead in the dirt and no use. So I told her everything.

Promise's mouth popped open. Shock would be an understatement. "You mean it? You in charge of this shit, now?" I lifted my wineglass and emptied it as an answer. Promise nodded her head up and down and I could see that she was proud. And honestly, I didn't know how to feel about that. "Damn, my sister is a motherfucking boss! These basic bitches ain't even ready . . . fill my shit up." She pushed her empty wineglass over to me. "You have made my day. My big sis the queen of these LA streets."

And that was the last word spoken on it. I pulled out another bottle of wine, we talked, laughed, turned on the music, and twerked. Surprisingly, I had Promise beat, hands down. All that practicing in the mirror had paid off. I was tickled with laughter.

Chapter 34

It was hot and LA was looking good and I was feeling even better. People were out and everyone seemed to have a smile plastered on their face. That too made me feel good. It always felt good when I didn't see any cops chasing someone, or the ambulance with its blinking lights and loud siren blasting, while some poor mother stood screaming over her blood-ied, bullet-ridden child. I turned onto South Main and pulled into the parking lot of Keisha's and Quincy's new nightclub. It was under renovation, and she had asked me to stop by to check out the place. And I was happy to do that; supporting my friends was also a must. Adjusting my Gucci eyewear, I made my way inside.

I immediately saw that work was still needed for the entrance area. It looked like some drywall had been pulled down and the floors were dated. Keisha had told me they were going for a modern, upscale look, so I knew this wasn't it.

"What's up, chic?" Keisha stepped out from be-hind the bar area, which was completely remodeled.

"I see you had your favorite part of the club re-modeled first," I joked.

"Shidd, you better know it. I need to be able to take a drink before I do anything." Keisha chuckled. "So what you think? They put this in two days ago. They had to pull up the floor and everything."

"I like it. What all is being renovated?" I questioned. From just a quick glance at the place, it was apparent that a lot had to be done.

"Just about everything you see in here. They starting on the entrance part tomorrow and the bathrooms. New flooring going in every inch of the place. The balcony area is up there." She pointed up over my head. I turned to see a circular area high in the air. From the design, I could already see the potential. "Up there gone be the VIP area, of course."

"I'm excited to see it once it's all done." One thing I knew for a fact was that if Keisha was opening a nightclub, it was gone be off the hook.

"I know, right. Shit bout to be ignorant off the hook." She cosigned my thoughts. "Come on, let's go to my office. I have a bottle of Hennessy. We can have a shot."

"It's too early for all that. What about a margarita? "I suggested. But I knew Keisha was not hearing me.

"Precious, get yo ass in here and celebrate wit' me."

I stepped into the nicely renovated office.

"This is nice." I glanced around in awe. The office was big. She had it painted off-white with a brownish-green accent wall that was beautiful. A plush couch with two accent chairs to match, and carpeted. "I see this was the second part you remodeled."

"Damn right. A bitch gotta be comfortable. I want

to be able to sleep in this motherfucker if I have to."
Keisha smiled.

"And thanks for the snacks." There was a table
with a spread of fruit, cheese, and turkey—you name
it. And of course that bottle of Hennessy and two
margaritas set up. I couldn't help but laugh.

"Yeah, I knew you would cry for that weak-ass
ladies' drink." Keisha giggled. It was good to have a
friend that knew you.

"Well, thank you." I stuffed a strawberry in my
mouth and grabbed one of the margaritas.

Keisha wasted no time pouring herself a shot; she
downed it in two seconds flat. "A bitch needed that,"
she commented and poured herself another.

"Well I guess since you have two areas done, I can
say it's coming along?"

"Thanks to me. I have been picking floor cover-
ings and ordering shit day and night. Dealing with
the contractors, which is a pain in my natural ass. But
Quincy been so busy he hasn't been around much.
At least not when it really counts. I ain't trippin'
though, as long as this shit get done for the grand
opening."

"When do you anticipate that to be?"

"Couple weeks, a month at the most. I still have to
choose a date, but I will by week's end. Once the contractors get in here tomorrow shit should be done
pretty quickly."

"Well, besides the business part of it all, how is
your relationship with Quincy going?" I didn't want
to ask that question, but I had to. Them opening up
a nightclub was cool, but if they were not together,
how would that work?

Keisha popped two bite-size pieces of cheese into

her mouth and chewed. "It's cool . . . we good. Things are getting better and I'm glad, because I didn't want to have to fuck Quincy's ass up. Sometimes I just get pissed when he ain't around for this shit. But I chill because I understand why. Because if he don't hustle, then some of this shit won't be possible. We good though. I love that big-head-ass nigga." Keisha smiled.

"That's what's up. I just want to see y'all win," I added. And I meant that. Black love was important. I missed DaVon so much. I sipped my margarita. "This is good. Did you make these?" I referred to my drink.

"Girl, hell no. One of my potential bartenders came in for an impromptu interview. I had him make them. He just left before you arrived."

"Hummph, I should have known you couldn't make them this good."

"Bitch, and you was right." We both laughed. "So how about you? How is it going with all this new responsibility you have with the operation?" I should have known she would bring that up. I still didn't like to talk about that with her. "You know ain't shit changed, I'm here for you," she once again insisted, as she had in the past. "I'm willing to help out anytime, always available to travel wherever, whenever. You know that DaVon was like family to Quincy, and when y'all started dating that instantly made you the same. So we got you."

I knew Keisha just wanted to help out, and I could appreciate that. But having her friendship was enough. I didn't want anything else coming in between that. The drug game could be really complicated and it was safer if our friendship didn't come into contact with that. "Listen, everything is in place with the operation and it's all good. Now we just waiting on this club. It's gone be a good look for the hood." I swiftly, and hopefully successfully, changed the subject.

I sighed inside with relief when she asked about Promise; my plan had worked. We could talk about anything but the drug game. "What's good with Promise?"

"She straight. Gettin' herself together in LA. You know it's different out here if you ain't from here."

"Hell, yeah it is. But she'll be a'ight. I seen her new whip though. Shidd, she lucky."

"That's my sister, you know I got her." My cell phone started ringing. Clip's name lit up, which meant it was business. "I gotta take this," I mouthed. "What's up?" I said into the phone. I got up to step away and walked out toward the bar. Clip filled me in on a late shipment. He told me he'd call me back in a couple hours once the shipment was in. We ended the call. I turned with the intent to join Keisha back in her office, but to my surprise she was standing close. I almost got the feeling she was trying to pry. I wasn't sure, but I hadn't even heard her approach.

"Everything good? Everybody a'ight? Promise ain't get lost, did she?" She gave a slight laugh that I didn't think was sincere. But maybe I was just trippin' off the fact that the shipment was late, because that pissed me off. Either way, I didn't like nobody sneaking up on me.

"Nah, everything all good. Listen, I have to get going. Keep me posted on the renovation." She agreed to keep in touch and I bounced back out into the LA heat.

Chapter 35

Promise had been staying with me for a while, but she was a grown woman. And while she had never said anything and seemed quite content living with me at the Bel-Air estate, I felt she would be quite happy with her own place. So I called a Realtor and set up a meeting to look at some condos that she might like. It didn't take me long to find some potentials. I called Promise up and had her choose one and sign the paperwork. She was overly excited and couldn't stop thanking me. Once again, I had to remind her that she didn't owe me any thanks; she was my sister. We were getting to know each other more and more each day. I loved her. And would always make sure she was okay.

Today was the day that she was moving in, and even though I would miss her and I hated being in that big house alone, I was excited for her. She had reassured me that she would stay with me several nights a week or whenever I wanted her to. But even I knew once she got her freedom I would have to push, drag, or pull her to my house. Keisha and I pulled up to the condo at the same time. Even though she was still busy with the finishing touches on the nightclub, she had insisted that she come along to help out.

"I love these condos," Keisha said as she climbed out of her sports Mercedes.

"I know, right. Wait until you see the inside. Is that a bottle of wine?" I questioned the bags in her hands. And if I knew Keisha, she had alcohol on her hands.

"Bitch, you know it is. And I brought glasses just in case. You can't move into a place without christening it with alcohol first. It's rules to this."

"I'm sure you believe that." I smiled as I led the way.

"Hey, y'all." Promise was all smiles when she let us in.

"I love your new place, Promise," Keisha commented. "And I brought wine to break the place in." She handed her the bags. "Oh, and there are glasses too."

"Well, let's pour up and toast." Promise set the bags down on her counter. I was shocked to see a tall, dark-skinned guy with a neatly trimmed goatee come from the back. Keisha and I both glared at him. "Oh, this is Ryan. Ryan, this is my twin sister, Precious, and a friend, Keisha."

"Hey, ladies," Ryan said in a deep, sexy tone.

"Hi," I said. Promise had recently told me she was dating a guy named Ryan. I just hadn't expected to meet him this soon.

"Umm-hmm," Keisha followed up. I could see the lust in her eyes for Ryan. I tapped her shoulder.

Promise giggled.

"Are you done?" she asked Ryan.

"Yeah. All the boxes are where you wanted them. I'll hit you later."

"You do that." Promise smiled at him.

"It was nice meeting you ladies." He nodded at Keisha and me before making his exit.

"Damn, he fine, Promise." Keisha wasted no time.

"Always. If I'm dating him, never expect nothing else."

"Where he from?" was my concern.

"Say he grew up in Inglewood. But he graduated from USC and is now pre-med."

"Damn, bitch. You pullin' doctors." Keisha seemed surprised.

Promise smirked. "He ain't a doctor yet. And what you think, I only like gutter rats?" Promise was still wearing a smile, but her tone said different.

I was glad he was not in the life. However, I still didn't know him, so I would keep my eyes on him if they continued to date. "He fine, Sis. I didn't know you had invited him over today though."

"He asked if I needed help, and since I had those boxes I let him. And that strong body came through."

"Where did you meet him?" Keisha continued to ask questions.

"I was at the gym bout a month back."

"The gym." I was stunned again. The house had a full gym. "Why not use the gym at the house?"

"Precious, I care a lot about this body. I need guidance while I work out; it motivates me."

"Shidd, I can only agree, especially if they got eye candy like Ryan," Keisha cosigned.

"Maybe you should join me sometimes. I mean your body already tight. But maybe you'll find a man." She eyed me.

"Nah, I'm good." I shut that down quick.

"Yeah, you could do better, Precious. Besides, you lookin' for street niggas. Them niggas who hang out at gyms be soft and shit. They could not handle a boss bitch like you, Precious."

I was confused about Keisha's comment. Not five minutes before she was praising fine niggas at the gym.

"Either way I ain't got time for a man. I'm good." I left it at that.

"I'll drink to that. Promise, go pour up them drinks and show us this crib before we start slaving for you."

"The liquor right, let's get to that."

After pouring up the drinks, we toasted to Promise's new place and started on the tour. I, of course, had seen it, but still tagged along. Keisha seemed to take in everything. Her eyes roamed the place as if it was guilty of something.

"Yo, I wish I had a sister to hook me up like this when I was out here struggling. Promise, bitch, you lucky. Shidd, I bet you feel like you hit the lottery since you ran up on Precious." Keisha tried to chuckle with her statement, but neither Promise nor I cosigned. For some reason, the comment didn't seem innocent to me. It felt slick and I wasn't feeling it. Apparently, Promise wasn't either; I could tell from the way her neck rolled around to Keisha. Thankfully, my phone rang.

"What's up?" I answered. Quincy was on the other line, so I knew something was up. "Right," I said to his comment. "I can be there in twenty. Text me the address." I ended the call. Both Promise and Keisha eyed me. They knew what was going to come out of my mouth.

"What's the deal?" Promise asked first.

"That was Quincy. I have to meet up with him."

"What's wrong?" Keisha's tone was demanding.

"I don't know, but I have to go. Promise, I'm sorry but I'll come back if it's not too late."

"Nah, you good. Handle your shit." Promise understood where I was coming from.

"A'ight, Keisha, I'll catch up to you later."

"Aye, I'll follow you to make sure you straight. Shit be crazy," Keisha volunteered.

I turned around to tell her that was okay and almost bumped into her, she was so close. "You can't go, Keisha. This is business."

Keisha gazed at me like I just said the dumbest shit she ever heard. Twisting up the corner of mouth, she sucked in her bottom lip. "Girl, that's bullshit. What do you mean I can't go?" She had an attitude.

I thought I had made myself clear with her in the past about the operation. Clearly, she did not get it. And at this moment I didn't have the time nor was I in the mood. "Keisha, check this. This right here ain't friend business, this crew business. Now I gotta go." With that, I turned to leave before I said something I could not take back. I didn't know what was up with Keisha, but her sticking her nose in my empire was pissing me all the way off.

As soon as I got to my car, my phone started ringing. "What's up, Clip?" I answered.

"Aye, I'm on my way to meet up with Quincy right

now. I told him to call you because I was on another call."

"He did. I'm on my way. But what is up now?"

"I don't know. Quincy just told me shit gettin' ugly and he needed me to get over there."

"I'll see you when I get there then." I ended the call. With a rapidly beating heart and uncertainty, I balled down the interstate. I still had bad nerves when it came to dealing with the business, because deep down I knew what came with it. Pulling over, I went into my trunk and into my secret compartment and got out my gun. I just felt safer with it on me.

The ride took forty-five minutes, but soon I pulled into one of our abandoned spots. Thankfully, Clip pulled in at the same time. I felt much better when I saw Clip. I always felt safer when he was around. Not that I didn't trust Quincy, but Clip and DaVon had been closer and I knew Clip had me no matter what because of that. Clip led the way up to the door. He gave the secret knock and Quincy opened the door.

There were only a few chairs in the room, but no one was there. "What's this bullshit, man? Why the fuck you got us out here?" Clip demanded. Clip didn't beat around the bush. He was serious and anxious at all times.

"Mane, y'all check this shit out." We followed him into another room where we found peons Derrick and Ray. At first, I was shocked but I quickly dismissed that. Both Derrick's and Ray's eyeballs roamed over the three of us. They both were tied to iron chairs with duct tape over their mouths.

"Fuck is this?" Clip asked.

"Both these niggas claim they got robbed for their product. Again." Quincy stressed that part.

"Fuck that! Who da fuck y'all think believe this shit. Derrick, ya shit was short two months ago. Is you a dummy nigga? Nah. Fuck this!" Clip rushed across the room. Derrick's bloodshot red eyes bulged. Clip punched him in his face. The look on his face read death. Blood splattered across the room.

"How much?" I asked. Not that the money mattered, I was just curious.

"Seventy-five G's apiece," Quincy said.

"How in the fuck did this shit happen?" I eyed both Derrick and Ray. I knew they couldn't answer with their mouths duct-taped. But the question had to be asked.

"These motherfuckers lying. I ain't hearing shit."

Clip glared at me. "Precious, it's simple. This shit ain't good for our image, but I think you know that."

"These niggas is dead." Quincy cosigned Clip's statement. There was nothing else to be done. But all decisions were mine to make, so they looked to me.

"Take off the duct tape. I want to talk to him." I pointed at Derrick.

Quincy tightened his lips and clenched the nine millimeter in his right hand tighter.

"Fucking talk," Quincy barked. "Unless these ill motherfuckers got seventy-five G's and some respect and shit to discuss."

Clip smirked. "Shidd for real, these niggas words just loud."

"Take the fucking duct tape off now!" I barked.

Quincy walked over and snatched the duct tape off with force. I could hear the tape peel from Derrick's skin. Once the tape was off Derrick took in a deep breath.

I looked at Derrick and I thought of DaVon, his

words, his encouragement, his way of dealing with all issues. See, when you looked at DaVon, you didn't see a killer. But that was never to get it twisted. He had blood on his hands because business was business. He made sure that I understood that. "I think you know there is only one way to solve this . . . that's money or the dope." I sighed, then ran my hand across my face. Not from frustration, but from amazement at their stupidity. I would never understand the thoughts of a thieving dealer. "Where the dope at?" I threw out.

Instead of answering me right away, Derrick threw his head back off his shoulder and shook his dreads out. Holding his head back, he sniffled and wiggled his nose. "Aye, you DaVon's girl . . . I remember you."

I hadn't expected him to mention DaVon's name. That stalled me for a brief second. Thinking of DaVon always took me to an emotional place. Now was not the time for that, and personally, I didn't appreciate Derrick having DaVon's name in his mouth. "Where is the fucking dope?" I said with steel in my voice. If he dared to say DaVon's name again I probably would shoot him myself.

"I don't fuckin' know. I keep tellin' this nigga we was set up." He nodded at Quincy.

Quincy seemed to slide across the room. His gun made a cracking sound as it connected with Derrick's jaw. Ray closed his eyes with defeat. It was clear he was worried about his turn. "Stop repeating those weak-ass lies . . . be a man and own up to ya shit," Quincy spat.

"Listen, fuck all this. Precious, let me light these niggas so I can go out and find where they hid ya shit." Clip eyed me with an imploring stare.

I turned my attention to Ray and nodded at him. "Take the duct tape off his mouth." Everything would move at my speed no matter what. "This probably will come as a shock to you, but I'm a high school graduate . . . meaning I have basic sense. So I won't repeat the question I just asked your boy here. You just answer it."

Ray twisted his mouth up, then spit up a wad onto the floor. It was so disgusting and unexpected that I blinked. His eyes were glued to me. "Mane, who the fuck is this bitch questioning me?" he barked.

All I heard next was a bang and Ray's scream. I saw the blood dripping down Ray's leg and realized that Clip had shot him in the knee. "Respect her," Clip said in a calm tone. Ray tried to squirm and fight to keep from screaming again, biting his bottom lip so hard blood seeped through.

I was tired of the whole scene. I looked from Derrick to Ray. "It's simple, Ray." I addressed him by name. "Give me my dope or the money and you go home tonight."

Ray shook his head from side to side, unable to control himself. "Augh!" he screamed out. His lips turned white from his pain. "I can't give you what I ain't got . . . why you don't ask that motherfucker." He tossed his head in Quincy's direction.

Quincy gave a slight chuckle. "Fuck you, nigga. You caught."

Ray stared at the blood running down his leg. "Mane, on everything I love. Fuck you and this bitch, shit."

Once again Clip rushed toward him. "No, stop, Clip." I intervened before Clip sealed his fate. "Give me your piece." I referred to his gun. I decided not to use mine. Clip didn't hesitate and placed it in the palm of my hand. I walked toward Ray. "Remember this, my name is Precious . . . not bitch." I pulled the trigger and shot him in the left foot.

"Agggh." Ray threw his head back, screaming. "Fuck you and that pussy-ass DaVon. I'm glad that nigga dead!" He spat at me.

Quickly I turned and glanced at Quincy, then Clip. I took one more look at Derrick, then Ray. Slowly, I passed the gun back to Clip and looked him in the eyes. "Finish this." This business was done.

Chapter 36

I had a headache, that much was for certain, and I couldn't take much more of the throbbing pain. Tired of lying down, trying to fight against the pain, I pushed my covers back and took small steps to the bathroom. The pain was so intense that it hurt to plant my feet on the floor. Fishing out my Aleve, I tossed two into my mouth and swallowed some water. Looking at myself in the mirror, I searched for any evidence that my head would explode at any moment. Fortunately for me, there was no such sign. Back in bed, I prayed for sleep to claim me, with the hope that when I woke up the headache would be gone. At some point, my wish was granted, but suddenly I woke up from a bad dream. The dream consisted of Derrick and Ray breaking into the house looking for me. They were dead; there was no chance that they would be breaking in on me or anyone else, ever.

It had been a few weeks since Clip and Quincy had killed them. And the last place I expected them to be showing up was in my dreams. I didn't regret their murder because I knew that it was necessary for business. But I wasn't sure how I felt about it so I didn't think about it much. I mean, why should I? There were rules and consequences, period. Pushing the covers back again, I sat up. That's when I realized for the first time since I had opened my eyes that my pounding headache was gone. The ringing doorbell grabbed my attention. Maria was off and I was not expecting any company. Throwing on my robe, I made my way down the stairs to the front door.

"Where have you been? I ain't seen or heard from you in days. And you haven't returned my calls." Promise stormed in the house.

I shut the door behind her. The burst of sun I received just from opening the door gave me a blast of energy. "I been meaning to. Just been so busy." I yawned.

"Too busy to call your own sister. Hopefully, it was G-fourteen classified."

"Not really." I laughed. "Come on, let's have an espresso or some." I headed toward the kitchen. I could not tell her about the killing of Derrick and Ray.

"Well, I know the street part of your life keeps you going." I was surprised yet glad to hear her say that. "I would never want to go into the hustling business, mainly because I know there are boundaries. But that damn Keisha clearly don't know about boundaries; she so damn worried about what is going on in your operation. Ever since you introduced us, I get a strange vibe from her." She shrugged her shoulders. "I don't know what's up with her. But I don't trust her." That part of the statement caught me off guard.

"What you mean? Keisha's cool people." I continued making our espressos. "I admit that she clearly wants to be involved."

"That's all you think?" Promise squinted her eyes.

"Yeah." I smiled.

"Fuck that. The bitch is sneaky. Watch how she move. I'm close to smacking' her ass in the face."

I couldn't help laughing when I realized what this was all about. Promise was still mad about Keisha's statements when we went over to help her move. I had never asked her how that went, but now was certainly not the time. Promise and Keisha both had strong personalities; they would always butt heads. "Both you two just got egos," I concluded. "But don't worry about Keisha, she chill."

"Whatever." Promise reached for her espresso.

"Get ready though, because the grand opening to her club is coming up. And you know you gone be invited. And even if you not invited, which you will be, you gone be my plus one."

"When is it?" She sipped her espresso.

"Not sure about the date, but a few weeks."

"Humph," was Promise's only comment.

I just smiled and started in on my espresso; the last thing I needed was my sister and my good friend beefing. That was sure to throw me right in the middle, and what was a girl to do? They say blood is thicker than water, but I never really had that problem because Dad had been my only blood. Having a sister was new. I eyed Promise with my cup of espresso directly in front of my face, the steam cleaning my sinuses. And I knew without any doubt I was my sister's keeper.

Chapter 37

Everything was still going good and things were falling into place. No one had made mishaps like Derrick and Ray. And even though we still didn't know what had happened to the dope they claimed they had been robbed of, things were moving along. Seventy-five grand really wasn't shit; we moved big weight on the streets. I was running an operation that was worth millions. It was simply the principle of the thing.

"Hi," I said to the guys on the cleaning crew who were emptying the building I had chosen for Promise's salon. I decided to stop by to see how the cleaning was going.

"Everything is going as planned," Wyatt reassured me. He was the guy who owned the cleaning company. "We should be done by the end of this week as planned."

"Thank you. I want the remodel team to be able to get started."

"That's not a problem. I'll give you a call in a couple days."

"Sure thing." I headed out to meet up with Keisha for lunch.

"I can't believe Mrs. Prompt is running late." Keisha started in on me before I could sit down at the table. We were at a Mexican restaurant and I was starving.

"Please don't start before I eat. I need the strength to go back and forth with you." I smiled.

"Well, I didn't order your food. But we got drinks though," Keisha said with excitement. The waitress approached the table and placed a margarita in front of me and one in front Keisha. "Yass, henna. Now my day can get started."

"Mine too. I was up early, and the only thing I had was juice and that was hours ago."

"That's the life of a hustler, my friend."

I didn't respond.

The waitress was back to take our orders.

"Bitch, you ain't gone believe this. Matter fact, sip your margarita before I spill this tea."

"Oh hell, what now?" I sat on the edge of my seat and sipped my margarita.

"Buffy's ass is pregnant."

Now that was a shock. I couldn't imagine her being pregnant, let alone having a baby. "By who?" My mouth was wide from shock.

"Bitch, who the fuck would know?" Keisha said. "I told that crazy bitch to go ahead and call Maury." We both burst out laughing at the same time. "I got to go to the bathroom. I feel ill." Keisha excused herself.

I ate chips and salsa and tried to soak up the information about Buffy. I had to see it to believe it.

"I guess Mother Nature is running life." Keisha approached the table. "My cycle done came on. We should just take this food to go. Quincy ass ain't there, so we will still be able to have girl time."

"I'm cool wit' that. We'll have her box this stuff up," I said, nodding to the approaching waitress.

As I pulled in behind Keisha, I noticed one of Quincy's whips out front. Him and Keisha both normally kept two cars at the house. They each kept one in the garage and one in front of the garage. Keisha only had the two vehicles, but Quincy had two more and he kept them in a garage somewhere else. But he must have been home if he had a car outside. Keisha must have read my mind when I climbed out of my car.

"Quincy must have come back," she said. "Hopefully, he just picking something up." Keisha unlocked the door and I stepped in behind her. She stuck her head into the living room area. "His ass must be upstairs."

"I'll take the food in the kitchen and set it out. I'm ready to eat before it gets cold." Keisha nodded her head and headed for the stairs. In the kitchen, I pulled the plates out of the bag, then reached in the fridge and grabbed a Coca-Cola. Keisha drank them like crazy, same as me, so I knew she would have some. I turned on the water in the kitchen sink to wash my hands. It sounded as if yelling was coming from upstairs. I turned the water off, but all I heard was quiet. Concluding I must have been hearing things, I turned the water back on.

I sat down and I heard what I was sure was people yelling. Stepping out into the hallway, it sounded harsh. Worried, I raced up the stairs to see what was going on.

"Whore," Keisha yelled. I stepped into the doorway and Keisha was attempting to jump across the bed. I nearly shouted from shock when I saw who she was trying to get to: Buffy standing by the window wrapped in nothing but a bedsheet. "Let me the fuck go, Quincy!" Keisha screamed.

"Calm the fuck down," Quincy said as Keisha kicked, scratched, bit, and squirmed trying to break his grasp. "Stop, mane, you know that girl pregnant."

Keisha's body seem to go limp for a brief second. "Niggas and you think I give a fuck." Keisha elbowed Quincy in the cheek and turned around and started punching him all over. Again Quincy got hold of Keisha. Trying to break free, Keisha started breathing hard. She glared at Buffy. "You fucking dirty, nasty, gutter bitch! How could you betray me like this? All that I done for you. But I shouldn't be surprised because I been knew you was a ho."

"Fuck you, Keisha. I'm just giving yo' man what you couldn't. A baby."

"Quincy!" Keisha shouted his name. A tear rolled down her cheek.

"Wait, naw, baby, she lying. That ain't my baby."

I had been so stunned at the whole situation in front of me, I was stuck in the spot I was in. Finally, my body came back to life. My only thought was to get Keisha out of there. I felt so bad for her. I tried to get to her, but she lunged for Buffy again. I tried to help Quincy hold her.

"Quincy, bring her out of here. Take her downstairs."

Still kicking and struggling to free herself from

Quincy's grasp, Keisha was not giving up. It was a struggle, but before long he had her downstairs. I had to plead with her to convince her to leave. Because if she stayed, someone was going to get hurt or she was going to jail. The one thing I knew for certain was that neither I nor Quincy wanted LAPD's finest to get involved.

Chapter 38

A long, hard week passed and Keisha was still at my house. To my surprise, she had calmed down about the situation, or least she seemed calm. The first two days she lay in bed all day and talked about killing them both. On the third day she showered, brushed her teeth, and cried. By the fourth day she declared she was a boss bitch, got up, got dressed, and went to her businesses. And as of today, she was still a boss bitch, but I knew deep down inside she still had to be hurt. I mean, I still couldn't believe it. Quincy and Buffy. Damn, that was fucked up.

"What's up?" Keisha entered the kitchen. I had just made a homemade pepperoni pizza, which I had been craving.

"Hey. You hungry?" I started slicing the piping-hot pizza.

"Hell yeah. That looks good."

"Well, here you go." I placed two slices on a paper plate and passed it to her.

"You made this from scratch?"

"Yep." I placed two slices on a plate for myself.

"Damn, Paula Deen in the house," Keisha joked.

"Some like that." I laughed. "For real, me and my dad use to make this all the time."

Keisha blew on a slice and bit into it. I had put so much cheese on the pizza, it stretched the distance from her mouth to the slice. "Oh, this shit bum. Cheesy and full of sauce just like I like mine."

I fake popped my collar. "Aye." Then bit one of my own slices.

"So I wanted to tell you thanks for allowing me to crash here and cry on your shoulder these past few days. I know a bitch ain't easy to put up wit'." She grinned.

"Aww, you good."

"Thanks for lying." She laughed. "But for real though, thank you. I'm going back home tomorrow."

"So soon?" I raised my right brow. "You sure you ready for that?"

"I'm ready." She bit her pizza again.

I hated to bring up the situation, but I had to ask. "What about Quincy and Buffy? You talked to them?"

"Talk to Buffy?" She twisted her face in a circular motion. "Fuck that bitch. But I did finally talk to Quincy. He been callin' since the first night I got here. He apologized . . . I guess as much as a guy can. I mean really, what he can say? That sorry shit don't carry no weight wit' me. But as for Buffy, I'm gone fuck that bitch up in due time. And that's a promise. Quincy claims he's done with her."

"Is that enough for you?" I asked.

"Yeah, because I ain't about to let no bum bitch like Buffy ruin my life. And trust, Quincy will pay. I will make him pay in my own way. He'll wish he never met that bitch." She smirked.

"What about the baby?"

"Precious, Buff is a ho and full of lies. That baby could belong to anyone in the free world. The bitch is a sperm bank; it ain't a nigga within a ten-mile range that ain't ran up in her."

And with that I knew her mind was made up about Buffy and Quincy. There were no more questions for me to ask and nothing else left for me to say. I would leave well enough alone.

"Now what I gotta focus on is getting this club business back on point for the grand opening. I want that to happen in two weeks tops, if possible. I'm about to boss up this money and shut this mother-fucking city down. You watch ya girl work."

"Aye, I'm here for that." I smiled. I would sit on the sideline and root her on while I ran my own life and business.

"These floors are nice," Clip complimented as soon as he stepped through the doors. I had asked him to stop by Promise's new salon so we could chat a minute.

"Yes, they are. They just finished them last night. That's why I wanted to come by and see them. So listen, I called you by here with a concern of mine. That concern is ya boy Quincy. I know you heard about his and Keisha's problem."

"Mane, who ain't heard? I think ya girl Keisha took out an ad in the paper or some." Clip chuckled.

"Maybe. But they problems is risky to our operation. Just like that"—I snapped my fingers—"Keisha is taking him back. And saying shit like she gone pay him back in her own way. I couldn't care less to be involved in their relationship drama, but I don't like the sound of that."

"Me neither. I'll talk to Quincy and make sure he keeps a lock on her. And I'll keep a lock on him."

He was speaking the words I wanted to hear. "That sounds like a plan."

Clip started looking around the place again. "So what's up with Promise? When you gone hook us up?"

"Boy, if you don't stop, I don't have nothing to do wit' that." I laughed.

"Hello, hello," Promise sang as she entered. I had given her the address and told her to stop by.

"Hey, Promise." I greeted her with a smile.

"What's up, Promise?" Clip wore a huge grin. I couldn't help but smile at him. He had it bad for Promise. And it was clear Promise didn't have a clue.

She looked around the empty building. "So what exactly is this place anyway?"

I wondered how long it would take her to ask that. "This place is your new hair salon. I mean, new once it's done being remodeled, of course." I handed her the keys.

Promise looked at me with her mouth open for a full minute. Then she stared at the keys in her hand. "What?" finally came out of her mouth. Tears ran down her face.

"Why are you crying?"

"Because no one has ever done all that you have done for me before." Promise fell into my arms and I hugged my sister. Tears stung my eyes, but I fought them back.

"What about me? I would like a hug," Clip joked.

We both looked at him and laughed. "Shut up," I said. I turned my attention to back to Promise. "This place belongs to you now. I want you to decorate it how you wish once the remodeling is done. So you better get those ideas together now."

"I am so on it." Promise looked at the keys in her hand and gripped them tight.

"Listen, if you need me to paint or something, I got you," Clip threw in.

"Nah, son. I'm good." Promise laughed.

"Besides, I would not pay you," I added.

"See y'all got jokes. It's cool . . . For real though. Promise, your place gone be dope. I'ma support you when it's done."

"Thanks, Clip." Promise smiled.

I had to stare for a second; I had never seen Clip's soft side. It was pretty sweet.

"A'ight. I gotta bounce though." Clip excused himself.

"Aye, my stomach just growled. We need to eat. Besides, the food gone get cold."

"Bring your starving self on in here." I grabbed Promise by the hand and made a dash for the food.

Chapter 39

"Damn, Sis, I'm really feeling your new Bentley. This shit is all the way tight. You gotta let me keep it for a whole day." Promise babbled as we pulled into the parking lot at Quincy's and Keisha's new club. Tonight was grand opening night, so it was going down. I had recently purchased a Bentley as a fun gift to myself and I too was loving it. And already Promise was trying to rob me of it. But I could not blame her. I smiled.

"How about baby steps? You know I let you drive into the driveway of my house and park." I laughed.

"Whatever. So controlling." She played at being mad.

"And you know it. Now let's party." We climbed out of the Bentley and made our way around to the front.

"Damn, I think everybody in LA up this piece," Promise said. The line was wrapped around the building.

"Follow me," I instructed Promise. "Mark." I addressed the bouncers in front of me. They all knew who I was.

"Precious." Mark smiled at me and removed the rope. "Come on in."

"Thank you. Remember her—this is my twin sister, Promise."

"Trust me, I won't be forgetting." Mark flirted.

"Nice meeting you, Mark." Promise giggled.

Inside, we headed straight for VIP. I looked up and saw the balcony, and it was shining like diamonds. True to her word, Keisha had made the place come to life. "This place is nice," Promise said as we stepped in VIP. "And the DJ lit."

"Aye!" Keisha sang over the music and swayed her hips. I had to pause a minute and take in the whole room. The seating area was classy and everybody looked the part. "What's up, bitches?" Keisha was hype; she came over and hugged both of us.

"Congratulations," Promise and I said in unison.

"Hey, this place is on point. I'm loving' it," I said.

"Yo, this gone be my new hangout. You gone have to put me out." Promise was now moving her hips to Gucci Mane's verse. "And this my shit. I swear, your DJ on fire."

Keisha smiled. "Yeah, that nigga lit. But you gone really turn up later. Quincy got 2 Chains coming through later; he gone do a walkthrough. Quincy says this should boost celebrity attendance."

"Keisha, you got to tell Quincy to put me on." Promise was ready to jump 2 Chain's bones. I had to laugh.

"Girl, you got Ryan coming through," I reminded her.

"Damn right I do. And that means what?" My sister was a daredevil. But hey, I couldn't hate. She was not married or in a committed relationship, so she was free to do what she pleased.

"What's up, ladies?" Quincy came over. "I bought a li'l something over for y'all to celebrate this special occasion." The waitress who was standing behind him passed him the bottle she was holding.

"Don Julio." Keisha chuckled. "You really must be trying to get us fucked up."

I laughed because I so agreed with her. "Quincy, ain't no way I'm fuckin' wit' that tonight."

"Come on, ladies. This is the time to get lit. Do this shit the boss way."

Promise grabbed a shot glass off the tray the waitress holding. "Fuck it. Pour up." She extended my glass at Quincy just as "Mask Off" by Future came on.

"Shidd, fill my shit too then. I ain't no prude." Keisha snatched her a shot glass next.

I was not changing my mind. That damn Don Julio was a beast. I'd had my share. Plus I was in the Bentley and no one would be driving except maybe Promise. And she would be toast after the shots. "Quincy, send ya girl a bottle of that Patron. I'm being a lady tonight."

"Aww." Keisha teased me.

"I got you." Quincy smiled before walking away.

"Keisha, these designs you used for the club are nice," Promise complimented. "You gone have to hook me up with your designer so I can use them for the salon."

Keisha's head seemed to jump off her shoulders as she turned to face Promise. "What salon?"

"Oh, you didn't know. Precious surprised me with a salon."

"Yep." I jumped in. I wasn't sure why I had not mentioned it to Keisha. I guess so much other stuff was going on until it slipped my mind. "'Bout to let her put her touch on LA," I said proudly. I could not wait to see Promise's success in the hair business.

Keisha, on the other hand, seemed a bit stunned. "Well, that's what's up." She smiled but it seemed forced. "I thought about opening up a salon. But Precious wouldn't go in with me." Keisha looked at me.

"I found out that Promise was a licensed beautician, even competing in hair shows. I had to help her fulfill her dream."

"Thank you again, Sis." Promise hugged me again.

Keisha eyed us and took another shot. "I'ma have to come through."

"Ladies and gents, ya man 2 Chains just stepped in the building," the DJ announced.

"Aye, I need you to walk to the front with me." Quincy approached Keisha and they rushed off.

"Ya girl seem a bit in her feelings about my salon," Promise announced. I guess she had noticed it too.

"I noticed it too," I admitted. "But she gone be okay. She just really wanted me to go in with her. She cool though."

"I didn't know she could do heads."

"She don't. She was going to hire some stylists."

"Hmmm . . ." Promise said, but looked over my shoulder. "There is Ryan down there; I'ma go meet him.

"What's up, Precious?" Clip approached me as soon as Promise wondered off.

"Sipping' this Patron and chilling'."

"Yo, when you gone hook me up?" He was back on that again.

I couldn't help but grin. "Clip, brush, her dude is here."

"That wacky-ass nigga that she down there talkin' to? Please, I don't take that shit seriously."

I laughed so loud and hard my stomach hurt. I saw Ryan and Promise approach. Clip stood stone-still in his spot.

"Ryan, you already met my sister, Precious."

"Yes, I remember. Hi again, Precious," Ryan said.

"And this is Clip." Ryan extended his hand for a shake. Clip put his hands in his pockets, nodded, and walked away.

Promise looked at me with a question in her eyes and I just smiled. "Ryan would like to try one of these Don Julio shots, courtesy of the owner."

"Sure." Promise reached for the bottle and poured up four shots. I watched as Ryan tossed back one shot and then another. Clip had been wrong, my man was not wacky. Promise took a shot.

Keisha stepped up. "Where the Don at? I need it."

"We got you faded," Promise said and filled some more glasses.

Keisha tossed back two shots and from there we all turned up.

Keisha raised her glass in the air. "Let's all toast to a successful grand opening." Everybody toasted except me and Promise because we didn't have a drink in our hands.

Suddenly, I saw Keisha's eyes land on Promise. "And let's all toast to Promise and her new salon."

Promise smiled at the mention of the salon. "Hell yeah, that bitch bout to be on fire."

A smirk spread across Keisha's face. "Girl, it must be nice to have a sister with the golden ticket."

Promise looked at me but no smile was on her face. She turned her attention back to Keisha. "What does that mean exactly? Because it sounds to me like you throwing shots."

"No, sweetheart, not shots, just observation." Keisha chuckled with sarcasm.

"See, Precious, this shit right here is called jealousy. Take it from me, Sis, this bitch right here is not friend material."

Keisha's whole face dropped. She jumped up from the seat she was sitting in.

"What you gone do, bitch?" Promise kicked off her heels.

Quincy stepped in front of Keisha and asked her to be quiet. "If you wasn't Precious's sister, I would beat your ass," Keisha said.

"Bitch, bring it," Promise said. Clip stood in front of her and tried to hold her back. She said, "What you need to be worried about is how yo' nigga fuckin' yo' ho-ass friend and making bastard babies."

Keisha went wild trying to break free from Quincy. Promise tried to push past Clip. I grabbed her, but she yanked free. Somehow, she jumped over Clip and past Quincy and punched Keisha in the jaw. Keisha tried to swing back, but Promise's fist landed against her face again. Quincy had been knocked down. Finally, Clip got his balance and snatched Promise back. I yelled for Clip to take her out of the club and I followed. The night was fucked and there would be no getting it back. Grand-opening fail.

* * *

The night had been long and the last thing I was looking forward to was my phone ringing so early in the morning. I glanced over and saw Keisha's name. Not ready to be bothered, I sighed. "What's up?" I answered groggily. I was truly sleepy.

"Precious, listen. I was so fucked up last night. My bad bout all that shit. It was them Don Julio shots. I don't know why Quincy bring that shit up in VIP," she declared.

What she said may have been true, but I didn't care. "You fucked up, Keisha, and just went too far. She ain't fucking wit' you no more. And I don't blame her. That shit you said seemed personal."

"But it wasn't. I told you, it was the liquor."

"Maybe. Either way, that shit was petty, and I for one don't have time for it. I got an empire to run." I kept it all the way real.

"I know and I'm sorry. Quincy was mad at me too for starting that shit and fuckin' up the grand opening."

Promise beeped in on another line. "Listen, I gotta go. We can chat later." I ended the call.

"You up?" Promise asked.

"Yeah." I was sure she didn't care one way or the other.

"See, Precious, I told you that Keisha's ass was jealous . . . Augh, fuck that bitch. She messed up my good time. Petty ass. I just can't seem to get a break from these bitches. Now some female calling' my phone talkin' bout she Ryan's wife and they got three kids. Bitch accusing me of breaking up they happy home." Promise started laughing.

This information was a shock. Ryan had fooled me. "Hell no. I thought his ass was legit."

"Legit as his ass could be, I guess. I swear these niggas a trip. But anyway all that bullshit aside, what about my budget for the salon? I got some designers coming through today. Can you make it?"

"What time?"

"Later, around three."

"Yeah, I can be there. I have a meeting with some people around one, then I'll stop through. And there is no budget. Get what you want, like I said before.

"Thanks, Sis."

Then I heard a voice coming from the background that sounded familiar. "Ain't that Clip I hear?"

"Precious, I gotta go." Promise rushed me off the phone. Making myself comfortable again, I prayed for sleep.

Chapter 40

I had no time to help Promise work on the design for the salon because I had been making a few runs with Clip on business. We had new moves on shipments and I wanted to see for myself that it was working. So I was dog tired and getting sleep whenever I could.

"Hello," I answered my cell. It was seven o'clock in the morning. Why I was answering a call with a number I didn't even recognize this early in the morning was a mystery to me, but it was too late now.

"Is this Precious?" The voice on the other end sounded shaky, like someone had been crying.

"Yes."

"Precious, this is Susanna. One of Maria's daughters. I was wondering if maybe she stayed out there last night?"

That question woke me up and I sat up in bed. "Uh, no. I made it in late last night and when I got here she was gone. When was the last time you or Rebecca talked to her?"

Susanna started crying. "I haven't talked to her since yesterday when she left for work. I started calling her last night but her phone just rang. Now it's not ringing at all, it's going straight to her voicemail. I haven't heard from Rebecca either." All of this puzzled me. I wasn't certain about Rebecca, but I couldn't see Maria not calling her daughter if she wasn't coming home. "I'm going to call the police." Susanna concluded.

I thought that was a good idea. "I'm going to come over." I ended the call. I dialed Promise and asked her to meet up with me at Maria's house.

When I pulled in I saw two cop cars parked out front. I decided to wait a few minutes to see if Promise arrived. She barreled around the corner minutes later.

I knocked on the door and a young woman answered. She resembled Maria a lot. "Hi, I'm Precious. This my sister, Promise."

"I'm Susanna. Come on in." We followed her inside. The cops looked at us. "This is Precious and Promise." She introduced us to the cops. "My mom works for Precious."

Susanna sat down to finish her conversation with the cops, explaining that this was unlike her mother and sister. After the cops left, we all sat and talked. Susanna shared that her brother Jose was on his way up from San Diego.

"Precious, my mom is always saying good things about you," Susanna shared. "She loved DaVon like a son too."

"DaVon loved her too," I said.

"She really likes that Cadillac you bought for her. She has so many rules; the biggest is no eating in it." Susanna gave a slight laugh.

"I was glad to buy it for her. I wanted her to have a safe, dependable ride."

"Well, thank you again."

Jose finally arrived, and Promise and I decided to go for tacos.

"This is so messed up! I just can't believe Maria is missing. The crazy part is, I been working so much I didn't even see her yesterday when she came in."

Promise shook her head. "I just hope she's found." Her cell phone rang and she stared at the phone then ignored the call.

One thing I knew for sure, Promise never ignored her calls. "I know that was Clip," I informed her. "Ain't no use in hiding. I heard your conversation at the club. So what's up with you two?"

"Shit really. We just kickin' it. He's actually really sweet. So I'ma see what's up with him." She gave me a sly grin. "One thing for sure, his ass is bangin' under them sheets."

I laughed. "That information I did not need to know."

"Shit, you need to hear that. It might encourage you to get some. Hell, it's been too long. I don't know how you do it." Promise looked at me like I was living the impossible.

"Easy. I try not to think about it. Truthfully, that's my only hope."

"Good luck with that. Aye, so I'm sending out invites for the salon's grand opening. I need a radio advertisement. And to have a decent run I need fifteen thousand."

"I got you, so let me know when you need the money. But right now I got to get out of here and go get some sleep. I am so tired."

"Do what you gotta do. Let me know if you hear anything about Maria."

"No doubt." I stood up to leave.

At home, I fell into bed and slept until my cell phone woke me.

I didn't even bother to look at the number. "Hello."

"Precious, they found my mother's car but no sign of her or Rebecca," Susanna cried into the phone.

My heart skipped a beat.

Chapter 41

Weeks had passed and still no word on Maria or Rebecca. It was simply unreal; it was like they had evaporated from the earth. Susanna said the police didn't have any leads or a clue as to what could have happened to them. Maria's car contained no evidence that would give them an indication as to what could have happened. Investigators weren't even sure if Maria and her daughter had been together when they disappeared. But they were still investigating all the possibilities. Susanna was a wreck. Jose had tried to get her to go back with him to San Diego, but she refused. She wanted to stay, in case Maria and or Rebecca returned. The good thing was that their house was paid off. DaVon had told me that he had paid her house off when it had once gone into foreclosure. So for the most part she only had utilities to pay. I wanted to help out, so I told Susanna I would continue to give her Maria's salary. Once Forensics was done with Maria's car, they had returned it. I tried to keep in touch with Susanna just so she knew I had her back. Maria meant a lot to us.

But I tried to put all that behind me. Promise had worked hard and tonight was her grand opening. I wanted to be sure it was an epic night for her, so I planned to be all smiles. When I arrived, the crowd was nice. I was overwhelmed with happiness. I just stood outside for a minute and read the name: Precious Promises Kept Hair Salon.

Promise was engaged in conversation with a few people when I made my way inside. I decided not to disturb her and grabbed a glass of wine. The place was just sensational. The front part was an open reception area with three big-screen TVs. Off to the left was the waiting area.

"You made it." Promise approached with the people she had been talking to when I came in.

"Promise, the place is so beautiful." I teared up.

"Thank you, Sis. I am so grateful for you."

"No, I'm grateful for you." We hugged.

"Oh, I want you to meet my team. Well, at least this is some of them." She introduced all three ladies as stylists who specialized in different things. "This is my twin sister, Precious, so whenever you see her, spoil her. No questions asked." All the ladies smiled.

I grinned and shook hands with all of them. "It was nice meeting all of you, and I look forward to seeing all of your work. On my head."

"No worries, I got you. I already have some ideas." Trice, the tall, dark stylist who specialized in cuts and sew-ins, beamed.

"Aye, I'll book you next week." I took her up on her offer.

"Congratulations." Clip stepped into our conversation. He wrapped his arm around Promise's waist. "The place is beautiful, and so are you."

"Oh please." I playfully rolled my eyes at him.

"Keep going, Clip, because you're right." Promise egged him on.

Stacy, one of the other stylists, giggled. "Promise, we're going to exit stage left."

"Oh, my bad. Y'all go ahead and mingle. Little networking and clients."

"And wine," Trice added. The other stylist agreed and they strolled off.

"Promise, I'm sorry I was runnin' late; my day has been so busy."

"Hey, don't worry. I get it. You're here now."

I stood there and sipped my wine and listened to them like I was watching a reality show. I grabbed another glass of wine as one of the waiters passed by.

"I can't stay. The streets still callin' me." Clip glared at me.

I sipped my wine. "Why you lookin' at me?"

"Just thought I might blame it on you. Since you my boss," Clip joked.

"Ha, whatever."

"Well, thankfully for you, I understand." Promise placed her hands in Clip's hands and kissed him on the lips.

"I swear, I ain't for this." I playfully rolled my eyes. "Get a room."

"And we will." Promise and Clip were face-to-face, smiling at each other.

"A'ight, babe. I'll see you later tonight."

"You do that." Promise seductively bit her bottom lip.

"Precious, I'll keep you posted. Stack the bricks." He winked, then bounced.

"Ugh. You two are all the way disgusting," I joked.

"Nah, we just downright nasty." Promise giggled. "So what you think of my team? Think they'll work out? I've never been nobody's boss."

"One thing for sure, you'll know in due time. But they might be cool. How many more of them are there?"

"I have one more stylist and the two receptionists. And I'll fill in as a receptionist as needed. I didn't want to bring in another person so we can keep costs down the first year."

"See, you already making good financial decisions. I think it's going to be fine. I was afraid of runnin' the dry cleaners but it's working out . . . you'll see." I watched Promise's facial expression suddenly change from a smile, to shock, then anger.

I followed her eyes and they led me to the front door. I watched as Keisha and Nicole strutted inside. Keisha had an unbothered look and Nicole, as usual, was a mirror of Buffy, dressed like a two-dollar hooker.

"What is that bitch doing here?" Promise's right hand slid to her hip. "Precious, I swear if that bitch ruins my grand opening, I will personally shoot her trifling ass." Promise seethed.

"Don't worry, if she does, you won't have to shoot her, I will." I sauntered off and stopped in front of Keisha. I had no idea why she was there or how she even knew about the event. So her appearance was a shock. "What's up?"

"I came out to support." Keisha smiled and I was not sure if it was fake or genuine.

"Keisha, you better not be on no bullshit. This is Promise's event."

"Hell no, I ain't here for that. Like I said, I'm here to support . . . and of course apologize." She allowed her eyes to roam the place for a second.

"Hey, Precious," Nicole said. Nicole and Buffy were really close, so I didn't even understand why Keisha was out with her tagging along.

But I didn't have time to worry about that—that was between them. Right now my concern was Promise. I focused my attention back on Keisha without responding to Nicole. "Keisha, I ain't playin'. Don't fuck wit' me."

"Precious, you should know better. I told you I was sorry. I feel bad about that shit."

Promise approached and stood next to me with her arms folded across her chest.

"Hey, Promise," Keisha said first. I was interested in what she might say next. "Promise, I know it looks crazy that I'm here and shit, but I wanted to support you. And also tell you I'm sorry about that bullshit I pulled at the club. I was on one. But I didn't mean none of that shit. You Precious's sister and she my girl, so I'm all the way cool wit' you."

"Well y'all here now, so drink up and schedule an appointment or something," Promise said.

"Damn right, I will. Yo, this place is the shit." She looked around again. "Hey, where's your bathroom? I was sippin' before I got here."

"Down that way to the left." Promise pointed.

"I'll go too. That gin runnin' straight through me." Nicole was just as ghetto as always.

"Well, follow me, bitch." Keisha led the way.

"Ugh. I swear, these hos." Promise giggled and followed. "Listen, I still don't trust that bitch or choose to fuck wit' her. But I'll keep my cool tonight cause I refuse to allow her rude ass to ruin my shit."

"Bet." I cosigned.

Chapter 42

"Hey, Clip." I answered his call a few days after the party. I figured something was up, someone robbed, short on product, or murdered. "Everything okay?"

"Operation straight." When we spoke on the phone we used codes, never straight discussion. That meant nothing was wrong on the drug home-front. Either he just wanted to discuss Promise, or operational changes to improve business. "We need to meet up later this evening. I got some news, so clear your schedule for me." Before I could question him, he ended the call. I started to call him back, but Keisha called on the line before I could.

"What's up? Don't tell me yo' ass still in the bed?"

"Nah, I'm up."

"So what's up with you today? Working at the dry cleaners?"

"Nah, I'm going to run by there though." I yawned.

"Good, since you not busy, stop by the club so we can catch up and shoot the shit."

"No doubt. I can do that." It had been a minute since we had hung out. Things felt a little weird after that stuff between her and Promise. Plus, we all had things going on. But Keisha was always funny and fun. I couldn't wait to hang out with her.

"Well, I'll see you then." Keisha ended the call.

Chapter 43

After a quick visit to the cleaners to go over the sales, I dropped off the deposit from the night before and headed over to meet up with Keisha at the club. The parking lot was empty at this time of day. I parked close to the door and made my way inside.

"Hey, Keisha!" I yelled out.

"I'm over here." She stepped out from behind a wall.

"Why you hidin' in your own club?" I joked. "And turn on the damn lights up in here. You tryin' to save money or something?"

"You got jokes. I ain't hidin' I was up in VIP. I thought about gettin' in one of the cages and practicing my routines."

"You mean the new being cheap." I continued to poke fun. "What routine you claim to be practicing?"

"A dancer. Girl, you know I'm the best twerker around. It's okay for you to admit it." She bent over and started twerking.

"No, you're not. So stop. Please." I threw my hand

up in a stop motion. "A big booty does not make you a natural-born twerk master."

"Aye. I knew you were jealous. It's cool. I'll teach you and we can get you some butt implants. No problem."

"Whatever." I laughed. "This booty has been voted perfect." I playfully slapped my butt. I enjoyed kidding around with Keisha. She kept me in good spirits. The girl was crazy and funny, with a great sense of humor.

"Come on, let's grab a drink and sit at the bar."

"I'm here for that," I cosigned.

"So I'm thinking I'm going to open up a second location."

"Dang, business booming like that?"

"Yep. Line around the corner all three days the club is open. We turnin' too many people away. We can't have that. We may as well take cash money and throw it in the trash can."

I nodded my head in agreement on that. If it made dollars, it made sense. "I guess if you think about it that way. Do you have any idea where you might open it?" LA was an oasis of open spots for clubs. The people never sleep and are always ready to party.

"Not sure just yet. I'ma start lookin' in two weeks though. Gotta get this done before the thrill is gone."

"How is the hair store doing? It's been a minute since I been by there. I need to grab some bundles though."

"Please do. You better support ya girl." She laughed. "The store all good though. You know money just rollin' in all over the place. It is what I wanted you know. Just might be able to get that house out in Bel-Air after all." She laughed.

"See, I knew you could. I tried to tell you." I looked at my phone. Promise was calling. "Hey," I answered.

"Just answer me yes or no," Promise whispered to me. "Are you alone?"

"No." It felt strange answering her this way and not knowing the reason.

"Are you with Keisha?"

That sent my question cells all over the place. I was alarmed and it probably showed. "Yes. Of course, I am," I answered.

"Precious, I need you to listen to me. Keisha is up to something. So I want you to get ya shit and get out of there. Clip called me and tried to explain some stuff and I really ain't all that sure because he was in a hurry. But you need to go."

"No doubt. I'll hit you up." I played it off and ended the call. A million thoughts crowded in on my mind. Confusion was at the top of the list. I looked up at Keisha, who was staring at me. "Listen, some shit just came up and I gotta go."

"Who was that? Everything cool?"

"Oh yeah. Just business, so I have to make a run." I stood up.

"Wait, you can't stay just a little while longer?"

"No, I have to go now."

"Come on. I wanted to finish tellin' you about the club and my new ideas." Keisha stood up too. Suddenly, she seemed nervous.

"We'll talk later. Thanks for the drink." I grabbed my Gucci bag.

"Quincy!" Keisha suddenly yelled. I turned to walk away. A hand went to my nose.

"Precious, Precious." I heard my name but couldn't respond. I felt like I was in a dream but couldn't fully wake up. "Precious." I heard my name again. I shook my head from side to side; my body felt so heavy and I was groggy. "Precious. Wake up." I felt my eyelids flutter. I tried to open them. My vision was blurry for a second, and then I was able to focus on Quincy, who was standing in front of me. I realized that he was the one calling my name.

"Quin . . . Quincy," I muttered, unable at first to utter the words.

"It's me. Now wake yo' ass up!" he screamed. "You ain't supposed to go to bed." I focused in on him and he smiled. Then I saw Keisha standing behind him.

Suddenly, I remembered her calling him, and that was the last thing I remembered. I then realized I was sitting in a chair. Looking down, I saw I was not re-strained. But Quincy had a gun pointed at me. Keisha stood next to him and he whispered something to her.

I thought of how I could break free from the gun pointed at me. "What's going on? Get that damn gun outta my face." I almost panicked, but tried to stay calm. Then I remembered Promise's call. The looks on Keisha's and Quincy's faces was slick; they were different, not my friend and employee.

"Precious, stop the dramatic shit. All those stupid-ass facial expressions. Just relax, 'cause you can't con-trol this shit." Keisha looked irritated.

"I could relax if my so-called friend would release me from my captivity. What bullshit is this?" I was angry. "Quincy . . . nigga, say some or do some. Why this?" I eyed him. "Tell me this shit a joke."

"Nah, I ain't no fuckin' comedian ya know." Quincy chuckled and I didn't find nothing funny. "But here is what you can do: You and I both know this game out here is a beast, right. So this shit gone be easy for you. Give up the name of the connect." He sniffed as if to clear his sinuses. "Do that and I will allow you to live." His tone was matter-of-fact.

I should have known that was what this was all about. Since DaVon had died, Quincy thought he was entitled to the throne. And for that he would betray me. I shook my head with disappointment. "I can't believe this," I said. Even more shocking was Keisha. How could she stand by and let this happen? "So, Keisha, you just gone let yo' man do this to your friend?"

"Like you just said. He my man." She folded her arms across her chest.

"Yeah, and I can't believe you gone stand by him after he slept with your best friend. And that's probably his baby," I declared with disgust. "You should want more."

"What I want, I will have. Never mind me staying with Quincy. We have a bond you could not understand. But if you must know, I cheated on Quincy with his brother and he forgave me. So of course I would forgive him for what he done. We gone be together always. We got something you miserable bitches will never have. And that's real love. Oh, and our new empire." She laughed. "If you bitches had just stayed out of my way. I tried to give you something to keep you busy. That's why Maria was killed."

"Are you sayin' y'all killed Maria and her daughter? She was the sweetest, nicest person in the world. She deserved better. And her daughter?"

"Her daughter was just a victim of circumstance. But you loved Maria, so I knew that shit would keep you busy for a minute," Quincy said.

"Fuck all that. You too full of emotion. You don't need to be worried about Maria and that daughter of hers. Bitch so sensitive but wants to run an empire."

"Bitch, fuck you sickos. You two deserve each other," I said, my tone full of disgust.

"Damn right we do. Now it's time for you to do what your man wouldn't," Keisha said, her face devoid of emotion. And at that moment I knew they had killed DaVon.

I glared at them both with disbelief. Who were these two people? I could for the first time see them for who they were. My heart was truly broken. DaVon had trusted Quincy. I focused in on him. "How could you kill your own friend?"

Keisha burst out laughing.

"Precious, is that what you think, that Quincy did it?" She continued to laugh. She smacked him on the shoulder in a playful manner. "Bruh, she thinks you did it." I watched her in disbelief. I had so much anger inside I could taste blood in my mouth. "You a stupid bitch, but I always knew that. Yes, I'm the one that killed DaVon. It was me. For my man I will do anything," she barked at me.

I tried to jump up, but Quincy pointed the gun at my chest.

"I'll fuck you up. Nasty ho!" I yelled.

"Bitch, you won't do shit. You think you entitled to this shit? No, bitch, I deserve what you got. I been about this life on these dog-eat-dog LA streets way before you came along. Yeah, while you were dry cleanin', making sure motherfuckers had extra starch, I was out here slangin' rocks makin' sure I ate . . . that's right, bitch, I been hustlin' since I was a teenager. Nobody ain't never gave me shit. And you think you can come in and just take over. You ain't no fuckin' hustler." She looked at Quincy. "Babe, I swear these bitches don't understand that tricks are for kids." She burst out laughing, then turned her attention back to me. "You see, this ain't Burger King, you can't have it your fuckin' way. I paid the price to be on top, but since I have a king, it's his turn. And I'll be damned if some soft bitch like you fuck that up. Now—" Suddenly she reached over and snatched Quincy's gun from him. Unleashing the safety, she pointed the gun at my head. I closed my eyes. "Now give up the connect," she demanded.

Quincy turned his back to check his phone and I took a chance. With all my might I charged at Keisha and I was willing to die. I heard the gun hit the floor and out of the corner of my eye saw a knife fall from her shirt. Quincy tripped over us as I grabbed Keisha by the head and pushed her to the wall. I landed blow after the blow to her face. Keisha pulled at my hair. I stuck my fingers in her eyes.

"Agh!" Keisha screamed. She lifted her right knee and tried to kick me in the gut, and fell. I climbed on top of her and punched her twice in the mouth. Blood wet my fist. "Quincy, get this bitch off of me!" Keisha yelled as I got the best of her. Standing up I kicked Keisha as Quincy tried to pull me away from her. Keisha made her way back to her feet and we went at it again. Quincy struggled to keep us apart.

Finally he separated us. We heard the click of a gun and Quincy paused. We looked to see Clip standing behind him, a gun to his head. "Drop that gun, nigga," Clip said through clenched teeth. I scrambled to the floor and grabbed Keisha's Glock.

Promise appeared and snatched the knife off the floor. "Are you okay, Precious?" I could see she had been crying.

"I will be," I replied.

"Mane, I tried to get here earlier. I figured this shit out this mornin', but I had to be sure I was right about these snake-ass lowlifes." Clip shook his head. "I also found out this nigga is the one who set up the robbery to take Derrick and Ray's money."

"Damn!" I screeched. "Ray was right. He tried to tell us that you knew." I squinted my eyes at Quincy. "You a fucking snake, my dude. That was them young niggas life that you took. When you knew it was shit."

"Nah, them niggas got took 'cause they was weak. The grind don't give a fuck! Them niggas forgot that." Quincy give a vile speech of nothing.

"Tell 'em, baby. Money is all that matters," Keisha added with a smirk.

"Bitch, I swear you disgust me. I knew not to trust this slut. I just knew it," I seethed.

Promise yelled, "Bitch don't have no conscience. Nasty, trick, ho." Promise rolled her eyes at Keisha.

"Bitch, shut yo' damn mouth with yo' stank ass. Broke, bum bitch," Keisha spat.

Suddenly Promise pulled a gun from her waist, rushed across the room and smacked Keisha in the face with the butt of it. Keisha wobbled backwards, hitting the wall.

"Bitch, I'll kill you," Quincy threatened Promise.

"Nigga, shut the fuck up. Disloyal weak ass," Clip said.

Quincy attempted to check Clip. "Nigga, kiss my ass. You ain't never been shit but DaVon's peon. Non-goal-havin'-ass nigga."

Pop, pop, pop. Without warning, Clip released three bullets between Quincy's eyes. His body swayed in a circular motion. He attempted to look at Keisha but fell face-first, silenced for good.

"*Agh!*" Keisha screamed as Quincy hit the floor and the blood drained from his lifeless body.

"Bitch, don't scream for him now. Wait . . . or are you screaming for yourself?" Promise chuckled. "Clip, please let me do this bitch."

"No." I stepped in. "This sick bitch is the one that killed DaVon."

"Mane, ain't no fuckin' way." Clip was stunned.

"Yep. So the bitch belongs to me. Clip, did you bring along any of that acid that you known for havin' all the time?" I had something special in mind for Keisha. Plain bullets wouldn't be enough for her. No, that would be too easy. I wanted her to suffer and reminisce on her mistakes that would leave her rotting in hell.

"No doubt." Clip looked at Keisha and nodded with a smirk. "It's about to be showtime, bitch." He turned on his heel to seek out my request.

Emotionless, Keisha stared at Quincy's lifeless body as if it would bring him back to life.

"No matter how much you stare at this fuckin' loser, he ain't coming back. So look up, bitch. New life is for you, and it's coming in the form of steam. You know, fried chicken." I laughed, but it came from pain and disappointment.

A tear slid down Keisha's cheek. "Fuck you, Precious! Wit' yo' weak ass!" Spit flew out of her mouth.

I could not believe I had hung around her, trusted her, felt bad for her, when her own man treated her like dirt. All the while she was stabbing me in the back, plotting on my man's legacy, with full intent to kill me. This was war, and I had the upper hand. "No, fuck you, bitch. You lost."

Pop! pop! I pumped a bullet in each one of her kneecaps.

"*Agh, agh!* Please, no, Precious! I don't mean half the shit that comes outta my mouth. Please don't kill me. I'm pregnant." She begged for her life and I was shocked. I came to the safe conclusion that she was confused and pathetic.

"So now you scared, ho. Ha-ha, don't make me laugh." Promise chuckled. "Bitch, you gone take this like a woman today. And I'ma watch this final episode. All I need is some popcorn. Ain't life a bitch?" Promise shook her head from side to side.

Keisha's eyes left Promise and focused on Clip and what was in his hand. She too had heard stories about Clip and the people he had tortured and/or murdered with acid. They were all horrific and scary-movie-award-winning. The fear in her eyes was real "*Noooo!* Precious. Please," she begged as she watched Clip pass me the acid. "What about my baby? It deserves a chance to live."

"What about DaVon!" I screamed at her. "He deserved better, but you or your thirsty-ass man didn't give a fuck, right? Huh?" I barked. "So, bitch, fuck yo' cheap-ass life, that baby probably better off. This is for DaVon. That bastard baby you carrying is just a bonus." I tossed acid on her like she was a slug on the ground. We all watched as she slowly burned.

"*Momma!*" Keisha screamed. The mention of her mother surprised me. The selfish bitch never even talked about her mother. With no sympathy, I tossed more acid on her and continued until the container was empty.

We watched as she suffered. It became difficult for her to breathe, and just as she sucked her last breath, I yelled her name. "Keisha." She attempted to lift her head. She made it halfway. *Pop! Pop!* I pumped two bullets between her eyes. Tupac said it best: *I ain't a killer but don't push me.*

Chapter 44

Two weeks later

The two weeks following all the drama had been the longest two weeks possible. I could still hear Keisha in my mind, unraveling right in front of me. Her words on how she killed DaVon and how she deserved to take what I had. I could not believe her betrayal, nor could I understand it. My dad had raised me and taught me a lot of things, but most of all he taught me how to love and how to care. And I carried that with me every day. I would never understand people who thought like Quincy and Keisha. They were just selfish, out for themselves, city slick people.

They were two people that I would never forget. They had come into my life at the lowest and took me back to that lowest point before they exited. DaVon had been my refuge after my dad; before he came into my life, I thought I would never love again. He had come along and made love safe for me again. And just like my dad, some lowlife had taken that from me. And the fact that they were so-called friends was the tragedy of it all. But I fought every day to move on, because I knew that is what DaVon and my dad would have wanted. They both had left me a legacy. And even though DaVon's legacy was illegal, it was a part of him. And I had to stay on my grind, or at least that's how I felt immediately after everything went down.

A week ago I woke up with a change of heart. I wasn't sure what it was, but it's like a feeling of freedom had come over me. I felt like I had always been tied to something. And I wanted to just travel. LA had so many memories. I loved my city but I needed a break. Penelope was in town and we got together and discussed the re-up. We had been bringing in so much money and were in such demand, we requested double the product. Penelope was impressed and made the phone call to make it happen.

Clip had been all smiles when the shipment came in. "Yo, this life is sweet. Al Pacino would be proud. If we move weight like this another round, we gone shut LA down. We already got this shit on lock." The look on his face was complete satisfaction, the same look DaVon used to have. They loved the game, thrived on it, lived for it. Then and there my mind was made up. I would walk away and hand the throne to Clip. DaVon would want that.

I had invited him out to the house to talk. Afterwards I had I invited Promise over to share the news with her. So my day was sure to be emotional.

The doorbell rang and I shuffled to the door. "This must be serious since I got invited to the mansion." Clip chuckled.

"Boy, don't start that. You know you family and always welcome. Bring yo' butt in here." I stepped to the side. I shut the door behind him. "Let's go down to the arcade room, shoot some pool and have a drink."

"Girl, you know you can't shoot no pool."

"I already schooled you and DaVon. How many lessons you need before you can be honest." I smiled.

"Aye, if you say so. What's that smell? You cookin'?"

"Yeah, I got my chef in the kitchen preparing some things. I got Promise comin' through later. We gone smash." I was hungry just thinkin' about it.

"What about me? I eat too."

"I can have her throw something together for you if you like."

"Nah, I'm good. Just pull out that Hennessy."

"And you know I got you." Down in the arcade room Clip headed straight to the fully stocked bar. The arcade DaVon had created was sick. He had all the games, including the original Pac-Man. He even had a mini bowling lane that used to be my favorite, but I hadn't played since DaVon was alive.

"You gone take a shot wit' me?" Clip asked. He poured a shot and downed it straight.

"Sure. Why not." I headed for the pool table.

"Mane, I miss comin' down here." Clip looked around the room, then hand me my shot. "We had so much fun. I be whoopin' everybody on Pac-Man and of course pool."

"Lies. You lost on both. But since you think you winnin', rack 'em."

"Oh it's on." Clip racked the balls. "Since you a girl, ladies first," he joked.

"A'ight. But you know how I get down. Right off

the bat I fly eight in the corner end pocket and six left cross." I smiled and shrugged my shoulders. "This what I do," I bragged.

"Stand still." Clip walked the table and sized up the balls and corners. "See, it takes patience and readiness."

"I'm sure." I grinned. He shot and missed.

I laughed. "You might suck at pool, but you a street genius." I put jokes aside. "I know you wondering why I brought you out here without warning. And I thank you for coming . . . I want you to know that I appreciate you. Ever since DaVon . . ." I paused. I hated saying what happened to him.

"Aye, you good, you don't have to say nothin'. DaVon was my big brother and you my sis. I got yo' back always."

"I know. And thanks. But you help me keep this operation going. Actually, you kept it going. I mean I had the connect, but you put in the street work and I don't take that for granted. The empire still growing. We larger than ever."

"No doubt. Man, DaVon would be so proud. And you, his lady, kept it going. Precious, you the classiest queenpin ever. I know you give me credit, but you been deeply involved. You a boss."

"This was all new to me. I stepped in to represent for DaVon. He was my man. And I loved him. There was nothin' I wouldn't have done for him. But now my work is done and it's time I pass the reins . . . to you, kiddo. This empire is now yours. Lock, stock, and key, effective immediately."

Clip just stared at me. I wasn't sure if he was happy or pissed. He looked down at the floor. "I know motherfuckers think I'm insane. And maybe I am, but never did I think I would have to take over this shit. Don't even know if I'm ready. But I don't want to let you down, Precious. I got this."

"Dang, you scared me for a minute. I thought you might turn it down." I breathed a sigh of relief.

"Nah, never. I love this shit too much. The grind, the mean, the grit, all of it."

"Well, it's yours. Let's toast." He poured us both a shot. We downed them. "Next week I'll set up a meeting with the connect. You already got the streets on point. They think you're in charge anyway. So the transition should be good."

"No doubt."

"Now that we got that straight, let me finish taxing you in this game. You may run the streets, but I run this pool table." I bragged for reasons he understood. We finished the game and I made good on my threats.

"Precious, I swear this steak was so good. Can I borrow your chef for a week or some? I'm tired of eating out and I don't have time for cooking . . . or more like I hate cooking," Promise admitted with a grin.

"Sure, you can borrow her. Just bring me a plate every day."

"I got you." She laughed.

"So listen. Shit changed for me tonight, and I got to let you know what's up."

Promise's eyebrows bent with worry. "You straight?" she asked.

"Yes, I'm good. But I'm leaving . . . moving away. I need a new start. I have to get out of this city for a while. Too much loss, you know. And not only that, I want to travel."

"You can't go. We just found each other."

"I know, but we'll see each other again. And you always welcome to join me. But you have a new business, and you have to be here to see it through. And what about Clip and your relationship?"

"There is no relationship with Clip, and we just havin' fun." She smiled. "But I can come out to visit you once a month. But when I get everything together I'm moving wherever you are. Hey, what about the dry cleaners, the hustle, this house?"

"All taken care of. I'm going to leave Katrina in charge and I'll drop in often. Wherever I am will be just a flight away. I'm going to shut both of the houses down for a while . . . and I turned the operation over to Clip. He the man now."

"Really. How does he feel about that?"

"He's ready. He been ready," I said matter-of-factly. "So celebrate with him."

"I'm supposed to see him tonight. I'll make something happen."

After dessert, Promise asked the chef to fix her a plate, then she bounced. I jumped in the shower. Exhausted, I fell into bed. I was trying to get some sleep but my cell phone refused to stop ringing. Reluctantly I reached for it and with my eyes half open, I answered.

All I heard was screaming muffled with crying. I recognized Promise's voice right away. "Promise, what's the matter?" Sleepy, I tried to sit up in bed. "Calm down and tell me what's wrong." I was nervous and my heart was racing.

"They shot him, Precious. Somebody killed Clip. He gone." She continued to scream the words that I couldn't believe and did not want to hear. My jaw dropped, and even though I wished this was a dream, Promise's piercing screams banging on my eardrums, along with the tears that stung my eyes, confirmed its reality.

Chapter 45

I could say I had no idea who had murdered Clip, but in this game, enemies came with a smile, bearing gifts and claiming loyalty. So it could have been anybody. One thing I knew for sure, when I found out who was responsible, there would be hell to pay. No questions asked. I knew there wasn't a hustler in LA that didn't envy me. Someone probably figured with Clip out of the picture, they had a chance to take over. But they had underestimated me. And the death of whoever tried to cross me would be my pleasure. But for now I had to keep DaVon's legacy alive. See, Clip was the only person I trusted with it, and now that he was gone there was only one thing left for me to do: climb back on top of my throne and adjust my crown. And with Promise's help, the streets of LA would not be the same as I reigned supreme and continued to hold it down as a Hustler's Queen.

DON'T MISS

The Hearts We Burn **by Briana Cole**
Kimera Davis thought she was finally free, until
her obsessed ex-husband ignited a spectacularly
malicious deception that's left her family, and her
best friend, Adria, reeling. . .

Property of the State **by Kiki Swinson**
Kiki Swinson's novels crackle with breakneck
triple-twists, no-limits characters, and an unfor-
gettably brutal portrayal of Southern life. Now
she shatters all expectations as a young woman
serving time must survive a prisoner-abuse
conspiracy . . .

Snapshot **by Camryn King**
An ambitious photojournalist. An uber-dedicated
enforcer. And an explosive, high-profile
scandal ignites Camryn King's explosive new
thriller . . .

ON SALE NOW!

Turn the page for an excerpt from these thrilling
novels . . .

Chapter 1

Adria

I never thought I would hate my husband. Well, maybe not hate, because that is such a strong word. Nevertheless, as I listened to his voicemail greeting message for the third time, I couldn't help but feel a strong emotion superseding anger. That's for damn sure.

I pulled the phone away from my ear without bothering to "leave a message for ya boi," as Keon had so eloquently instructed in his greeting. I knew he was doing it on purpose, and that's what was eating at me. He couldn't feign ignorance with this appointment. I made sure of that. We hadn't been speaking, but I had reminded him all week and even this morning before he left for work. So how convenient was it that his phone was off when his truck should've been parked in this deck right along with mine.

Three months. It had been three months since our lives had changed so drastically, three months of this bullshit, and time was doing nothing but driving us further and further apart. I rested my head on the back of the seat and glanced out at the traffic clogging the city streets of Atlanta. Somewhere, a horn blew, a siren wailed, and a slew of pedestrians hurried along the sidewalk through rush-hour congestion, probably to make it home to their families. I swallowed a wave of envy. If only life were still that simple for me. I was too busy dealing with my own losses, my husband included. Fact was, he was showing me he didn't care, and I was slowly adopting those same sentiments.

The phone suddenly rang in my hand, which startled me. Sure enough, Keon's number flashed across my screen. I quickly picked up.

"Where are you?"

"Damn, good afternoon to you too, *wife.*"

I rolled my eyes at the smart ass comment. "Keon, today is not the day. Where are you?" I knew what he was going to say before the words even filtered through the phone. Same shit I had heard for our last two sessions.

"I have to work late. Sorry." His tone was anything but apologetic, which only heightened my anger. Maybe hate was the right word after all.

"Keon, I thought you said you would be available. That's why we scheduled this appointment today for this time. Because you said it was convenient for you."

"Why you acting like that, Dria? Therapy was your dumb-ass idea anyway."

"My dumb-ass idea?"

"Yeah, you're the one with whatever mental shit you got going on and I'm trying to work with you—"

"Boy, don't act like you're doing me any favors," I yelled, not bothering to calm my tone. "You act like you're not even in this marriage. Like none of this is important to you."

"You tripping. All because I think therapy is bull-shit?"

"No, you know what? This whole damn relation-ship is bullshit. Keep doing you, Keon. And I'll be sure to do me without you. See how that feels." I hung up and immediately powered down my phone, cursing as my fingers trembled over the buttons. I knew I was arguing from another place because those words had felt completely empty. But as I shut my eyes and struggled to keep my blood from boiling over, regret began to ease its way into my subcon-scious. Not for the argument. Hell, that had become too common between us these past months. No, re-gret that I had walked down the aisle to give this man my heart again. Til' death do us part, my ass.

Sighing, I slid weary eyes to the clock on the dash. 5:08, already well into my allotted grace period, so I needed to get inside if I still wanted to be seen today. I grabbed my purse and stepped out of the car.

I bundled my jacket tighter against the September chill as I made my way across the parking deck. The therapist's office was in a high-rise in the hub of downtown Atlanta. But since it was adjoined to other doctors, realtors, and finance companies in the building, I certainly appreciated the discretion.

I stepped into the elevator and jabbed the button for the seventh floor, maybe a little too forcefully, as a sharp pain pierced my thumb. When the doors closed,

I could only stare at my piss-poor reflection in the mirror finish.

I still carried baby weight, hadn't bothered to try and get rid of it. Though I still looked the part, to my despair I was very much not pregnant. The realization had sadness extinguishing my anger and I touched my belly. Ghost flutters or something. My OB-GYN had told me it was common to still feel like my babies were kicking or rolling around in there. My head would want to feel there was still someone in there. My heart would *need* to feel it. But I was empty. In more ways than one.

The doors opened to reveal a narrow hallway with watercolor paintings flanking one side and floor-to-ceiling windows along the other. At the end of the hall, a door with the words Waller Family Counseling etched in the glass automatically slid open to welcome me into the quaint lobby.

The receptionist looked up and smiled. "Good afternoon, Mrs. Davis," she said, sliding the clipboard across the marble desk in my direction. "How are you today?"

I wondered if she really expected a truthful answer to that question. I'm sure it was automatic, but would she be surprised if I actually told her how I really felt one time? *I feel like shit, thank you very much for asking.* But my lips thinned into a polite smile as I scribbled my name on the sign-in sheet.

"Fine," I said instead. No need to blurt out my frustrations to the poor little intern who made coffee and answered phones. Her little college courses probably hadn't prepared her for an Adria Davis. I would do enough of that in just a moment.

Dr. Waller was a brown-skin sister who wore a short

curly afro and not a stitch of makeup other than lip-gloss. I always thought she looked entirely too young for this job, like she needed to be taking notes in a black history university classroom instead of being burdened with the world's problems on her shoulders. But she was kind and patient, which kept me booking session after session, even if it didn't initially feel like I was getting better.

"Adria." She hugged me as we stood in the doorway, a genuine embrace like best friends. I held on a moment longer, inhaling the nostalgia of that familiar feeling, before I let go.

"I'm sorry I'm late, Dr. Waller," I said as she closed the door behind me.

"Evelyn," she corrected.

I nodded. "Evelyn."

We sat together, side-by-side on the plush leather couch overlooking the city skyline. In front of us, a recorder and two cups of water sat on the coffee table. Evelyn crossed her legs and folded her hands in her lap.

"Where is your husband?" she asked, though I'm sure she knew my answer.

"He's working late."

"Do we need to reschedule?"

"He'll probably be working late then too."

Evelyn nodded her understanding and remained silent, watching me gather my thoughts.

"That's why I was late," I went on, the argument festering fresh in my mind. "He's just being so damn difficult about this whole thing."

"I want to hear about that," Evelyn said. "But first, tell me about a good time with your husband."

I sighed, already recognizing her tactic. She liked

to do some kind of sandwich-method, start with something positive, then let out all my negative energy, then end positive. As irritating as the strategy was, the shit was effective. I let out a breath and closed my eyes.

"You look so beautiful, Mrs. Davis," Keon murmured, the words causing my body to heat with anticipation. I did a seductive sway of my hips, slowly peeling out of my wedding dress. The hotel room was nearly dark, illuminated only by candles my husband had placed on the bedside tables. His naked frame looked delicious lying on the white sheets and rose petals, and the light from the flame flickered across the hungry gaze on his face. He licked his lips and I wanted to cream right there.

"I'm in love with you, Mr. Davis," I said, crawling up from the foot of the bed.

"Oh, yeah?"

"Yeah."

He kissed me, caressing my lips with his tongue. "Damn, I'm gon' get you pregnant tonight, girl."

I laughed and let him roll on top of me. This man of mine. My forever. Mr. Playboy, who I had waited through woman after woman while he got his shit together. Always his little booty call. Finally his wife. It was about damn time.

"He's dealing with it," Evelyn said, her gentle voice breaking my memory. "In his own way."

"I'm the one having to deal with it," I said on a frown.

"Adria, he lost his daughters, too. And a sister,"

she added at my continued silence. The last sentence had me wincing. She was right. Kimera was his sister, but she was my best friend. As much as it pained me to admit, it was easier to not think about her. Not thinking about her made it easier to not blame her, nor feel guilty about blaming her, since she had lost her life. More memories flooded through me, threatening to swallow me into some kind of black hole.

"Tell me about Kimera," Evelyn said. "Before . . . everything."

For the first time, I reached for my water and took a desperate swallow. Despite the fruit I knew Evelyn infused with the water, it remained tasteless, the liquid seeming to hit my stomach without touching my throat.

"I had known Kimmy since middle school," I started. "The girl was a mess, even then. Always seemed to be in some kind of trouble. But I loved her. More like sisters than friends. I used to tell her she never took anything serious, but that was just Kimmy. The epitome of living her best life. But we were always there for each other. I never even really came out and told her I was feeling her brother because honestly, I knew I was being stupid for that boy. Somehow, she always knew though. Just like I knew she was in love with Jahmad, Keon's best friend. But Keon and Jahmad were both young and seemed to always be in some kind of competition on who could sleep with the most girls."

The statement came out snarky but that didn't change the facts. Restless, I rose and wandered to the window.

"Jahmad hurt her so bad when he moved away. It was clear he had just been using her for sex, hell, just like Keon was doing to me, but me and Kimmy, we were built different. I dealt with the shit, but my girl, it changed her. There were times I didn't even recognize her . . ." I trailed off at the thought.

"Changed her how?"

"Kimmy met Leo," I said simply. "And well, you know the rest."

Of course she did. I had hashed out the past two years for Evelyn over the past five sessions. How Kimmy had met Leo, a man with two wives. How his long money had prompted her to enter the poly relationship as wife number three, because she would be able to get her hands on enough money so we could open our cosmetic store. The fact that Leo had been harboring a huge secret, and that secret resulted in me and Kimmy being kidnapped and tortured for nearly a week. That was three months ago, but it seemed like yesterday.

Pain snatched me from darkness, piercing my body like a thousand blades stabbing from flesh to bone. Everything was throbbing, and a slight ringing in my ears seemed to overwhelm the quiet conversation. Someone was talking. No, several people, in hushed whispers, as if they feared disturbing me. But as the raw memories came barreling back, licking the recesses of my subconscious, I knew it was too late. I was well past disturbed.

I moaned, not bothering to open my eyes to face the dark realities. I was in this mess because of Kimmy—being held hostage, deprived of food, and subjecting my babies to this torture. I hadn't done anything but be a good friend, but now . . . A noise ripped through my thoughts, followed by silence. I could feel eyes on me. Then,

"Adria?" Keon. My husband's voice held the weight of uncertainty. "Babe? You awake?"

I lifted heavy lids, squinting against the sudden glare of the hospital room lights. One by one, the other figures came into view, first Keon, then my mother-in-law, First Lady Davis. And judging by the man in the lab coat at the foot of my bed, my doctor.

He came to the side of my bed, a gentle smile on his lips. "Mrs. Davis," he said. "I'm Dr. Hinton. Can you hear me okay?" He plucked a pen-like object from his breast pocket and shined the light in my eye.

"What happened?" My voice was hoarse, unrecognizable. I cleared it, bracing against a headache that was beginning to intensify.

"You're in a hospital," Dr. Hinton. "We've been treating you for about eighteen hours, but it's good to see you finally came through. Are you in any pain?"

"Yeah."

"On a scale of one to ten?"

"One hundred."

Dr. Hinton chuckled, though I didn't see this shit as humorous. He scribbled something on a notepad, then checked some fluid in the IV bag near my bed. "We'll increase the dosage of morphine," he said. "And I'm going to check on your MRI and ultrasound results."

Ultrasound? My hand went to my stomach in alarm. "Are my babies all right?"

Dr. Hinton's eyes lowered before glancing to Keon on my other side. The panic rose with this silent exchange of information.

"Babe," Keon's voice cracked. "They did everything they could—"

"No!" I shook off his hand and lifted the sheets to eye my stomach. I still had a pudge. My babies were okay. They had to be. "They're fine," I said, sinking back into the pillows in relief. "Thank God."

First Lady Davis turned her back to me, shielding her face from view. I looked back to Keon.

"They're all right," I said with a small smile. "I'm all right. We're all right."

He shook his head and my heart fell as the first few tears rolled down his cheeks. "No," he said. "We're not."

"Do you feel like it's Keon's fault you lost your babies?" Evelyn's voice again cracked through my sordid memory as I struggled to blink back tears.

"No," I shook my head, my voice surprisingly forceful. "No, of course not."

"Then why are you so angry with him?"

"I'm not angry with him. I'm angry with . . ." I trailed off, my heart not allowing me to utter the name. I shouldn't have been angry with Kimmy either. But how could I not? Still, how could I place the blame on a ghost? Yes, my babies had lost their lives in this mess, but so had Kimmy. And my nephew Jamal. So really, whose burden was worse?

"You told me a few sessions ago that you were Christian," Evelyn said. "Have you been praying about this issue?"

I didn't respond, afraid to let Evelyn know I hadn't cracked open a Bible, nor said anything to God since the good pastor, my father-in-law, was killed. I didn't like to admit I had turned my back on Him, but I couldn't really see where He had helped me in any way thus far.

"I want you to go home, and read Psalm 73:26," she continued, scribbling her instructions on a notepad. "And I want you to write down a list of everything you have to be thankful for. I want us to do a little exercise next time you come in."

I shook my head, already dreading the assignment. "Come on, Evelyn. You know that's not what I need."

"What do you need, Adria?"

"Can't you just write a prescription?" I said instead.

"The antidepressants? You're not due for a refill yet." Evelyn stared at me a little longer, making me uncomfortable under her scrutiny. I averted my eyes.

"I know. I just wanted to see if you could write something stronger," I lied. "I'm not sure if it is really working for me."

"Let me be the judge of that," she said with another one of her signature smiles as she handed me the scratch sheet of paper. Defeated, I rose to leave. A sudden swell of anger had me mumbling a quick goodbye before nearly running from the room. Dammit, I had been out of pills for two days, a supply that should have lasted me the rest of the month. I had figured Evelyn could just call in some more to my pharmacy, so I hadn't prepared for her refusal. But fine, let her be on her Dr. Phil rampage. I knew someone who could get me that same medicine for cheaper anyway.

Chapter 1

Time's Up

"Misty, time's up," Agent Sims had said, his handcuffs dangling in front of him.

"No." I shook my head as tears sprang to my eyes. "I have to make sure my mother is okay. I can't just leave her like this."

"We'll take care of her. But, right now . . . 'You have the right to remain silent. Should you give up that right, anything you say can and will be held against you . . . '"

I opened my eyes after replaying one of the worst days of my life. My chest heaved and the air around me felt heavy. I felt like my body would collapse, just like my whole world had days before Agent Sims had taken me down and handed me over to the local cops for my ex-boyfriend Terrell's murder. On one hand, I was grateful that Sims had saved me from being taken by mafia guys that wanted to kill me, but on the other hand, facing down a long prison sentence wasn't ideal.

Damn! I had fucked everything up. Everything about my life had gone in a totally opposite direction than what I had planned. One seemingly foolproof plan to steal drugs had sent my entire life on a crash course with disaster. Murder, mayhem, and now my arrest had been the result of my plan, instead of making money and getting rich quick. Call it karma, or just straight bad luck—whatever it was, I was knee-deep in it now.

Goose bumps cropped up all over my body as I thought back to watching my mother scramble for her life. Knowing that it was all my fault she'd been kidnapped and held hostage made it even worse to bear. My whole plan to trade my life for my mother's had fallen apart, even though a small part of me knew that Ahmad, the bastard that had held my mother hostage, wasn't going to trade my life for hers as easily as he'd made it seem. Ahmad was ruthless and he was out to avenge the savage killing of his family, which he blamed on me.

I swear, this wasn't how my life was supposed to end. And now I was sitting in lockup, waiting to be arraigned for murder. *Murder! Me, a murderer?* I had worked so hard in school and struggled in life to be successful. And all for what? To end up in jail facing a real-life prison term.

I'd been racking my brain thinking of all sorts of ways I could get out of this situation. But Agent Sims had warned me that the local detectives had clear and convincing evidence against me. I was officially doomed. When I get convicted, because I am sure it will happen, I know that I will probably spend the rest of my life in prison while my mother is out on the streets alone. Who would protect her now? I was locked up. Carl was dead. My grandmother and cousin Jillian were gone. My mother was alone with a bag of money and an entire organized crime family out to get her so they could exact revenge against me. My mother's safety preoccupied most of my thoughts.

I had bitten my fingernails down to the quick and could barely keep still. I hadn't eaten since I'd been arrested. Sleep was a thing of the past; I hadn't gotten one solid hour. Every time I closed my eyes, all of the craziness played out in my mind's eye, over and over. My life had turned into a real-time nightmare. One thing after another had me wanting to end it all, again. I thought about it and could actually see myself going through with it, all over again, but the thought that my mother would really be left with no one in life kept me from doing it. I let the tears that I'd been hiding run down my face this time.

As different officers moved me through the process, my head pounded with all sorts of thoughts. I had had enough of hurting people that I love and getting hurt as well. At one point, I even wanted to die myself. The whole plan was to trade my life for my mother's, but then that plan blew up in my face. I mean, I can't win for losing. Nothing I do ever comes to fruition. *Ugh!*

The time came for me to be moved from the holding cell in the precinct, where those backstabbing detectives dropped me off, to the county jail until my initial appearance and arraignment could finally be scheduled. When the police officer pulled me from the cell, he escorted me down to the first floor, where the inmates were processed in and out to be transported to jail. He handed me over to a white man and white woman dressed in regular clothing and a dark blue jacket, which told me right away that my case had been turned over to state authorities. I was handed a brown paper bag, escorted to a back room and was told to change. Without saying a word, I took the brown paper bag, which contained my belongings, and went about changing. Immediately after I finished, both feds, the man and the woman, handcuffed my wrists and placed shackles around my ankles.

"Ouch!" I bellowed as I looked down at the cuffs around my ankles.

"Are the cuffs too tight?" the female asked.

"Yes, but you already know that because y'all do this type of stuff on purpose," I answered with an attitude.

She didn't get rude back; she just smirked like she knew that I was going to have many more complaints ahead. Once she loosened up the cuffs, she stood straight up and placed her hand around my arm. She waited for her partner to give her the signal that they could head out.

"We're ready for the other inmate," the male fed told the precinct officer.

That alarmed me a little bit, because I thought I'd be in the black jail van alone. I'd heard horror stories about inmates assaulting others in those van rides. My stomach cramped up. This was going to be the worst part of my life; I could already tell. I had done a lot of things, but I was not cut out for the prison system.

"Opening doors!" the officer yelled out, and then the metal door let out a loud buzzing sound and the lock on the door clicked.

"Step out into the hallway," the officer instructed. I couldn't see who he was talking to, but I was still nervous. I heard chains slide across the floor as the other female inmate made her way out of the holding cell. And when she appeared from behind the beige painted metal door, I immediately looked at her from head to toe. She looked completely out of place. I had to admit she was pretty with delicate features and looked more like a celebrity than a prisoner. She didn't look like she belonged there at all. I could see the male officers ogling her, and I can't lie, it made me a bit jealous that none of them had had that reaction to me when I was brought out.

The male officer instructed the pretty female inmate to walk toward us. The second she got within arm's reach of us, she was told to walk side by side with me and follow the lead of the female state officer that was about to transport us down to county. This is what they meant by *chain of custody*. Even though the agents had taken me to the local precinct, as feds, they were still responsible for turning me over to county. Chances are I wouldn't stay in county. I was facing down state time, for sure.

While the female officer led the way down the corridor, all three of us followed. We went through several metal doors, and when one closed shut, we had to wait for the other door to open. The security at this place was in full force. I couldn't see anyone escaping if they wanted to. Trust me, I thought about all types of ways I could get out of there.

After the last metal door opened and closed, we ended up in an underground garage. While I was being escorted to a black van with darkly tinted and caged windows, I saw two uniformed police officers escorting a young guy toward the door we had just exited. He looked like he had been roughed up, given the fact that he had a black eye and blood all down the front of his shirt. I winced just looking at him. These officers didn't care. Police brutality was an issue in our area, for sure, and I was seeing it first-hand. That's exactly what I was afraid of too.

The guy they were moving whistled and catcalled us when he saw the other female inmate I was with. The officers holding him yanked him by the hand-cuffs and told him to shut his mouth. The guy laughed like he didn't even care. It was obvious he had given up after being beaten and held. He probably knew his life was over, just like how I felt.

Both of the cops that were moving us along chuckled at how rough the officer was with the guy. I personally didn't think that shit was funny or amusing. Like I said, police brutality was an issue, and I was praying I didn't have to endure any of it.

"I see you got yourself a fake thug with a big mouth," the male cop with us called to the other officers.

"You're right about the 'big mouth' part, but we busted his stupid ass on weapons charges, so you might be making a trip back this way to pick him up too," the same officer said.

The male cop looked at his female partner and

smiled. "The more the merrier. These people keep us gainfully employed with their stupid behavior," he replied, and then laughed.

He meant it too. The more black people they locked up, the more money they made off of cheap labor and off of their jobs. Locking people up was the new form of slavery, I was convinced. I knew all about it, which is why I'd always tried to keep my ass out of jail or prison.

Right after, the male cop with us turned his attention back toward me and the other female inmate with me. He opened up the side door to the van, grabbed a footstool from underneath the seat, and then told us both to climb inside. He didn't give us a bit of help and it took me a few times to get up into the van, since the handcuffs kept me from having good balance.

"Sit on either side and not together." The female cop droned her instruction like she had said that same line a thousand times a day.

After we both struggled into the van, we took our seats and were strapped down with seat belts. The male officer hit the side of the van to signal to the female cop that we'd been strapped. "Animals ready for transport," he said. I was screaming in my head, *Who the hell you calling an animal, you racist!* But I didn't dare say anything at all.

"Ready to get on the road?" the female called out.

"Ready," he commented, and then he smirked at us and slammed the side door shut. He used a key to lock the outside of the door and then he climbed into the passenger side of the van. I could see the backs of their heads and out of the front windshield, but other than that, we couldn't even see outside. I was hoping to see some trees and anything that might cheer me up.

I still couldn't believe I was strapped down in a fucking jail transportation van with metal bars protecting the window, handcuffed and shackled like I was a part of a freaking chain gang. I was definitely out of my element. The girl that sat across from me seemed super calm. A little *too calm,* really, for my liking. I started thinking about the way I'd gotten here, and I just chuckled under my breath at how stupid I'd been.

With a look of aggression, the girl turned her focus on me. "What's so funny?" she asked.

I stretched my eyes and looked over at her like she was crazy. "Nothing that has anything to do with you," I came back. I don't know who she thought she was with that question. I turned my focus to look out of the windshield as the van exited the precinct. I didn't want any problems before I even officially got locked up.

I turned my thoughts to the day and what I might be doing if I wasn't locked up. I thought about all of the people out in the world going about their daily routines. They were free to do whatever they wanted to do, and I envied them. Knowing that I may never be able to spread my wings again was a thought that began to cut me deep in my heart.

Thinking back to when I first fell into that trap of getting involved with the feds, and that prescription ring operated by my former boss at the pharmacy, brought tears to my eyes. I had had it good before that. My life had been turned upside down and now I had the very likely prospect of life imprisonment dangling over my head. I thought about how unfairly I would be treated once I went to trial. There was just no way I would get a fair trial based on the fact that the media had dragged my name through the mud as a killer. Terrell's family had made sure of that, especially his mother.

While I was in deep thought, I noticed the girl across from me fidgeting with her handcuffs. She tried to do it discreetly, but my peripheral vision was working overtime. She was moving her cuffed hands up to her face and back down and she repeated it several times like it was a tic. I looked directly at her and she looked at me. She didn't say anything at first, but I think she noticed that I was getting suspicious and might tell on her. Because of that, she started making small talk with me. I knew it was a distraction, but I went along with it.

"What's your name?" she asked. Then she smiled.

I guess it was her way of changing how she approached me a few minutes earlier.

I gave her direct eye contact. "Misty," I muttered, and quickly turned my eyes away and looked down at my hand.

"That's it . . . just Misty?" she asked.

"You don't need my whole government. You work for the FBI or something?" I asked, annoyed. I wasn't no punk and she needed to know it. And besides, I had too much shit on my mind than to be answering a whole bunch of questions. And especially by a chick that's in the same predicament as me.

"Nah, I'm just asking, that's all," she said.

"What's your name?" I asked. I figured why should she only know my name.

"Shelby," she answered.

"That's it . . . just Shelby," I came back at her with the same comment she'd given me. Touché.

Her eyes grew two inches wide at my little dig. "You don't look like someone I'd expect to see locked up, Misty. I like that name, by the way," she said, and then giggled.

Okay, this chick had to be high off something. I gave her an expression of disbelief. I know she wasn't talking. She looked glamorous as hell even locked up. I could look at the nail tips on her hands and see that they were done at one of those high-class salons and not by the Vietnamese ones in the hood. Even Shelby's eyelashes were the high-priced mink ones that were applied one hair at a time. Her hair extensions were laid so well they looked like they had grown out of her scalp. She was high-class, and there was no doubt about it. I knew a lot about how chicks looked when they had a little bit of money, and Shelby definitely had money.

"You talking? You look like you need to be in somebody's magazine or walking a runway, so the feelings are mutual. I'm just as shocked as you are. There is no damn way I expected to see someone like you sitting up in here. You didn't see how many men were staring at you as we got led out to this van? Shit, you could've probably got that guy up front there to set you free—he had so much lust in his eyes for you," I said. "So now you tell me, what the heck is a fly chick like you doing locked up like an animal?"

She let out a long sigh and hung her head a little bit. She knew damn well I was right. "Let's just say, it's complicated, and you probably wouldn't believe my story even if I told it to you," she replied with a forlorn look on her face.

"I'm sure. You'd probably feel the same way about my story because sometimes even I can't believe it," I replied.

"Well, it was nice meeting you, Misty," she said as if she was about to go somewhere.

"Huh? What do you mean 'was'?" I asked. "Looks to me like we going to the same place right about now . . . county lockup."

"You'll see," she replied, and then she smiled once again, like she knew a secret I would never find out.

Then she did that weird thing again where she held up both of her hands with the handcuffs and put them to her mouth. It looked to me like she took something out of or put something in her mouth.

I crinkled my brows, but I didn't dare ask her what she was doing. I just wanted to mind my damn business. I just wanted to go home, honestly.

"I'm glad you didn't ask any questions," Shelby said after a few long minutes.

"What you do is your business, I'm no snitch," I said nonchalantly. I wasn't about to let her drag me into anything illegal she was doing or about to do.

"Well, I appreciate that, and you'll find out soon enough what's going on," Shelby said cryptically. "Just understand that I don't have anything to lose. That's all I'm going to say about it," she said with a lot of mystery behind her words.

"What does that mean?" I asked. I wanted to know.

"I murdered my parents and I'd do it all over again," she blurted, changing the subject.

"Oh my God! Are you serious?" I asked her, feeling my eyes go big. This bitch was crazy. I thought what I was in for was bad, but at least mine was self-defense. This was crazy. Who has the guts to kill their fucking parents? Well, unless they're pedophiles or physically abusive. Other than that, you've got to be a very sick individual to commit a heinous crime such as that.

Instead of responding verbally, she nodded her head kind of somberly. Shit, she looked really sad, like her life was surely over, and I kind of agreed. I thought that murdering your own parents was as low as you could go. I immediately reflected on my crime and suddenly my whole mood changed.

"You all right?" she asked me in a weird tone.

I don't know exactly how she wanted me to react to her telling me she had murdered her own parents. I turned my focus back to her and said, "Not really. I can't imagine what would make someone kill their own parents. I'm in here dying to see my mother one last time, so I just can't understand it. I know people with terrible parents, and they wouldn't dare kill them. So . . . no . . . I'm not all right."

"I guess you'd have to know my story before you could judge me, right?" she said, and then shrugged her shoulders like she didn't care. "Every parent is not the same. I may look like I had it all, but you have no idea and neither do these people trying to keep me locked up for the rest of my life. I won't let them do it. I'd rather die."

I shook my head and then I turned my focus away from her. I was no longer in the mood to talk to her. I had enough problems of my own. And I had already made up in my mind that this chick, Shelby, was crazy as hell. The one thing I didn't need to do was get into it with anyone crazy.

I could hear the two cops up front having a conversation, but I couldn't hear exactly what they were saying. Periodically I noticed the woman look at us through the rearview mirror like she was making sure we hadn't jumped out, which would've been impossible, anyway.

After a long period of driving, I saw Shelby start to nod, her head jerking down and then back up. I just chalked it up to her being tired. I noticed that the van had slowed down. I leaned to my left and looked straight through the windshield and saw that we had come upon railroad tracks. The gates were down on both sides and the lights flashed on and off, but there was no train in sight.

I heard the female cop sigh really loudly while the male cop made a loud outburst. "Dammit, I thought we would make it around it. This could be like an hour sitting here," he snapped.

"You think it takes that long?" the female cop asked him.

"Hell yeah," he replied, annoyed.

As the van came to a complete stop at the railroad tracks, I went to say something to Shelby and noticed that she was hanging way over at the waist. The only reason she hadn't slid to the floor was the fact that she was chained to the seat in the van.

"Shelby?" I called to her in a harsh whisper. I didn't want to be loud and bring attention to us back there. She didn't answer. "Shelby," I called her again, this time a little bit louder. Still, nothing. Then, as I listened to the cops complaining, Shelby's body started to jerk. I jumped back.

"Oh my God!" I gasped. "Shelby!" I called out, this time louder and with more force. I didn't care if the cops heard us.

"What the hell is going on?" the male cop called back to me.

My body started trembling as I watched Shelby's body convulse and white foam started bubbling out of her mouth. "Fuck! Shelby! Oh my God!" I screamed this time. Now I really didn't care. Something was definitely wrong with this girl.

Both cops turned in their seats at the same time.

"What the hell are you screaming about, inmate?" the female cop yelled out.

"You better shut the fuck up if you know what's good for you," the male cop followed up.

All of a sudden, we all seemed to hear a strange sound at the same time. Shelby's body started convulsing even more violently, causing a loud banging in the van.

"Help! Help her!" I yelped. Not only was white foam bubbling all over Shelby's face, blood started to leak out of her nose. "She's dying! Help her! Oh my God!" I wailed. I started stomping my feet, the only power I had to make them understand that something was seriously wrong.

I saw the male cop scramble out of the driver's seat. I continued to scream, and so did the female cop, but only she was telling me to shut up and calm down. She tried to be the voice of reason, but I was too inconsolable to listen to her. There was a damn girl dying right in front of me, as if I hadn't seen enough death and destruction in my life. I watched in shock; and my heart was beating so fast, it hurt. I looked over at Shelby with a look of pure terror etched on my face.

"Oh my God . . . she's dead! I know it!" I screamed out. I was nervous as hell because we were helplessly shackled in the back of the van with no way for me to help her and no way for her to be saved. The inside of the van suddenly grew overwhelmingly hot and the air felt stiff. I heard another loud bang on the van, and I started saying a silent prayer that they were going to help her. This would be a fucked-up way to die for anyone, even an inmate that these cops cared nothing about.

The back doors to the van flung open. I jumped so hard, I almost pissed and shit on myself. The male cop was standing there, breathing hard with a beet-red face. "What's going on, inmate!" he screamed.

It was clear that he didn't believe me and thought maybe we were just trying to make a distraction. I mean, who could blame him? Convicts do it all the time in the movies. But this time was the real thing.

"See for yourself! She's dying!" I belted out. I was crying by then. Seeing someone die like that was a crazy experience. The male cop scrambled his ass into the van. He looked horrified. He pushed Shelby back up into a sitting position. I was in shock, to say the least. Her face was completely different. She had foam coming out of her mouth, blood out of her nose, and her eyes were all white. She looked like the girl in the movie *The Exorcist*. My heart dropped and I quickly closed my eyes. I knew that if I didn't, nightmares of her face would haunt me for months, just like Terrell's did.

"What happened here?" the male cop asked me.

"How am I supposed to know?" I replied with an attitude. "She was sitting over there one minute, and the next minute, she was nodding and then this. I have no fucking clue what happened, but I will tell you being in here with a dead person is not cool for me."

"Did you see her take something?" he asked, his voice getting a bit more frantic. He needed answers.

I thought about what I would say, and whether I should tell him about seeing Shelby fiddling with her hands and handcuffs, but I didn't want to be set up to be any kind of witness. The cops and the feds had set me up one too many times and I didn't trust their asses as far as I could throw them. And that wasn't very far.

"I told you what I saw! I saw her sitting here one minute, and the next minute, she was like that!" I screamed out. That was it, I almost fainted right there in that van. Sweat broke out all over my body. This girl was dead, right then and there, right in my direct line of vision, and we seemed to be in the middle of nowhere. How much more drama can I take?

"I feel a faint pulse. We need to call a medic!" the male cop yelled up to the female as he touched Shelby's neck.

A feeling of relief came over my entire body and my nerves kind of simmered down a little bit. I was hoping Shelby was still alive and it seemed that she was . . . for now.

"I'll call for one, but that means we still have to wait for this train to pass!" the female cop yelled back.

"Looks like you're going to have to sit in here with her until we can get a medic to come. If she dies . . . well, then . . . she dies," the male cop said, then shrugged his shoulders like he didn't give a damn about Shelby.

There was complete silence. If this was any indication of what I was in for, I didn't know what I would do with myself.

After what seemed like an eternity, an ambulance finally showed up. "One female, no pulse!" the first medic yelled out.

I wanted to scream, *Of course, she doesn't have a pulse now! You bastards took forever to come save her!* But I just sat there, shaking and looking at Shelby. Her lips had turned completely purple and so did her fingernails. They took another thirty minutes before they even un-strapped her from the van seat. This is how messed-up they treated inmates, like we weren't even human be-ings.

After what seemed like forever, they finally took Shelby's cold, dead body out of the van in a black body bag. They pulled it right past me with no regard for my mental state at that point. They left my ass, shaking, crying, and in handcuffs and shackles. No one even cared. To them, I was just another fucking criminal awaiting my fate for killing a nigga. It didn't matter that I was trying to defend myself. All they knew or cared about was throwing another black per-son in jail so they could throw the book at you.

"Hopefully, we make it to county with at least one," the asshole male cop joked with his partner.

"She looked spooked, so we better hurry up be-fore we have a cardiac arrest on our hands," the fe-male cop joked back.

I didn't find anything about what they were saying funny. I also didn't find anything about my situation funny. Little did I know, life had just begun to get in-teresting for me.

Excerpt from *Snapshot*

Chapter 1

The Bahamas. Sun and sea. Gentle breezes. Tasty drinks with floating umbrellas. Paradise. Kennedy Wade thought about the refreshing drink brought by the kind boat captain as she placed her foot on the boat's gunwale and braced herself against the boat's gentle rocking to snap a round of pics. She was relieved that the showers from that morning had passed over the island, leaving behind fluffy cumulus clouds floating in a bright blue sky. She looked forward to enjoying her last day on the water, as she'd intended. For the past two days she'd crisscrossed the island, documenting its beauty, and writing up the accompanying article for a spread set to appear in the *Chicago Star* newspaper's upcoming Memorial Holiday Sunday edition. But today was for her. As she took in the beauty of the Caribbean, with its pristine white beaches, turquoise waters, and verdant countryside, a rare, philosophical thought assailed her. Kennedy wasn't necessarily religious, and had no real concept of heaven or hell, but if for whatever reason she landed in the latter, at least she would have caught a glimpse of paradise.

"What are you doing, girl? You're supposed to be relaxing."

Kennedy smiled. Clinton's lyrical phrases drifted toward her on the wings of the wind. The boat captain had helped make the time pleasurable during her ten to twelve-hour work days. He regaled her with colorful stories about famous people who'd visited the island and engaged in shenanigans they hoped would stay there—just like Vegas.

She lowered the camera. "Taking pictures like this is relaxing." Not like the other days, while waiting for the right light or searching for the perfect shot, then returning to her room to spend another few hours crafting the words that would bring the reader fully into this idyllic world. "Today I can just take in the beauty and capture the magic when it happens." She looked beyond Clinton and motioned with a nod of her head. "Like that."

Raising her camera, Kennedy placed the colorful lines of a perfect rainbow squarely in the middle of her lens. She adjusted her aperture to enhance the color, then engaged her long-range lens for a clearer shot. She took several frames, pulled out a bit to include a small island, and shot a few more. Her finger hovered over the shutter when a flash caught her eye. *What was that?* Instinctively, she pushed the shutter in rapid succession before lowering the camera, squinting as she shielded her eyes from the sun. They were a good distance away from the island, which was dense with brush and tropical trees. She looked for Clinton, who'd returned to the helm, then back at the rainbow. It had shifted and begun to fade. She joined the captain up front.

"These smaller islands all around. Are they inhabited?"

"Some of them, but not these out here."

"Are you sure?" She nodded toward the rainbow, now behind them. "What about that one, directly in front of the rainbow?"

"Someone owns it, but as of right now it's uninhabited."

"I could have sworn I saw a flash while taking pictures."

"It could be anything," Clinton said. "Most likely something reflecting against the sun."

"Like what?"

The captain shrugged as he waved to a tourist boat passing by. "We've had hundreds of years for all kinds of things to have washed up on these shores."

"That makes sense." Kennedy spent the better part of an hour photographing the beauty that surrounded her. Satisfied, she sat on a bench facing the water and rested her head back to look at the sky. "This is the life right here, my friend. You are so lucky to call this home."

"Easy enough for you to do too, if you want it. Plenty of people want their picture taken. You could set up a little stand on the beach, get a printer, make it work."

"You make it sound so easy."

"Everything's easy in the Bahamas."

Probably true, Kennedy imagined. Not like back in Chicago where freelance photographers and writers outnumbered White Sox fans, making both industries dog-eat-dog. Or where she'd just unraveled herself from a complicated relationship that had continued long past its expiration date. Even in paradise, there was no escaping serial liar/cheater, Will's incessant texts begging to be given one more chance. She'd blocked his number, but he'd only used a friend's phone or bought burners to continue his pleas. It would be a hassle to change a number she'd had for more than a decade, but maybe that time had come. Because after too many chances to count, Kennedy was done with the brother named Will. Done with him, and for the moment, done with thinking about him. She reached for the decadent rum punch she'd saved for this moment, settled herself against the bench's far side, stretched her legs out and allowed the water to rock away the stress of the past few days. She thought of her friend Gwen who worked in advertising for the *Star,* and had given her the inside info that led to this plum assignment and her being rocked like a baby in the ocean's arms. She needed to find a gift of thanks before leaving the island.

"Wake up, sleeping beauty. It's time to go ashore."

I went to sleep? Kennedy blinked her eyes against the setting sun as she righted herself on the bench and accepted Clinton's outstretched hand.

"I can't believe I was that tired."

"You've been working hard, lady."

"I know but still . . . I planned to see more on the return trip than the back of my eyelids."

"Plus," he added, with a nod toward the empty glass that set on a table. "You were sipping at sea, and you know what they say?"

"No, what do they say?"

"Bahama rum packs a punch."

Said with such infectious glee and in that rhythmic accent, Kennedy joined Clinton in laughing out loud. While doing so she noted his pristine white teeth, the dimple peeking through a five o'clock shadow, and the cute little crinkles surrounding his sparkling onyx eyes. To make sure she was healed from Will, she'd sworn off casual dalliances and one-night stands. Was she sure that extracurricular was out?

His voice dropped an octave as he added, "And rum is not the only thing packing."

One thought kept Kennedy's resistance from breaking. That same type of package is what had kept Will in her life for two years—a year, ten months and two days longer than he should have stayed. Yes, she was sure.

"Your offer is tempting," she replied with a smile to not leave his ego bruised, then reached inside her pouch and pulled out a tip.

He raised his hands. "Oh no, that's not necessary, beautiful lady. Squiring you around was my pleasure."

"And mine, too, especially since you arranged for me to be your only passenger. That cost you sales."

"Not really." Clinton glanced at Kennedy and continued a bit sheepishly. "Today was my off day. So, your lone fare is more than I would have normally made."

"Clinton! You shouldn't have used your free day for me."

"Like I said, it was my pleasure."

While appreciating the obvious flirtation from the Caribbean cutie, Kennedy knew the teasing was as far as she'd go. She reached into her purse again and pulled out another bill to add to the one in her hand. "I'm greatly appreciative. It was a wonderful ride." She held out the money. "I insist."

"Okay, beautiful lady. Thank you."

They stepped on to the landing. Kennedy hugged Clinton, allowed him a selfie and took one of her own, then strolled down the ramp to a line of awaiting taxis. Feeling the captain's manly muscles reminded her how long it had been since one had been inside her. It heightened her awareness of the island men's looks. Suddenly, they were all gorgeous, including the dark chocolate bar who smiled and opened his cab door so she could slide inside. *Must be that packing punch rum.*

The hotel was only five minutes away. On the ride there, she planned out the rest of her evening—order room service, do a final read through of her article before sending it off to the travel section editor, upload photos to her cloud accounts, enjoy an eight-plus hour date with her pillow. She entered the lobby and walked over to the concierge.

"Hello, Hank."

"Hello, Kennedy. How are you today?"

"Deliciously tired. I spent the day on a boat."

"Ah, the water. A great lover."

"The best. A perfect way to enjoy my last day here."

"Leaving so soon? You only arrived."

"I feel that way, too. I'll be back."

"And staying with us, I hope."

"Most likely. You guys are amazing."

"What can I do for you this evening?"

"Recommend something great from the room service menu, or a restaurant nearby that delivers?"

Hank looked aghast. "On your last night in paradise? Oh, no, my lovely lady. You mustn't spend this last night all alone in your room. At the very least you should enjoy a delicious meal and glass of wine while taking in a view of all that you're leaving. I know just the place to recommend, only a short, five-minute walk from our front door."

"I'm exhausted, but your suggestion is hard to resist."

"You won't be sorry, I promise you."

Kennedy watched as Hank pulled a card from several stacks on his station. She accepted it, gave a wave and headed to her room. After checking off the items on the evening's to-do list, all except the pillow date, she took a quick shower and donned a striped, cotton mini and flat leather sandals adorned with shells. Simple silver hoops and bangles completed the outfit and a quick shake out of her natural curls, a dash of mascara and a swipe of pure plum lipstick completed the look. She grabbed her pouch, checked for her ID, debit card and cell phone, and after a quick internal discussion decided to leave her digital camera in the room.

Five minutes later, and Kennedy was glad she'd taken Hank's advice. The shower had revived her and now a warm breeze caressed her clean skin. The azure blue sky had slid into indigo. Stars twinkled and disappeared as she joined tourists and natives strolling down the paved pathway. As she reached the steps leading to the restaurant on a hill she paused, pulled out her cellphone, and captured the moment. Once inside she was quickly seated on the establishment's veranda where a row of seats faced the ocean. She ordered the seafood dish Hank had recommended and took the server's suggestion for a fruity white wine. While eating, she became engrossed with the latest news on social media, DMing friends and posting pictures of the island taken with her cellphone. So much so that she didn't notice the handsome stranger who had been seated beside her until he spoke.

"I hate eating alone," he began without greeting, while looking out on the waves gently crashing against the shore. "But if I have to do it, having a gorgeous woman beside me makes it infinitely more satisfying."

Only then did he turn toward her with a smile.

Well, damn. Kennedy was prepared to be aggravated at the tired line, but the man was gorgeous in a way that was free and unscripted, a face that suggested, "I woke up like this."

"Thank you."

"I was thinking about ordering that dish. Is it good?"

"It's delicious. The concierge recommended it and he was spot on."

"Where are you staying?" Kennedy told him. "How have I missed seeing you?"

"You're staying there, too?"

"For the past week, though mostly I've been down at the beach soaking up the sun. What are you doing here if I may ask, and more importantly, why are you eating alone?"

Kennedy turned and swept her arm across the occupied tables. "I'm not alone."

The stranger smiled, revealing pearly whites that sparkled, just like his eyes, the color of the sky in her earlier photographs. The brilliant shade of blue against tanned skin, combined with a head of thick and curly brunette hair, and Kennedy once again considered ending her penis drought.

A server arrived, set down a drink, and took the man's order. Afterwards, he held out his hand. "Jack Sutton."

She picked up a linen napkin and wiped her hands. "Kennedy Wade."

"Nice meeting you, Kennedy."

"Likewise."

For the next forty minutes the two casually chatted. Kennedy learned that Jack was an engineer from Rhode Island, recently divorced, taking his first vacation in more than three years. He was intelligent and funny, easy to talk to, and seemed to genuinely listen as Kennedy talked. When he suggested they split a dessert, she agreed. When he offered to pay the tab, she said yes to that, too. When he asked her to join him for an after-dinner drink back at the hotel, Jack was three for three. They sat in the cushy chairs of the lounge in the lobby and swapped tall travel tales. A yawn reminded Kennedy of the next day's early rising. She finished her decaf caramel coffee and reached for her bag.

"Thanks for a great evening, the dinner and the conversation. I enjoyed it."

"Are you leaving?"

"Yes," she said, and stood.

"Then so am I." Jack also stood and reached for his wallet.

"Oh, no. You did dinner. I've got this one."

"Are you sure I can't talk you into extending the evening? The company is amazing and it's a beautiful night."

"I agree on both counts, but tomorrow's alarm rings early. I have a plane to catch."

They bantered back and forth a bit more, but Kennedy wouldn't change her mind. After paying the tab, the two walked to the elevator and got in. Jack's finger hovered over the floor buttons. "Which one?"

"Seven."

He pushed seven for her floor, and ten for his. Later, when asked, that would be the last thing she remembered that night.